IRON BOUND

THE THIEF'S TALISMAN: BOOK TWO

EMMA L. ADAMS

1

Even humans know that making a deal with any faerie is a one-way ticket to trouble.

There were no exceptions to that rule. All faeries, from the highest Sidhe to the lowest hobgoblin, were hardwired for trickery and deceit, despite not being able to tell a lie. As a half-faerie changeling, I had more cause to know that than most, and yet here I was, bargaining with a Little Person for free passage back into the mortal realm. To say my life had gone off the rails lately would be an understatement.

The bearded man paused before saying, "For my favour this time, I'd like you to bring me two shoelaces."

I blinked. "Shoelaces? Seriously?"

"Yes." Like all the Little People I'd met, he was of average height with reddish skin and a long beard. Whether they were identical siblings or products of some kind of cloning spell, I'd learned not to ask. I couldn't tell a single one of them apart, anyway, and they all seemed to know which favours I owed the other ones.

"All right… shoelaces it is."

I used the rift to travel to the mortal realm so often these days, the Little People had stacked up a list of no fewer than fourteen favours I owed. I'd been afraid he'd ask for something impossible. Shoelaces, though, I could manage without having to return to my thieving ways. Admittedly, I'd almost relish the challenge after weeks cooped up in the palace I'd inherited from my deceased mother, along with the title of Lady Whitefall of the Unseelie Court.

I might be the only half-blood heir in Faerie, but I still wasn't gifted with the Sidhe's ability to walk between realms. Neither was Viola, my friend and servant of the Whitefall family. We shared the same magic, thanks to my mother thinking it was amusing to demonstrate her power on a soldier from the Summer Court, replacing Viola's magic with part of her own. Viola had been trying to leave the Hornbeam family's army anyway, but a lifetime of servitude to my family hadn't been on the plan, though, and nor had being separated from her girlfriend, Rose. The Sidhe might not be able to lie, but that didn't stop them being deceitful monsters who played the same cruel games with half-bloods as they did with humans.

"Will you be using the rift, too?" the Little Person asked Viola.

"No, I just came to say goodbye to Raine."

We both knew better than to walk in the woods alone, even now the threat from the other families in the borderlands seemed to have subsided a little. I didn't mind the company. Viola was my closest friend these days, and since my arrival in Faerie, she'd surprised me with her warm and welcoming nature, even if she did insist on naming all the spiders which lived in the palace dungeons.

We left the Little Person's house and headed down the

path into the woods. Like all of this section of Faerie, it didn't appear to belong to either Court—the neutral temperature, dense undergrowth and thick mist swarming the path signalled neither Summer nor Winter. Here was the territory's edge, right at the back of the borderlands at the edge of Faerie. Through the trees, the path back to the mortal realm beckoned. Smoke swirled between thick ancient oaks, sending chills down my arms. In a realm where nothing and nobody died—in theory—the trees were older than even the Sidhe, and seemed to whisper secrets to one another as their branches rustled. I took in a breath, and approached the smoke at a jog.

As I did so, someone took hold of my arm.

In that instant, white light swallowed both of us up, immediately depositing us on cold, damp grass. I yanked my hand away from my unexpected fellow passenger, and found myself staring into the laughing eyes of Cedar Hornbeam, right-hand-thief of the Hornbeam family.

"Oh, it's you," I said, as though he hadn't scared the crap out of me. "Maybe warn me before you want to hitch a lift?"

"I thought I'd surprise you." He straightened up in his usual graceful manner that made us half-faeries the envy of humans.

"Any reason you followed me here?" I brushed grass from my "human" clothes, jeans and a thick coat, mostly for show. I generally didn't get cold—one of the perks of being half Winter Sidhe. If anything, I felt more energised when the air was cool and biting, and snowflakes swirled in the air. Where I'd grown up in the mortal realm, winter was characterised by grey skies and rain, but I still got a boost now I had magic.

Cedar dusted off his pristine coat. "I have an errand to run in the mortal realm."

"Thievery?"

"Surprisingly not."

I opened my mouth to ask what, then thought better of it. Cedar was likely bound by a vow not to tell me his plans. I didn't *think* Lord Hornbeam had decided he wanted to steal my power as his wife had, but I assumed the polite distance Cedar had kept between the two of us over the last few weeks had to do with not wanting to piss off the new leader of the Hornbeam family. That, and the fact that I'd accidentally killed the last one.

Typically, the rift had dumped us on a hillside just outside the city. We walked downhill until the ground levelled off, bisected by fences and low walls dividing fields outside the town. Cedar didn't speak for a few minutes. He looked tired, half-moon circles under his eyes and the light of his usually evenly tanned skin dulled to pale grey. He had pointed ears, jet-black hair that swept to shoulder-length, and hazel eyes that hid his status as a Summer half-Sidhe. The one flaw in his appearance was the jagged scar on his right cheekbone, which served as a human touch to his otherwise entirely fae appearance.

Cedar finally caught my gaze. "What have you been doing lately?"

"The usual," I said. "Exploring the palace, reading my mother's old books—the ones not written in ancient faerie languages, that is."

"No more clues?"

He meant about why my mother had died. "Nope," I said to Cedar. "Obviously. All traces of her death vanished a long time ago." There was no harm telling him what he and the other families already knew. Lady Whitefall's death had heralded my return to Faerie, to be tested by the talisman containing her power. I'd won it, over my other half-siblings, and the magic had become mine. Two of said half-siblings were dead, one after failing the talisman's test, the other because he'd chosen suicide by touching iron over murdering me on Lady Hornbeam's orders.

Perhaps it was guilt over his death which drove me to search every one of the ancient books in the palace library for clues on our mother's strange death. Not only had she not been carrying her immensely powerful talisman at the time, she'd died with witnesses, none of whom could explain what had happened. Add in the fact that Sidhe could permanently die now, without being reborn as they'd been before, and it was a mystery I couldn't resist. It wasn't like the palace came with any other forms of entertainment.

Of course, I also had a second mission—to find out how to undo a faerie vow—but Cedar didn't know about that one.

"Perhaps the answers are in the palace rather than at the site of her death," Cedar offered.

"Maybe I haven't found them yet. Leaving a neon sign flashing with the word "clue" isn't her thing. It took a year for Viola to unravel the information leading to the heirs." Meaning me.

His brow furrowed in thought. "Maybe try questioning others who knew her."

"That's part of the problem. If she had friends, they aren't showing up now. Viola doesn't know." I shrugged. "Not much else to do. I'm here for my dad, and then I'll get back to it after the holidays."

"Holidays," Cedar repeated, like it was a foreign word to him. Faeries—at least the ones I'd interacted with—didn't subscribe to particular holiday traditions, and their calendar was different to the one I'd grown used to in the mortal realm.

"I take it you don't get time off?"

"What would I do with it?" He sounded so perplexed, I laughed.

"I don't know, whatever you do in Faerie. Dad and I used

to watch TV, when it was working. If you like going out, there are night clubs or…" What did Faerie have that was equivalent? "I don't know. Parties."

He smiled. "In Faerie, revelry is a very serious game."

"Think I got that part." Considering someone had tried to assassinate me at the first ceremony I'd attended in Faerie, I wasn't keen to attend another faerie celebration. Though if my timing was right, it was close to the winter solstice this week.

Cedar seemed to relax a little as we walked, closing the distance between us, his gaze skimming my human-style coat as though searching for something. "You don't carry the talisman?"

"Hidden." I'd grown used to holding the sceptre within sight, but I wouldn't be able to carry it so openly in the mortal realm. A talisman was a sign of power, a challenge, and proof that I no longer belonged amongst the regular half-bloods. Even Denzel, my former best friend, who hadn't spoken to me since I'd implied that hanging around with thieves and vagabonds like him was likely to end up with someone dead, considering I was now royalty. When all the half-bloods had been invited to claim their heritage in Faerie as part of a bargain Ivy Lane had made with the Sidhe, I'd never expected to be allowed in at all, let alone as the leader of a powerful family. My old life and this one went together about as well as Summer faeries and a blizzard.

As we neared the town, the sounds of, well, revelry, drifted over the frost-coated rooftops—if I had to guess, I'd come back on the day of the solstice itself. Here in the middle of England, the only place covered in actual genuine snow was half-blood territory, thanks to the concentration of Winter magic due to reach its peak. I shivered as it traced through my body, rejuvenating the empty numbness that had filled me far too often since I'd used the talisman against Lady Hornbeam. Cedar, as a Summer half-Sidhe, wouldn't feel a thing. Summer and Winter were supposed polar opposites, but in this realm, they lived on the same territory, in an area sustained by their magic which mimicked the seasons outside.

Sure enough, half-blood territory was wrapped in a full-on blizzard. Winter faeries ran shrieking through the snow, drinking in the magic pouring out of the very air. The ponds had frozen, to the annoyance of Summer nymphs and selkies who usually swam there.

Cedar jerked his head in that direction. "Why not join them?"

"Maybe later. I need to check on Dad first."

I slowed down my pace anyway, letting Winter's magic wash over me. Cedar glanced sideways at me but didn't speak. I wondered if he picked up on my magic the way I sensed his, whenever there wasn't any other magic interfering. Even now, with the air humming with Winter magic, the slightest trace of his Summer magic brushed my skin. Mine, I could hardly sense at all.

"Is it normal for magic to take a while to recover from using a powerful spell?" I hadn't meant to speak aloud, but I didn't have anyone else to ask, and it'd been bugging me for weeks.

"Yours?"

I shrugged. "It's okay when I'm around Winter territory."

"The spell you used was strong, even by Faerie's standards, and you aren't used to handling that level of power."

Considering I hadn't had magic at all until the talisman had chosen me, I'd figured that much out myself. Especially after being virtually comatose for a week following the incident. I'd heard of magical burnout, but not on this scale.

Then again, I didn't know anyone else who'd got halfway through one of the most powerful spells in Faerie, a spell that shouldn't even exist. Much less a half-blood who shouldn't have been able to use the spell to begin with.

The scene revisited me in my nightmares every time I closed my eyes. The moment when Lady Hornbeam had reached into my soul and yanked out my magic. When I'd realised I couldn't fight and *let* her take the power, swamping her own enough to stop her spell and land us both in front of the Hornbeams' iron prison. And when I'd used what was left of my strength to push her into the path of the tornado our colliding magic had unleashed.

I'd killed a Sidhe. The beings which, up until very recently, I'd thought were immortal. Lady Hornbeam had deserved her fate. She'd kidnapped and tortured humans for hundreds of years, punished her half-blood children by forcing them to carry iron, and tried to kill me for being the only half-blood who'd dared to take the talisman of a Sidhe. Didn't change the fact that the Summer Court would want my blood if they knew.

Cedar and I lapsed into silence as we entered a residential area. The city had taken a severe hit in the faerie invasion of the mortal realm twenty-two years ago, and the remaining suburbs had formed a town divided between supernaturals and regular humans. Not that you'd know it looking at the streets bright with decorations. A fair number of human habitations we passed were draped in flashing lights, which seemed to fascinate Cedar. He stared at a particularly bright display, in which the human family had covered the entire front of their house in a motif of Santa's North Pole, complete with reindeer.

"What are those supposed to be?" He indicated the diminutive people carrying stacks of glowing gifts.

"I think they're Santa's elves."

"Elves?" he asked. "They don't look like elves."

"Not the faerie sort."

"Hmm." He carried on walking, burying his hands in his pockets. "What's this Christmas for, exactly?"

"Human religious thing. Some humans. And not really religious. I don't even know." I hadn't quite figured out what the faeries' religion was, only that their ancient gods had died out a long time ago. Everyone worshipped the Sidhe, and the Sidhe pretty much worshipped themselves. Maybe you didn't need to have faith in a higher power if you possessed the ability to rearrange the whole universe whenever you felt like it.

I'd never understood mortal traditions, but anything that made Dad happy made me happy. Usually I stole something nice for us. This year, I could take him genuine icicles that never melted or lights that shone forever—but that wasn't wise. I sometimes forgot the effect faerie magic had on mortals, especially ones who'd fallen victim to it before. Every day the guilt that I hadn't told him about my mother's death grew deeper. Her leaving him in the mortal realm had broken his heart and fractured his mind. Sometimes living between these two worlds felt like walking on thin ice.

"I'll see you later, Raine," Cedar said as we reached my road.

"Sure." I waved him off, skipping down the road to home. *Home.* Our rickety old house had a more welcoming air than the icy palace on a good day. A small red-brick building divided into flats, it lay slightly apart from its neighbours, the other floors unoccupied at the moment. The downstairs floor lights were off. That wasn't a good sign. Dad didn't leave the house much—I'd ordered all our groceries to be delivered, and the mercenaries guarding the house were supposed to stop him from wandering off. Over the last few weeks, I'd searched the palace for anything I could safely sell in this realm without it turning into leaves, and sold a few artefacts on the black market to fund twenty-four hour bodyguards. Better than depending on Robin, my ex, for charity. We hadn't seen one another since he'd apologised for nearly killing me while under Lady Hornbeam's compulsion, which was probably for the best.

I nodded to the latest mercenary guard—a skinny human of around eighteen, wielding a sword twice the length of his arm.

"Has he left the house?" I asked, and the poor kid jumped a foot in the air.

"Ah. No… Lady Whitefall?"

"Call me Raine." I went by my human name in this realm, but apparently word had started to spread amongst the human mercenaries, of all people. "Word of advice: get a smaller weapon. They won't see it coming."

He nodded and stepped aside in a sweeping bow as I approached the house. All right, then. I didn't look *that* much like a Sidhe, who inspired humans to throw themselves at their feet, did I? Living in the faerie realm had changed me, certainly. Wielding her magic, even more so. But here would always be my home. I unlocked the front door, hoping I wouldn't find Dad in one of his moods. It was impossible to find the right way to announce I'd be coming home when our clocks and Faerie's were wildly out of sync.

Dad sat in his usual armchair, and didn't look up when I came in.

"Hey, Dad," I said, smiling brightly. "Thought I'd come home early and—"

He looked at me with wide, haunted eyes. "Tell me they're wrong."

I stilled, my heart sinking. He did this sometimes—asked questions that made no sense, referring to the years in my mother's palace he couldn't recall. She'd wiped both our minds when she'd left us back in the mortal realm, three years after she'd kidnapped my father as a human prisoner, but the memories found their own ways of coming back.

"Dad, we're here. At home. Nobody's going to hurt us."

He shook his head. "They're lying to me," he said. "They're telling me she's dead."

2

M y body locked into place, fear slithering down my spine. "You're mistaken," I said quickly. "Imagining things. It's okay. Nobody's dead—"

"Your mother is *not dead*. They said you knew."

Shit. "Who told you that?"

I hated lying to him. But his mortal mind was susceptible to faeries' tricks, and he'd been through so much already that I'd refrained from telling him about my mother's death, skirting around the subject the best I could. I pretended she was too busy with the Court and her duties to come to the mortal realm. Dad had tried to follow me to Faerie three times, only for me to gently take him back home. I'd known this day was coming.

He half-stood, a manic gleam in his eyes. "I told them," he said. "I told them she's not dead, because my daughter's with her, and the Lady is teaching her to be one of *them*. It's the truth."

I took in a painful breath, my eyes stinging. "Dad. Please don't..."

"You told me she was with you."

I shook my head, tears leaking from my eyes. "I'm sorry, Dad. I didn't want to hurt you. She didn't—she died a year ago, and I never knew."

"She's *not* dead." He stood abruptly, kicking the armchair and swearing in anger. I tensed, backing away, preparing to move anything breakable aside—except the shelves were empty, as was the coffee table. His beloved book collection lay scattered on the floor.

"Dad, *please.*"

He didn't get close enough to grab me. His knees gave out and he fell to the floor, writhing as though in unimaginable pain. I grabbed his shoulders, not having a clue what to do. I lifted his head, and stared into eyes laced with blue, like impossibly bright veins.

Her magic.

"Dad!" I gasped. "Please, *please* calm down."

His fists struck the floor and he screamed a horrible noise I'd never heard from a human before. Blood dripped from his nose and mouth, his limbs twitched, and the blue veins spread from his eyes across his face.

"Dad!" My vision was blurred, tears streaking my own face. I'd never felt so terrified and helpless, not even in my time as Lady Hornbeam's prisoner. "Please."

I folded him into my arms, like I could hold both of us together. *Magic, help me!* It was her magic—the same magic I had—that was attacking him, but I couldn't undo the spell, not if she'd already used it. And the only kind of magic I knew how to do was transforming things. Not helpful in this situation.

"I—I..." His voice faded, his eyes closing.

"Dad—*no.*" I sat rigid with terror, my arms still around him. I didn't dare move. One minute passed. Two. His heartbeat steadied, but didn't stop. He was unconscious, not dead. But if he woke...

I stood shakily and opened the door to my room. Maybe my collection of contraband contained a spell that might help. I'd stolen magical items before.

But my shelves were empty, the contents destroyed. Shattered glass jars, broken charms, and other debris littered the floor.

I let the door fall shut. Shaking all over, I sank into the vacated armchair. *Think, Raine.* Okay, so I had nothing here. I'd have to buy something from the market. I scrubbed my face, wiped my eyes, and lifted Dad back into the armchair as carefully as possible.

"Raine!" said Cedar from the other side of the flat door. "What's going on?"

Dammit. He just had to get involved. Had he followed me home? Sidhe's blood, had *he* told Dad the truth?

"Raine?" Cedar called. "Are you okay?"

"No." I crossed the room and opened the door with shaking hands. "No, I'm not. My dad—someone told him the truth, and I think he's dying."

"Told him what?"

Oh. Cedar didn't know my situation. I kept forgetting he and I had been strangers before all this had happened. He'd never seen into my messed-up home life. Which meant someone else must have told him.

"My mother kidnapped him, and she used some kind of magic on him to stop him remembering the years he lived in Faerie. When he found out she died, her magic made him have—like, a seizure, until he passed out. I need to find a witch."

Cedar barely blinked. "Why a witch?"

"Because he nearly *died*. If he remembers it when he wakes up, I can't—I can't let that happen. He's all I have."

It was a desperate plan, but unless I found a way to shut the memories off, they'd literally kill him. My own magic didn't remove memories—I had no clue how my mother had done it. But there were witch potions that could achieve a similar effect.

He studied me, then nodded. "I can watch him. I don't know about human magic, whether it'll be enough, but using another faerie spell on him would not be wise."

"Thanks." I wiped my eyes, and went into the bathroom to make myself look vaguely presentable. The market wasn't the most hostile place in town, but it was unwise to walk there with my eyes puffy with tears. I cleaned myself up and grabbed a handkerchief to cover my white hair, as I used to do. What with my plain clothes and the hidden sceptre, I looked like the thief I used to be, not a Lady of the Faerie Courts. I went back into the living room to find Cedar standing beside my father's chair, still as a statue.

"I'll be fifteen minutes, at most. If he moves—please try to stop him hurting himself."

"Of course."

I half-ran outside, sprinting to the road's end, only slowing when I reached the market which had sprung up on a grassy area between half-blood and mage territories. Bright under the dull grey winter sky, the stalls were a riot of colour and noise, draped in tinsel and enchanted floating baubles.

The goblin market was staffed by an ogre called Ug who grinned at me, waving.

"Hey," I said. "I don't suppose there's a witch around today?" The market varied, and new stalls sprung up each time I came here. It was mostly humans, perhaps surprisingly, but there was no distinction to human eyes between the genuine spell stores and the ones selling fake antiques. Luckily, I was familiar enough with the place to know the difference.

"Third on the left," said Ug. "Name of Langley."

"Cheers." I walked to the left, no longer able to hurry now

the holiday crowd surrounded me on either side. The world that had once glamoured itself to hide from humans lived alongside them now, and apparently every single one of them had come to the market today. The crowd surged and bustled with noise and the occasional yelp when one of the ogres accidentally knocked someone over, or a human got too close to a thorny Summer faerie. I finally managed to slip through to the store I wanted when someone grabbed my arm.

"You," hissed Twill. "You thieving bitch."

"I didn't steal anything," I protested. "I was trying to buy something, actually."

"Your reputation precedes you, thief," he said. Twill had once been one of my suppliers, until his greed and desire for my talisman had caused him to attempt to kill me. I'd hoped he'd forgotten his grudge and would leave me in peace. No such luck.

He whipped out a sharp stick and jabbed at me, catching another half-faerie instead, who screamed. The weapon was iron-tipped. He'd *designed* it to hit faeries. And considering I was the only faerie enemy he had, he'd apparently nursed his grudge for a while.

I danced out of reach, realising I'd unintentionally drawn a crowd. I wanted to transform the stick into a live snake and watch it throttle him, but my magic couldn't turn an inanimate object into a living animal. Pity. He deserved it.

Instead, I splayed my hands and blasted him with magical energy. Blue light froze the moisture in the air into icy shards aimed at his face. He ducked, arms raised to shield himself, and fell sideways into the nearest stall. The surge of energy from using my magic again washed away my lingering anger and guilt over Dad. Snatching the weapon from where he'd dropped it, I snapped it into two halves, and hit him across the face with what was left of it.

"Need a hand?" Ug the ogre parted the crowd easily, his hulking body knocking into several stalls. Humans and faeries alike scrambled to get out of the way.

Twill lay in a heap on the floor, groaning. "Ug," I said. "Please throw him out."

"With pleasure," the ogre rumbled, doing exactly that. He bodily grabbed Twill and hurled him over the roof of the nearest stall. I heard a crash and a yelp from outside.

"Thanks." I ducked my head and did my best to ignore the crowd, so they'd stop staring. Sure enough, within seconds, everyone forgot the commotion, caught up again in the curiosities of the market.

On the other side of the stall I'd been aiming for, whose occupant was hiding behind a giant carved troll skull, Twill's store was unguarded.

Oh, screw it.

I slipped behind the stall, scanning the shelves. He didn't always get his hands on genuine enchantments, but there were a large number of potions in the back, all labelled. I found the one I needed—for memory loss—and slipped it into the pocket of my coat. I gave the stall one last glance to make sure he didn't have anything too dangerous or illegal, then I returned to the crowd and let its momentum carry me back to the entrance.

The potion I'd chosen was a mild one, designed to calm the mind and remove unwanted thoughts. Because my dad hadn't actually seen proof my mother had died and was convinced she was still alive, hopefully it'd be enough. It'd last a few weeks, and as long as I kept the bottle out of his reach, I'd be able to reapply it.

I extricated myself from the market, and sprinted in the direction of home.

My hands shook as I unlocked the door. "Dad?" I called, hoping he hadn't woken up. Cedar wouldn't know how to restrain him, and my mother's spell might rebound on both of them. But he remained in the armchair while Cedar re-stacked books onto shelves. If I glanced at Cedar at the corner of my eye, reading the back of one of Dad's paperbacks, he'd have appeared entirely human. In this realm, he didn't quite fit. Like everyone who'd spent more time in Faerie than here, he'd picked up their mannerisms so thoroughly I couldn't put my finger on what it was that made him stand out. The way he moved, maybe. He saw me looking and returned the book to the shelf.

"Oh. Thank you," I said awkwardly. He'd also turned the rest of the non-broken furniture in the living room the right way up, and cleared anything that couldn't be repaired into bin bags he must have found where I kept them in the kitchen. Miracle of miracles, the TV had survived the ordeal intact.

"Are these books yours?" he asked, picking up another one.

"Dad's, mostly. He taught me to read, though." I crouched beside the armchair. "I'll get him to drink this when he wakes up. It's a temporary solution—anything stronger would make things worse. I just hope it works."

Cedar glanced at him. "Your mother did that?"

"You live in Faerie. I don't know why that's a surprise."

He blinked, then returned to tidying the bookshelves, his silence speaking for itself.

"Sorry," I said. "I'm just having a really crappy day."

Cedar said, "I apologise for being callous with my questioning. I was just curious as to why she would have let him go. Most mortals…"

"Don't survive that long. I know. I suppose she used the same spell on me, but I don't remember it."

"Your blood is stronger."

"He's been fine until the last few years. Someone told him

she died, and it must have set off the spell. Believe me, I'd like to know who."

"Your friend… Robin, was it? He knew."

"He did. I guess I never specifically said not to tell him, but it's downright careless." I sighed, contemplating the state of my room. "You don't have to help clean up, Cedar. I know you have some other mission to be on. I think it'd be easier if just I'm here when he wakes up."

Cedar paused. "Do you want me to leave?"

I turned to him. "Not that I don't appreciate the help, but why did you come here? Or am I involved in this mission of yours."

"Not exactly," Cedar said. "I sensed when the magic acted on him. That's why I came back. But to answer your question, Lord Hornbeam did ask me to invite you to our Court."

Another vow? The last one had nearly killed both of us. "Is this a compulsory thing, or…"

"No, of course not. Lord Hornbeam just asked me to pass the message on. He's aware the solstice is an important time for your people in the mortal realm. I wasn't supposed to ask you until you were back in Faerie, but I thought it couldn't hurt to give you an advance warning."

His expression betrayed nothing, but he'd risked enough to stop me from getting killed on his territory before. Surely he thought about it at least as often as I did… though for all I knew, it wasn't the first time he'd been forced to hurt someone under the influence of a vow.

Maybe he was here to assassinate someone.

"Then why are you here?" I asked, curiosity overcoming common sense.

"To keep an eye on the solstice celebrations for signs of trouble," he said.

I frowned. "The solstice? What does that have to do with the Hornbeams? They don't celebrate."

"No, but many half-bloods from the families come back into this realm at this time of year. When one Court's power vastly outranks the other, it's always wise to be on one's guard. Are you going to the solstice ball?"

"Why?"

"You mentioned your magic isn't as strong since you drew it out of the talisman. I think you're suffering from burnout after using so much of it at once, and there's no better way to replenish it than a gathering of Winter energy. There'll rarely be a better chance, save for the Court itself."

He might well be right, but given my track record when it came to celebrations on half-blood territory, I'd probably be best sitting this one out.

"I don't think so," I said.

"I could escort you."

I stared at him for a second. "A Summer faerie in a sea of Winter half-bloods? You'd get eaten alive."

A smile curled his lip. "You don't have much faith in me, do you? I'm capable of disguising my allegiance. It's one of the things that makes me so very good at what I do."

"So much humility." I shook my head at him. "Why would you want to come? It's out of your territory. You wouldn't get anything out of it."

"Maybe I have some spying to do. If the families are planning anything, one of the best places to amass power is such an event as the solstice. I'm expecting trouble."

"You're really selling this to me."

"It's up to you."

Hmm. The Mage Lords and the non-supernatural authorities kept a close eye on half-blood territory on the solstice days, in case the party got out of hand and wrapped the city in a five-day blizzard as it had on one memorable occasion. Unlike Faerie's Gatherings, there wouldn't be any scheming families either. Just Winter half-bloods getting drunk on power.

"Okay," I found myself saying. "But not too late. I need to be back with Dad."

"Of course."

"And you're really okay with wandering into the middle of Winter's event?"

"I've been undercover before. I'll pick you up later this evening, all right?" He approached the door, opening it. "Let me know if you need anything."

"Sure." Dad was beginning to stir. As his eyelids flickered, I placed the potion in his hands.

Cedar closed the door behind him, and Dad sat up, blinking at me.

"Dad," I said. "You're not feeling well. Drink that, okay?"

He looked at me blearily. "Raine?"

"You fell down and hit your head," I told him. "That's a potion which will make it better."

To my relief, he accepted the potion and drank it down. His head slumped forward, but he looked back up at me a second later, his vision clear. "What happened here?"

"An accident," I said, but he'd already dozed off again. *Good.*

I ran into his bedroom and set about fixing everything he'd broken—luckily, the furniture was screwed down and I'd long since removed anything he could hurt himself with, so all I had to do was put his clothes away and flip the bedside table the right way up.

I saved my own room for last. It wasn't pretty. I threw my remaining clothes back into the drawers—I'd left most of my human clothes here, because I had an extensive wardrobe in Faerie and my magic allowed me to transform my clothes whenever I felt like it. But everything else I owned was a lost cause. Crying over broken things I had no attachment to was pointless, so I salvaged what I could and shoved the rest into black bin bags to dispose of. Really, he'd done me a favour. It'd been a while since I'd been forced to sort out my treasure hoard. Finally, I yanked the shoelaces out of an old pair of boots and shoved them in my pocket to take back to the Little People.

Back in the living room, I found Dad awake and fiddling with the TV remote. As usual, he'd forgotten to turn it on. I darted over and did so, then joined him on the sofa.

"Dad," I said. "I'm going for a job interview on the other side of town, okay?"

He glanced my way. "What job?"

"Shift work, with the half-faeries. So I might be working odd hours."

He grunted, half asleep. I didn't know how lucid he'd be while the potion worked its magic, but I hoped he'd remember later, when I disappeared again. I needed to get more consistent with my excuses.

I heated a microwaveable meal for him and went back to my room to get ready for the ball.

In the mortal realm, I usually dressed to blend in and avoid drawing attention. Anyone who looked at me could immediately tell I was from Winter. My bright blue eyes— brighter than any human's—shone with the magic I'd inherited. I had bone-white hair, pointed ears, and a tallish slim frame built for acrobatics and climbing things. I didn't clean up too badly, but I just plain couldn't be bothered putting in any effort with my appearance. Luckily, with the magic I'd inherited, I didn't need to.

First, I changed into old clothes, just in case my magic decided it was funny not to change them back afterwards. Then I concentrated on the humming in my veins, the power in my blood. Blue light glowed from my palms, rippling up my arms, my body, and my clothes shimmered, went transparent, then turned into something else entirely. I'd envisioned a dress that clearly said, "Winter faerie", and that's exactly what I'd got. It appeared to be made of endless overlapping snowflakes, shimmering with blue light as my magic faded. Another disguise, a costume, but one more eye-catching than the role I usually played. The sceptre completed my ensemble. Even though it didn't contain the essence of my magic any longer, the blue gemstone gleaming at its end looked like it belonged to a queen.

There was a knock on the door. Steeling myself, I walked out to meet Cedar.

3

Being escorted to a ball by a faerie noble had never been a dream of mine. While my fellow half-bloods had dreamed of being spirited away to Faerie and worshipped by a court of adoring fans, I'd hoped to avoid it forever. The real thing was nothing like the stories. Even half-blood territory, where it was supposed to be safe, I'd nearly been speared by iron arrows shot by assassins at the last occasion I'd attended.

My body tensed when Cedar and I drew nearer to the gate. He wore his usual elegant clothes, unadorned so as to hide his Court allegiance. Nobody would know he was from Summer, as long as he didn't use magic. I knew for a fact he carried iron weapons, but not visibly.

I didn't, for once. My magic would be more than enough to take down any threats. My veins hummed with power, my skin tingling, and I consciously let blue light shimmer up my arms. If I drew the guards' attention, they wouldn't look twice at Cedar. How he'd got his hands on an invitation, I had no idea.

Two green-skinned, giggling teenage female Summer

faeries with thorny hair wandered up to the guard at the gate. One of them placed a hand on his arm and whispered in his ear.

"No Seelie," he growled.

"But—"

She yelped as he hit her with a handful of Winter magic, and the two of them slunk away.

Friendly.

I took in a breath as the guard spotted Cedar and me and we walked closer. He could hold his own if it came to a fight, anyway.

There was no need to worry. The guard took one look at me, muttered "Whitefall," dipped his head and moved aside to let us pass.

"That was unexpected," I whispered to Cedar, once we were safely inside.

"They know you. Everyone does."

"I like to forget that sometimes." Luckily, the party was too spread out for all attention to focus on us. The Seelie half-bloods were presumably hiding indoors with their heaters turned up to full power, because the main area of half-blood territory was one hundred percent ice-cold Winter magic. The air shimmered with perfect snowflakes spiralling in patterns and clinging to bare skin. Though it was already dark outside, light encased the territory in the form of sprites and piskies flying around holding lanterns, and perched in the bare-branched trees. The grass glimmered with frost, the rivers were frozen in ice, and Unseelie had come out to play in all its glory. Magic filled my veins with energy, and I tilted my head back to let the snowflakes land on my face.

Cedar's hand rested on my arm, causing me to look at him. His face was flushed from the cold, but his eyes glittered with amusement. "I knew you wouldn't regret it."

"All right, Mr Know-It-All," I said teasingly. "So you're my date?"

His lips parted a little. "Date? The humans… right, of course. I haven't spent enough time in the mortal realm to be entirely familiar with their ways."

"You're saying you don't know what a date *is?*"

"Of course I do. It's just not something we really do over in Faerie. Choosing a partner, yes. Rituals—not so much."

"Can't imagine there's much opportunity for entertainment in the Hornbeams' Court."

I'd dated Seelie faeries before—to most of us, magical compatibility was the most important aspect of choosing a partner and it wasn't Court-dependent—but I'd never had one escort me to an Unseelie-only gathering before. I hoped Cedar knew what he was doing.

He took my arm and we walked towards the nearest table. I knew he was only pretending to be my partner as part of the act, but it was fun to pretend for a second that I was here for my own amusement, like the others, not on a potentially deadly mission.

Cedar lifted a glass of clear liquid, examining the contents, then handed it to me. "Pure Winter power. Don't worry, there's nothing in it."

"You can tell if something's poisoned?"

"Yes, I can. You'd be surprised how often it used to happen at Gatherings."

"No, I probably wouldn't." I drank down the liquid and shivered as magic resonated through my bones. "I don't suppose it's a good idea for you to drink that."

"Winter power? It wouldn't harm me, but I think I'd prefer elf wine." He picked out a glass of a darker red liquid instead.

"No elf wine," I said firmly.

"Oh?" He tilted his head. "Is there a story there?"

I had no plans to dance on any tables, so I said, "I'd prefer to remember tonight, that's all."

He smiled, taking it as a compliment I hadn't intended. Or maybe I had. What was one night in the scheme of things? I was due some good luck. Never mind that he was supposed to be my mortal enemy according to the Courts' doctrine. Then again, also according to said doctrine, a half-blood couldn't inherit a talisman.

"Doesn't the cold bother you?" I asked in a murmur.

"Not as such. These clothes are warmer than they look."

"Hmm." I allowed my gaze to drift up his silver-cuffed black coat, which fitted his slim form perfectly. I inched closer to him, feeling lighter-hearted than I had in weeks even with the hundred worries knocking at my door. While I recharged my magic, there was nothing wrong with getting to know my companion a little better.

"So," I said, "what's the most fun thieving job you've been on?"

I didn't know whether he liked discussing his past as Lady Hornbeam's thief, but he gave me a good-humoured smile.

"That's a trick question." His tongue ran over his lips, dyed red with faerie wine. "I'd say our chase over the rooftops is in the top five."

"Only five?" I said.

"I might graduate you to the top three, but there was an incident involving stealing a prized bottle of elf wine from a bunch of drunk leprechauns caught up in some astonishing debauchery."

"Okay, maybe I don't want to know that."

He grinned wickedly. "You did ask."

"Yes, I did."

Music started to play, the weird type of faerie beat I couldn't attribute to one particular instrument. Like a piano and harp accompanied by the humming of the magic thick in the air.

"What about you? You stole from humans, right?"

"Mostly," I admitted. "I tended to stick to stealing from people who deserved it, or who wouldn't miss what I stole. Sometimes when we ran out of food, I raided the mages' warehouses. They always have more than they need, so…" I shrugged. "You have to be on a register to get rations, and I didn't want people poking into our lives. Nobody can know what made Dad the way he is."

And now I'd gone and darkened the mood again. *Way to go, Raine.*

Cedar's forehead pinched. "I'm not sure I entirely understand how humans can't help him."

"Because our magic isn't like human supernaturals'," I said. "What the Sidhe do—you must know, we can barely look at the bastards without getting a headache. Humans have it worse. He lived in her palace for the first few years of my life, and those years are—gone. For both of us." I drank down another cup of Winter power, but this one didn't give me half as much of a buzz.

"I apologise for upsetting you, Raine. I was just curious about your time here living with humans."

"I didn't spend that much time with humans," I said. "I mean, I went to school. Sometimes. Dad didn't make me. He taught me to read, though. Then he couldn't work anymore, so it was up to me to work for both of us. I worked a lot of different jobs. My last one, I lost when my human colleague thought it was funny to put iron in my pockets."

His eyes widened, shocked. "The humans allowed that?"

"There was no proof. It was a crappy place to work, anyway. Have you always worked… you know, as a thief?"

He nodded. "Since I was a child, yes."

"And now you work for Lord Hornbeam." I wanted to

find out why he was really here, but his vow would doubtless get in the way.

"I do," he said carefully.

"Your vow passes onto the next family head, right? So, your stepfather. Not your father..."

"No, my father was a human who died many years ago."

I didn't need to ask where his mother had found him. Just like mine, she'd have captured him from the mortal realm. We had that much in common, at least.

"And yes," he added. "It does, but I am under no orders to steal from you this time, nor do I intend to."

Glad we cleared that up. "I wouldn't have brought you here if I thought you did."

His mouth tilted up. "I seem to remember I was the one who brought *you* here."

"To get me drunk on Winter power?"

He moved in behind me. "To get you to loosen up." He lightly wrapped an arm around my waist, his strong grip entirely too appealing. *This isn't what I came here for.* Even if he was playing a part, I didn't need to get distracted.

"You didn't answer my question," I said.

"Hmm?"

"Most fun thieving job you've been on. There has to be one. It also has to be pretty damn good to beat our rooftop chase."

He laughed, the same laugh I'd liked when we'd first met. "When I was a child, I gained a certain reputation when I stole from the Seelie King himself. Luckily, he interpreted it as a childish game. I most likely couldn't get away with the same now."

"The Seelie King?" I twisted around to stare at him. "You're having me on."

"I'm doing no such thing."

"Did Lady Hornbeam really think she could get away

with that? I suppose she *did* think you could steal a talisman, of all things."

His smile vanished. "Yes. She certainly had ambitions."

"Sorry," I said quickly. "I didn't think."

"It's fine. I was lucky he didn't turn me into a tree."

"Lucky." I shook my head at him. "And I thought I was pushing my luck stealing from the mages." I looked around in case anyone was listening, and spotted an improvised dance floor where a number of half-faeries swayed to the eerie music, wings glittering, skin speckled with falling snowflakes.

"You like dancing?" he asked, following the path of my sight.

"Like it?" Like was too small a word. I'd *lived* it. "Sure. Why?"

He leaned close to my ear. "I heard a rumour that you caused a sensation in half-blood territory the night after you came back from Faerie the first time. I strongly regretted missing the show."

His proximity, and the subtle scent of his magic, sent warm shivers down my back. But his words only served to remind me that his motives were unclear, that bringing me here didn't mean he wouldn't use me for his own ends. I stepped away from him.

"I'm not here to entertain anyone. That was a mistake."

"I didn't mean..." He paused, remaining close enough behind me that I could feel his warmth through Winter's chill. "I've very much enjoyed our time together tonight, Raine, and I thought you might like the chance to join me on the dance floor before we return to our former positions."

I turned to face him. "As mortal enemies?"

"Yes to the mortal part, but never enemies, Raine."

Not if a vow forces us against one another again.

I shoved the thought firmly away. He sounded sincere enough, and one dance wouldn't matter.

His gaze held mine. "I feel it remiss not to tell you that you look particularly stunning tonight, Raine. Even more so than usual."

"Please." I rolled my eyes. It was normal for faeries to throw extravagant compliments at one another. Humans, in my experience, not so much. "I'm the one who's supposed to be drunk on Winter power."

"Was that a yes? To the dancing?"

No. I shouldn't. I'd sworn I'd never play this game again. No dancing. Not the faerie kind, with magic and muddled senses and year-long mistakes. But he was right here, and just for once, I wanted to forget my obligations.

"Yeah, why not."

We joined the crowd, only attracting a few looks. The Winter faeries were too set on amassing power and recharging their magic to care that Lady Whitefall was amongst them, and I was hardly the only half-Sidhe present. Still, this was the first time I'd felt anything resembling self-consciousness. Maybe because I'd never known anyone in the faceless crowds who'd watched my show, but I very much wanted to know Cedar. As a thief, trained to move with precision, he was in his element. My feet found the rhythm and moved in step with him as magic flooded my veins, pouring off the crowd and our collective magic. Yet beneath that, Cedar's magic—so different from Winter, scented of lightly burning candles—drew me in. His hands circled my waist, holding me against him while we swayed in time with the music. The sound had slowed to a slow tune resembling a dirge, lost beneath the pleasing hum of Winter magic, and the even more pleasing buzzing sensation when it rubbed against Cedar's.

He had snowflakes in his hair. I reached to brush them

away, and his forehead rested against mine. "This feels like a night for breaking the rules," he murmured.

Of course, that's when the screaming started.

I spun around, magic springing to my palms, as the crowd parted, everyone running in the opposite direction from the dark shapes which had appeared amongst them like living shadows. A sluagh in the form of a skeletal woman bore down on three screaming teenage winged fae. I ran in their direction, shooting magic from my palms. With the power fuelled by the collective torrent of Winter magic inside the territory, the attack was brighter than I'd intended, blasting the sluagh halfway across the dance floor.

Other shapes appeared from the clusters of trees: shadowy beasts. The sort that usually preyed on humans, not half-bloods at the height of their power. Too many to fight at once. When I dragged my eyes away, I spotted Cedar swiftly moving in the opposite direction.

"Hey!" I ran after him, ducking around a troll. The problem with being in an Unseelie gathering was that there was little distinction between the attackers and the victims, aside from the shadowy beasts. "Where are you going?"

"They're Grey Vale beasts," he said, not breaking stride. "I have to find where they're coming from."

"Since when was this *your* job?"

But of course he'd been sent here for a reason. He had a job, and the notion was enough to send any lingering aftereffects of our connection fleeing. *Why did I let myself think he was here for my sake?*

Answer: *because it would have been really, really nice to have one day of my life which didn't end in bloodshed and screaming.*

Cedar halted, cursing under his breath, when three hellhounds ran into the clearing.

And hellhounds, I added to my mental list.

Panic erupted. Even the more powerful half-bloods ran

away from the hellhounds—after all, their deadly bite could kill a half-blood or human in a few hours. I used the humming magic in the air to turn my dress into an armoured outfit not unlike Cedar's, and approached the first hellhound at a run. In the space of a second, all three of them turned their attention onto me at once.

The hellhounds charged. They looked like wild boars, and that's more or less how they moved—with no regard for anyone in their way. Teeth snapping, drool hanging from their jaws, they ran swifter than you'd expect for beasts that size. My magic attack bounced off the first one's face. *I knew I should have brought iron.*

Cedar apparently hadn't made that error. He moved smoothly, whipping out a long knife—exactly how he'd sneaked it in here without anyone sensing it was a mystery. Ducking under the hellhound's gaping jaws, he sank the blade into its neck. Blood splattered the snow, but its companions didn't stop. I was forced to dance around them, firing magic from my hands. Every attack I sent at them fizzled out on contact like I was blasting them with air rather than powerful Winter magic. Apparently it didn't affect them —maybe because they were from Winter, too. *Fine. I can improvise.*

I walked backwards towards the nearest patch of trees, not missing a step, then shot magic at the draping tree branch over my head. It spun in the air, turning to a spear-sharp point, and I grabbed it one-handed, hurling it at the oncoming hellhound. The spear struck it in the head, causing its huge body to collapse.

Cedar spun around to look for the third one. It'd disappeared as though into thin air. *Huh?*

Wait. Hellhounds *could* do a weird disappearing trick— and here, where Winter magic was stronger than ever, it'd be even more effective.

I took one step in Cedar's direction and the hellhound appeared on top of me—literally. I fell beneath its furred body, gasping in pain as its weight cracked my ribs underneath my armour. Coughing, struggling for breath, I rolled to the side, trying to push it off me. Its teeth tangled in my hair, its drool making hissing noises when it connected with my armour. With my hands pinned, I could only direct my magic at the ground.

The surface froze when my magic hit the earth, turning it to ice. The hellhound skidded, its weight momentarily lifting to allow me to slide out from underneath it. Gasping, I came upright, an excruciating pain in my ribs. I lunged for the tree-spear and stabbed the beast in the eye. The hellhound collapsed onto its front, dead.

"Crap." I dropped the branch and doubled over in pain. "Ow."

"Raine!" Cedar ran to my side, crouching down to help me up.

"I think my rib's broken," I coughed. The hellhound had cut my hand up, too, and the wound glowed… green. *Oh, no.* Hellhound drool was as toxic to half-bloods as it was to humans.

"The hellhound's drool got into your wound," he said.

"Really. I had no idea." I tried to straighten upright but fell to my knees on the ice I'd created, gliding ungracefully to a stop at Cedar's feet. "I need a faerie healer—witch spells and human hospitals aren't designed with us in mind." I leaned on Cedar to get to my feet. "We'll have to go back to Faerie."

4

I looked up at Cedar, whose expression was grim. "Wait. I don't suppose there are any Sidhe to hitch a ride with?"

Going from Faerie into the mortal realm was relatively easy. Getting back, though, required standing in the middle of a field in the rain and waiting for one of the Little People to show up. Walking miles outside town with these injuries would be impossible. And with hellhounds still stalking us, the odds of us escaping disappeared by the second.

"No, but I know a shortcut." Cedar took my hand and pulled me after him. The party had well and truly ended, and faeries ran screaming in all directions. Fuzziness crept in at the edges of my vision, blurring the chaos around us.

We ran, dodging the crowds—or rather, Cedar ran, and I fought the shakiness in my limbs and stumbled after him. Rather than going out the gate, he aimed for the hedge. Before I could ask if he intended to walk into it, he raised a hand and the hedge parted, letting us through. *Hope nobody saw him use Summer magic.* Not that the crowd would have noticed, because they'd split in a frenzy of panic. Screams, and the sound of magic colliding, rent the air like fireworks. Trees fell, smaller fae disappeared beneath trampling feet, and shrieks of delight came from a few stray redcaps who hadn't been allowed in. They loved any kind of carnage.

We ran around the outskirts of half-blood territory, alongside the hedges. At the end, trees blocked the path.

"Nobody goes into that forest," I told him. "Not if they want to walk out alive, anyway." Rumours whispered that a clan of witches lived in the centre, and dark fae inhabited the rest.

"We're not going that far in."

He directed the trees to part and let us through, and darkness closed over us.

He might be taking you into a trap, came an unwelcome voice in my head. With my vision blurred and my limbs slowly giving up on me, I couldn't be in a worse position if I'd tried. Add in the darkness and the crowding undergrowth, and I might as well have wandered into the forest alone on someone else's territory. Rustling and yowling noises suggested a mix of Summer and Winter faeries.

"Here." He indicated a gap between trees, where a house was nestled. "We need assistance. Please—"

"What the devil is going on out there?" A bearded man appeared from the shadows—a Little Person, but not like the ones I'd met in Faerie. His beard was made entirely of moss, as was his straggling shoulder-length hair, and his face was moon-pale.

"Hellhounds," Cedar told him. "Attacking the solstice celebrations."

The Little Person's gaze fell on the crescent moon mark on my jaw. "Her."

"Don't tell a soul," said Cedar. "The hounds are after us."

"I heard them," he said. "The rift is supposed to be for emergencies only, Hornbeam."

"She's dying. We need to leave this realm, now."

"Only for you, Hornbeam."

Dizziness swept through my head. White light enveloped us, and the next second, we stood on a forest path. Cedar hadn't let go of my hand. He pulled me along the path, and within seconds, warmth washed over us.

We're on Summer's territory. To be specific—the Hornbeams'.

My experiences with this part of Faerie weren't pleasant, to say the least. The Hornbeams' territory didn't look like the Summer Court, which was a riot of bright colours and flowers and sunshine. We'd landed in a thick, tangled forest, allowed to grow wild to discourage trespassers, and with virtually nothing to indicate we were on Summer's part of the borderlands and not Winter's, except maybe it was a little warmer.

"What's the Vale attacking for?" I asked. "I thought it was closed. But you knew it was coming, right?"

Cedar glanced at me, worry knotting his features. "It was. The Grey Vale isn't under the rule of a single person, it's a place where anyone who doesn't play by the rules ends up. Those hellhounds, though, they were sent by a specific individual."

"And they targeted me. They can't be after my magic, right? It's not like they can steal the talisman."

Cedar shook his head. "No, but taking you out would throw the rest of the borderlands into disarray."

"What a waste. If they wanted the talisman, or my magic, why not come and steal it themselves?"

"Because whoever sent those hellhounds wants to destroy the Courts. My own family is effectively at war with them."

Wait, what? "Why come to the mortal realm, then?" The world spun, blue fuzziness edging into the corners of my eyes. *Stay conscious, Raine.*

"Because of the solstice. I suspected they'd make a move against the Courts, but I didn't expect them to target an event with so many faeries present."

I groaned, fingers digging into his palm in an effort to stay awake.

"Hold on, Raine," Cedar said. "We're close to your territory—" he cut off in a hiss of pain. "If you manage not to break my fingers."

"Sorry." I grinned at him, suddenly finding this whole situation absurdly funny for some reason. Possibly because of the effects of the toxic hellhound drool. "This is a really crap end to our date."

"Raine!" Viola's voice drifted through the trees, and she appeared edged in blue, before I fell down...

———

The next second, I lay on soft blankets on a bed the size of a bouncy castle, and just as springy. Not that I felt much like jumping. The room spun in gold-plated circles before settling the right way up. My mouth tasted like I'd washed it out with pond water.

Opposite me stood Viola, tall and thin with curly black hair and angular, pretty features. Her pet sprite, Volt, hovered above her head, a semi-transparent creature made of blue light.

"Viola." I lifted my head feebly. "Hi. Guess who nearly died again?"

"A *hellhound?*" she said. "How'd you manage to find one of those in the mortal realm?"

"Three of them attacked Winter's ball," I told her. "They're not the first ones I've met... Cedar mentioned—wait, where is he?"

"He left. Said he had to report to Lord Hornbeam."

"Guess he's required to mention we ran into trouble." I sat up to properly examine my hand. A jagged line indicated where I'd been bitten, but the wound had sealed.

"You've been unconscious for a while," she said. "I brought you inside. It's nearly five in the morning."

"It was daytime when I came here." I leaned against the mass of fluffy pillows. "Is there a way to calculate the time so I can be with my Dad at Christmas? Because every time I come here, I lose at least a day."

"I don't think so." Viola frowned. "Raine... there's a problem."

A slight tremor in her voice made me lean forward. "What happened?"

"Rumours got out that Lady Hornbeam's death wasn't an accident." She looked down. "The Courts know."

My heart sank, and my sweat-drenched limbs trembled as though I'd been hit with a dose of the poison again. "You mean they know I killed—"

"Not you specifically," she said quickly. "They knew Lady Hornbeam was dead, but news travels slowly, especially from out here. Lord Hornbeam apparently discouraged rumours. But Rose was here, and she said that more than a handful of people have guessed that the only thing that could have killed her is either one of her own people using iron against her—or an enemy Sidhe. And who's the newest person to enter the Courts?"

"Shit." I flopped back onto the bed, my hands shaking. "Please don't tell me they blame me for Lady Darkwater, too. Because her death happened the same day."

"It did," said Viola, "but the only witnesses were from the Hornbeam Family. Nobody from what's left of the Darkwaters would dare challenge them. However, Lord Hornbeam would have good reason to want you off the playing field."

"No kidding," I said. "I'm *not* playing with the Sidhe again.

I'm done. Retired. As for the Court, I think I'd rather have a second round with the hellhound than set foot there."

"They haven't summoned you yet," she said. "But if they do, they don't take no for an answer."

"Awesome." I heaved a sigh. I should have known that murdering Lady Hornbeam, even by accident, was bound to have consequences. But Sidhe's bodies were consumed in magic after they died, effectively removing the evidence. Viola and Cedar had been the only witnesses, and neither of them would have told Lord Hornbeam the truth. *Or maybe he would. After all, vows make it impossible to say no.*

Volt the sprite settled on my head and patted my hair. Possibly, it was meant as a comforting gesture.

I looked at the ceiling. "Cedar already said Lord Hornbeam wants to see me, but he hasn't issued a formal invitation. Guess I can expect one of those soon." And say goodbye, possibly permanently, to my budding friendship—of sorts— with Cedar. If he really had betrayed me to Lord Hornbeam, he wasn't worth my time, but was there any area of my life the Sidhe hadn't tried to ruin?

"Maybe." Her eyes were wide, anxious. "I'm not sure if they make exceptions in the case of self-defence. Sidhe shouldn't even be able to die. I don't know how much the Courts know about *that* yet. It won't change the punishment, though."

"Death or exile." I grimaced. "Maybe both."

"Exile means death anyway, unless you go back into the mortal realm. They probably won't let you, though."

"Nope. It'll be a one-way ticket to the Grey Vale." I sat up properly, dislodging Volt, who flew away with an aggrieved buzzing noise. "That's where the hellhounds came from. Someone sent them to target me. Did Rose mention her family's at war with the Vale outcasts? Because that's what Cedar told me."

"She said there'd been a few incidents, but Lord Hornbeam's keeping it quiet. She didn't use the word *war*, though." She ran her teeth over her lower lip. "I didn't realise they'd go to the mortal realm, too."

"Why do *they* want me dead? I know I pissed off the Courts, but the Vale? Or is it because they wanted to join the 'let's kill Raine' club?" I rolled my eyes at the ceiling. "If anything, I'd expect them to want me as an ally. My talisman's insanely strong and possibly evil. So are they."

"Vale faeries don't have magic," said Viola. "They *shouldn't*, anyway. It's stripped from them before being exiled. Of course, the only ones who survive exile do so by stealing magic from others."

"Which is illegal here," I added. "So how did Lady Hornbeam get away with it?"

"I have no idea." The corners of her mouth tugged down. "It's not like the Courts came inspecting. Otherwise they'd know what your mother could do. It might be that they do, of course. Most rules aren't enforced. Like everyone knows the Sidhe aren't *allowed* to capture humans. They never have been."

"But they do it anyway," I muttered, my mind on the Grey Vale, and the beasts that'd attacked us. A year ago, an army from the Vale had attacked the mortal realm for the second time and almost wiped us out. Dad and I had hidden in a safe house, and dozens of half-bloods had died. If the same happened again, how many more would suffer? Was the mortal realm on the brink of another attack?

"Why does nobody in Faerie talk about the Vale, anyway?" I asked. "It's pretty well known in the mortal realm."

"Because we don't speak of exiles. It's seen as bad luck— or the Sidhe think so, anyway," said Viola. Above her head, Volt buzzed in agreement. "Besides, as far as I last heard, the path between there and the mortal realm is supposed to be closed. So either it opened again, somehow, or the Vale beasts were already there, in the mortal realm. I wasn't there, so I wouldn't know."

"I didn't see where the hellhounds came from," I admitted.

"Because you were too busy dancing with Cedar?" She winked.

I groaned. She'd been trying to poke me into pursuing him for weeks. We'd had a… moment, or two, during our stint on Hornbeam territory, but had hardly had any time alone together at all. Not enough to discern whether he'd actually been interested in me, or just wanted my talisman.

"Was that a yes?" she asked.

"No. I mean, we danced, but it wasn't anything special. And then the hellhounds showed up. As far as dates go, I've had better."

"But you did call it a date."

"He's Lady Hornbeam's son."

Her brow crinkled. "I didn't think it mattered."

I shrugged. Court allegiance didn't matter. Belonging to an enemy family who wanted me dead did. "Would you say the same if he's the one who takes me to my death in Summer?"

"That won't happen," she said, her voice steely. "We'll stop them first."

"Your vow to my family doesn't obligate you to jump off a cliff for me," I told her. "Seriously."

Her mouth twitched. "If you died, your sister June would be my new master. I'd rather avoid that, to be honest."

She laughed as I swatted at her.

"Yeah, all right," I relented. "She was a piece of work. Wonder where she is now."

"Probably not arguing about the ethics of dating someone from the Summer Court."

"You really won't quit." I groaned. "You're supposed to tell me *not* to let an untrustworthy member of the enemy's Court into our palace."

"I think you're the one who's supposed to give *me* orders." She grinned.

"What, my mother didn't ask you to let any of her lovers from the enemy Court inside?"

"Actually—"

"Nope," I said. "You know what, I don't want to know. She was my mother, and that's creepy even if she *was* a centuries'-old Sidhe."

Viola laughed. "You do make the palace more exciting."

"Yeah, maybe. Am I ever going to get to meet Rose? She's never here when I'm around."

"That's because you're rarely here," said Viola. "Maybe you should go back to the mortal realm while all this blows over."

"That was the plan. I owe Dad a Christmas visit, even if…" *Even if I have to erase his memory. Just like mum did.*

A lump grew in my throat and I blinked rapidly. "Even if I can't stay long," I finished.

Viola looked at me curiously but didn't comment. "Okay. Let me know when you're leaving. I had to throw away your clothes, by the way. The hellhound drool ate holes in them."

"Yay."

When she left, I climbed out of bed and headed for the shower to wash off the smell of the hellhound.

My suite here was ridiculous. An over-sized four-poster bed draped in silver-leaf-patterned curtains took up half the room. Thick cream-coloured carpet blanketed the floor, covered in fitted wooden furniture in honey-coloured tones including a wardrobe containing whole outfits magically fitted to my size. The en-suite bathroom had surprisingly modern fixtures considering electricity wasn't a thing here in Faerie. Enchanted glowing stones fitted into the walls provided enough light, while I hadn't the faintest idea how the plumbing worked.

More than once, it'd occurred to me that whoever had designed this palace had borrowed elements from the mortal realm, or at least the part of it I lived in. Not that I'd ever set foot in a palace in that realm, so I had no point of comparison. In any case, the water was warm, my clothes were dry, and I didn't at all feel like I'd nearly died last night.

Once I'd changed, I left my room. The palace was a maze by design, only navigable because of my magic. I'd just point at the wall and open a door wherever I liked. Countless rooms provided accommodation for an entire assembly of guests, but I hadn't invited any visitors aside from Rose and Cedar, who weren't technically supposed to be here anyway. Still, I got to make the territory's rules. Not my mother. Even though I had yet to figure out how to remove the spell that kept a bunch of people imprisoned in the form of ice statues in the entrance hall.

"Raine!" Viola called. "Someone's at the door."

Did something else happen? I'd opened a door into the entrance hall, so I walked through, my steps echoing on the polished floor. Another knock came from in front.

Cedar began to speak before I'd fully opened the door. "Lord Hornbeam wants to see you," he said. "Immediately."

5

So much for going home. I frowned at Cedar. He looked like he hadn't slept all night, and his greyish-white complexion didn't help the shadows under his eyes. "What happened to you?"

"Nothing," he said. "Lord Hornbeam requires your presence. He suggests you get a move on."

He moved stiffly aside as I followed him out into the courtyard. Viola appeared behind me. "What—?"

"Lord Hornbeam," I told her. "You don't have to come. In fact, it's probably best if you stay here. I won't be long."

"No," said Viola. "Don't. You *know* how dangerous it is."

"I wouldn't ignore a summons from Lord Hornbeam," said Cedar. "He's not as formidable as his wife was, but he has ways to make you present yourself before him which will make you wish you'd obeyed him from the start."

"Tell him he can bite me," I said. "I don't suppose you planned to tell me the Seelie Court suspect I killed—"

"That's what he wishes to speak with you about," said Cedar. "He also told me the Court would be interested to hear if you fail to show up for a meeting."

My blood went cold. "That sounds like a threat."

"Lord Hornbeam doesn't do things halfway," said Viola, looking distraught.

"I thought he was the harmless one, compared to his wife."

"Comparing which Sidhe are the least dangerous is like comparing which swords are the least sharp," said Cedar. "It doesn't mean you can't cut yourself on them. And you committed a crime, in his eyes, even if you likely saved him from being another of her victims."

"He handed his magic to her," I said. "Fine. I won't be afraid of someone who ran from a fight." Never mind that I'd run from plenty myself, and I'd rather go back to sleep than walk into enemy territory with someone who'd deceived me *again*. He was a tool of the Hornbeams. When would I learn?

Before leaving, I used magic to turn my clothes into the same armoured gear I usually wore in Faerie—dark coloured, thick yet flexible material designed to hide my Court, protect my body and allow for maximal movement. I used to feel naked not carrying iron, but after the boost my magic had received in the mortal realm, my skin still hummed and a faint blue glow surrounded me. The Summer faeries would know who I was. Maybe I wanted them to.

Cedar gave me an approving look, which I ignored.

Finally, I took the sceptre from my pocket, though it was pretty much only a prop. It'd look weird for a Sidhe not to carry a talisman, even if it wasn't the source of my magic.

"All right," I said. "Let's go and speak to Lord Hornbeam. Viola, I'll see you in a bit, okay?"

"Sure," she said, with a cheery wave. "Don't die!"

"Don't jinx it," I told her, putting on my brave face. I was an equal to the Sidhe, and I'd be damned if I let Lord Hornbeam intimidate me. *At least Lady Hornbeam isn't there.*

"So," I said to Cedar as we walked into the forest. "What does he want?"

"He wants me to invite you to speak with him about recent events."

Meaning the part where I killed his wife. We hadn't left my territory yet, but I glanced around in case anyone was listening in. Nobody came near the palace anymore—the stormy aftermath of the magic I'd used fighting against Lady Hornbeam saw to that—but if I'd been called back onto enemy territory, it was a safe bet people here still wanted me dead.

Like the prince of the Hornbeam family, Aspen, for instance. He'd be the likely heir, as Lady Hornbeam's son. Then again, so was Cedar, and he'd never mentioned it. She'd showed no more affection towards him than she did towards her other soldiers.

Cedar seemed tenser than he had in the mortal realm, like he didn't feel safe even on his own territory. I didn't know why it bothered me so much that he walked stiffly, as though hiding some kind of injury. Lady Hornbeam hadn't exactly treated him kindly, from what I'd gathered.

"Come on," I said, recognising the shift when we passed onto his territory as my magic faded slightly. I could use magic anywhere, but could only rearrange the paths on my own territory. The forest didn't *look* any different, though— the borderland part of Faerie was pretty uniform no matter where you stood. "You might at least tell me what I should prepare for. What kind of magic does Lord Hornbeam prefer?"

"Lord Hornbeam is a strategist, more than a fighter," he said. "When it came to brute force—and magic—his wife could easily best him. But he's used to avoiding trouble. That the Vale's beasts keep appearing and attacking people on our territory is an annoyance that will be paid in blood."

"I don't understand what that has to do with *me*. I'd have thought he'd be happy she died."

He gave a short laugh. "If he was unhappy, you wouldn't have got away for as long as you did. Lord Hornbeam wishes to ask for an arrangement with you, of some kind. I can't say I know what, but he doesn't want to kill you. Otherwise, he'd challenge you directly."

"Really. He seemed pretty cowardly to me. Running away from his own wife."

"Not cowardly as much as practical. He never could have beat her. She was…" He paused.

"Power-crazy?"

"Yes. And dangerous even to the Sidhe."

"Because her moral compass broke a few centuries ago. Cedar… *why* do you still work for the Hornbeams? Couldn't you just walk away?"

"No," he said. "To be free of the Courts is to be an exile. The only alternative is living in the mortal realm. This is my home. Thieving and spying are what I'm best at, and from what I can tell, the humans approve of neither of those things."

Dammit, Cedar. I'd been all set to put him back in the "enemy" camp, and then he'd gone and made me feel sorry for him again. I might have fallen into this world by accident, but I'd been lucky to be given a position of relative freedom. Even if people did want me dead for it. His resignation to being bound to the Hornbeams forever was a different story.

Instead of responding directly, I said, "Someone hurt you, didn't they? You're limping."

"No," he said, unconvincingly.

"I thought you didn't lie."

"I don't like to," he said. "I did tell you my territory was effectively at war with the Vale. A rogue troll attacked me when I was patrolling last night."

"So iron wasn't involved? Lord Hornbeam isn't taking a leaf out of his wife's book and torturing his own people?"

"Don't say a word to him," he said. "Your own freedom is hanging by a thread. I don't think you know what death at the hands of the Seelie Court would be like. It'd be worse than anything the families might dream up."

I closed my mouth before I said something Lord Hornbeam might overhear. He must surely know what my magic could do. Maybe he wanted an alliance, or to recruit me. He couldn't bind me with a vow, so all he could do was threaten me. *I won't submit to him. Never.*

Cedar slowed when we reached a fence made of gold thread entwined like barbed wire. Leaves grew on the wire, which shouldn't make sense, but this was Faerie. Behind the fence were rows of carefully cultivated flowers in dark shades. Apparently Lord Hornbeam liked gardening. This area had been entirely empty when I'd last come here.

When Cedar and I had been forced to fight to the death.

I clenched my hands to stop them shaking.

Rows of plants that didn't exist in the mortal realm exuded an eye-watering stench, and not a particularly pleasant one. I blinked, my eyes stinging. "What's that for? If you stuck that on your arrows, the enemy would run for miles."

Cedar didn't laugh. "The plants are for a certain purpose."

"Hmm." The smell caught in my throat and made me cough, and I clenched my teeth to keep from having a choking fit in front of the guards. Two armour-wearing female faeries stood outside the gate, each with a crossbow strapped to her back.

"Thief," one of them said tonelessly, her hand clenched at her side. The other gave Cedar a wary look. *They're scared of him.* According to Viola, the thief had been a legend before he'd been exposed publicly by Lady Hornbeam, and forced to do battle with me in a public arena.

"I'm escorting Lady Whitefall to speak to Lord Hornbeam," Cedar told the guards.

"He said you were," remarked the woman on the right. "Doesn't look like much, does she?"

I narrowed my eyes at her, keeping a firm grip on the talisman as I followed Cedar through the gates. A path flanked by drooping plants led to the golden palace I hadn't got a close look at before.

Wait. The smell… it *was* familiar. It'd been there when I'd touched a poisoned arrow at the Gathering, shot by a Darkwater assassin actually working for the Hornbeam Family.

Was Lord Hornbeam responsible?

I'd guess *yes,* just to avoid being disappointed later. I dug my hands into my pockets, retrieving my thick gloves and putting them on in case anything else was covered in poison. This wasn't the time or place to take chances. Cedar gave me a sideways look of acknowledgement, but didn't speak.

I'd thought my own ice palace was huge, but the golden monstrosity in front of me appeared even larger. Its walls were polished to a dazzling sheen, reflecting the forest back at me as we approached. Wide golden doors opened to allow us through. Inside, two small bark-skinned creatures bowed and ducked aside to let us pass. Brownies. They must be servants of the family.

Our footsteps echoed against the polished floor. The inside of the palace was marble twined with gold, more like pictures I'd seen of human establishments than I'd expect from the Summer Court. Everything I'd heard about Summer told me their magic was to do with making plants grow, and that the energy of living things sustained it. This palace was a facade with nothing living inside it at all. Except…

A door materialised on my right. Cedar tensed, then turned in that direction, dipping his head. "My lord."

The golden-plated walls paled in comparison to the person inside the room. Even if I hadn't seen Lord Hornbeam before, I'd know him for one of the Sidhe in an instant. They simply weren't made of the same stuff as the rest of us. The world—or at least their territory—literally revolved around them. Sidhe magic was strong enough to fracture mortal minds if you looked upon it too long. Impossibly bright green eyes fuelled by powerful magic shone from a face too radiant for this world, made of a material other than skin and flesh and bone. My breath stopped, my gloved hands clenched the talisman, and instinct told me to bow my head in the same gesture of respect as Cedar had.

I didn't. Whatever he wanted to see me for, we were equals as heads of our respective families—however much he and his wife had openly loathed me for daring to bring my mortal taint to their level. He should blame my mother instead, for not naming a pure-blooded heir.

Silence reigned, thick and humming with power. The Sidhe had a sort of contained glamour that altered depending on who looked upon them. I didn't know what they looked like to one another, but any mortal who looked at them saw an approximation of what frightened or awed them the most. Half-bloods were a world apart from humans, but Sidhe—they were a whole *planet* away from the rest of us.

Or so their magic wanted us to believe. In reality, they were just overpowered immortals with a god complex, and I'd already proved they weren't as unbreakable as they pretended to be. If they were, none of us would be here in this room.

"Lord Hornbeam." I broke the silence first. "To what do I owe the pleasure?"

"Half-blood," he intoned, his gaze sliding from me as though I wasn't worthy to look at. "I see you came without a fight. That makes matters much easier."

"Probably because I had no choice," I said through gritted teeth. I sensed Cedar's eyes on me, but didn't look away from the formidable figure in front of me. He wore gold and black armour, closely fitted, but too polished to have been in a fight lately.

"You should be more careful when you speak to me." His words were slow and edged with menace. But my own magic wrapped around me like a comforting presence. I drew in a breath.

"What exactly is it you wished to discuss with me?" I asked.

"Your attitude, for a start," he said. His voice was lovely, like a melody, soft and enticing. But all Sidhe sounded like that. Everything about them was designed to convince you of their absolute power. His wife had let me believe that up until the second I'd realised I *could* overpower her.

"You threatened to report me to the Summer Court. If you expect me to worship you after that, you're mistaken."

"One would think you'd be more inclined to avoid such a fate." He tilted his head. "I didn't get the chance to have your full measure before, and after the incident at the Gathering, I certainly didn't expect my wife to see fit to put you under the full test of her power. She was powerful, but terribly flawed. She saw everything through her ego, and that cost her. Unfortunately, your actions have put me in a dilemma. I'm sure you know what it looks like. A Sidhe perishes at the hands of a half-blood with no true knowledge of our realm. I have to handle the situation in an appropriate manner."

"Then get on with it," I said. "Challenge me. You might as well, if you're so convinced people are going to call your family weak for losing their leader to a half-blood."

Despite what Cedar had said about him being a strategist, I half expected him to order me to fight him there and then. Instead, he shook his head. "There should be no more faerie deaths in the borderlands. Certainly not while so many enemies threaten us from the outside. I never agreed with my wife's methods, and her habit of hoarding the talismans of others made her vulnerable in the end."

I blinked at him. "You're not going to kill me?"

"I have no plans to at the present moment. However, don't underestimate my power nor my position, Miss Whitefall."

"Lady," I said.

My breath stopped as he unleashed his formidable Sidhe stare on me again.

"Call me by my proper title," I said to him.

"You're playing with dangerous forces, you foolish human child," he said. "It's clear my wife's death was an accident, whatever your intentions were. That's the only reason I have spared your life so far."

"Look, you didn't even like her, did you?"

"Do humans normally ask total strangers such personal questions?"

"No, but I'm not one. And she tried to kill me. Does the Court know that?"

His mouth twisted. "There could be evidence from a hundred people that you were attacked and defended yourself. The family heads themselves could argue in your favour. You could have intangible proof—and you would still be executed for your crime, because the murder of a pure Sidhe by a half-blood is unforgivable no matter the circumstances."

My throat went dry, my pulse racing. "She killed Sidhe herself."

"Can anyone prove that?"

"Isn't there a single person who'd testify against her? She's dead. She can't punish them. Even vows don't work if the person asking for the favour has died."

"You do understand some of our ways," he mused. "You were raised in a barbarian environment, so I suppose your lack of social graces can be excused somewhat."

"Barbarian?" I glared at him. "You don't know the first thing about humans, or half-bloods. You care for nobody but yourself."

"I've met enough of you."

"You mean kidnapped and threw people in cages."

All the air seemed to leave the room as though a thousand people had sucked in a breath at once—even though the only people here were me and Cedar, and he hadn't made a sound.

Lord Hornbeam tilted his head on one side again. "You care for the mortals?"

Ah, hell. I'd walked right into that one.

"Nobody in particular. Just pointing out why I don't trust you not to attack me, whatever you promise. What exactly do you want from me?"

A moment passed while he studied me with those impossible green eyes. "I was curious about the death of your mother for quite some time. As her body was consumed by her own magic at the time of death, it was impossible to verify the cause. The body of a chimera was found not ten feet away, injured by the weapon she was carrying, so the Courts' official report is that the beast killed her. I think there's more to her death than that."

I waited in silence, not taking the bait. How did he know more than me about the circumstances of my own mother's death, when it hadn't even been on his territory?

"Well?" he said.

"Well what? I wasn't here. I don't know any more than you do."

"My thief informs me that you're investigating the matter."

Dammit, Cedar.

"Obviously I'm curious," I said. "She was my mother. I never knew her."

"But you *did* know that she left her talisman behind, along with most of her power, the day she died."

He knew that? I supposed it wasn't hard to guess. After all, if she'd taken her talisman with her when she'd died, someone else would have ripped it from her hands before her body was cold. Then again, if she'd had the talisman, she'd have been more than a match for a chimera. Assuming that was her actual cause of death. With no body, nothing was certain. But none of this was Lord Hornbeam's business. At all.

"Obviously," I told him. "That's why I inherited it. But I'm not a Sidhe, and you probably know more than I do about who would have had a motive to take her life. If it wasn't an accident."

"Perhaps I do," he said, "but your magic gives you access to avenues the rest of us are unable to penetrate. I'd advise you to apply yourself to the matter."

"You want to know how and why she died? Just... out of curiosity?"

"Yes," he said. "I do. Things might get uncomfortable for you if you fail to bring me information."

And there was the threat. "I don't understand what it is to you. She's not the only Sidhe to have died."

"She isn't," said Lord Hornbeam. "She *is,* however, the first of the Sidhe to die and remain dead, without being exiled."

I feigned ignorance. "You just mean the border families, right? Sidhe in the Courts have died before."

"Not frequently," he said. "As to the border families, no,

she wasn't the first to die. But she did not return. The natural order of things has broken, and for the survival of us all, I would dearly love to know the truth."

"Wouldn't we all." Typical. Like his wife, he was scared of dying. Okay, he'd lived for over a thousand years, but if anything, that ought to make him less afraid of his eventual end. Maybe I just didn't understand the Sidhe, but neither did I understand what I could possibly do to find out why the Sidhe could die now. I wasn't one.

"I'd advise you to check your manner of speaking, Raine," he said softly. "The Sidhe of the Summer Court will not forget your crimes, if they find out. Word travels quickly."

Damn him. He had me backed into a corner.

"All right," I said. "I'll carry on investigating."

"Report to me in three days," he told me. "I'll trust you'll have more information by then."

I can't make any promises. But the threat was clear. I'd have to drag up some information, or face being exiled to the very realm which had attacked me last night.

"Take her home," he told Cedar.

"Yes, Lord Hornbeam."

6

I strode out of the room, fuming. "He can't *do* that," I
hissed to Cedar. "It's none of his fucking business who
killed my mum."

Cedar put a hand on my arm, a warning to be quiet. Oh,
right. Mr Creepy Omnipresent Sidhe might be listening in.

An arrow zipped past me, clipping my arm. Iron's presence cut through the humming sensation from the palace
combined with the heady rush from boosting my magic. The
arrow had barely nicked the skin, but my heart thundered.

I dodged another arrow which skimmed through the air,
whistling past my ear. All the Hornbeam soldiers used iron
arrows, a weapon that was supposed to be considered an
insult to the Sidhe, and deadly to all faeries. I didn't know if
they were shooting to kill or just to give a warning, but I
refused to be cowed.

Two arrows struck the ground on either side of me.
Worry for Cedar made me spin around, but he'd stepped
aside, narrowly missing being hit himself. Either they didn't
care if they struck him, or they knew he was fast enough to
get out of the way.

More arrows embedded themselves in the ground, where they remained, protruding like bristling spikes in precise patterns. The archers apparently had an infinite supply, and loaded their bows with fast, deadly precision. Rows of arrows circled me, boxing me into the small space remaining in the middle of the wooden floor. Fury jolted through me and I raised the sceptre high, though I couldn't transform iron, nor the palace that was fuelled by the enemy's magic.

Blue light covered me, transforming my already armoured clothes into a thicker, untouchable material. Maybe even strong enough to repel iron. I looked up at the lead archer. "Do your worst."

The last arrow left its bow, aiming at my heart.

I kept very still, holding my sceptre as a shield. At the last possible second, the arrow veered to the side, landing behind the closest circle.

I stepped forwards and kicked it.

As though on cue, the arrow fell into its neighbour, creating a whirling domino effect which spiralled through the endless circles, toppling each arrow in perfect sync. The rattling seemed to take an age. There were hundreds of them.

I stood rigid in the centre, surrounded by fallen arrows.

"I'm disappointed," a voice remarked. "I didn't know you were so easy to back into a corner, *Lady* Whitefall."

I knew that voice. It belonged to a half-Sidhe man with curly black hair, bright green eyes like his mother's had been, and a cruel smile. He waved a hand, and the archers dispersed, leaving us alone. Aspen Hornbeam was a prick of the highest order, as well as being the heir to his stepfather's throne now his mother was dead. He'd tried to kill me with iron once already, as a test.

This wasn't a test, it was a show of intimidation. His archers might have killed me at any moment. He knew it. They knew it, too.

I gave him the finger.

He hadn't grown up in the mortal realm so he probably didn't understand the gesture, but my body language made it clear I was insulting him. I wanted to rip his smirking face off, but as far as I knew, he was Lord Hornbeam's favourite. Fighting him wouldn't end well for any of us.

"You filthy mortal," he said quietly. "My stepfather should never have given you the chance to live. You're a murderess. A Sidhe killer."

"It's not my problem that you Hornbeams die so easily."

He inhaled sharply. "You will pay for those words with your life."

"Aspen," said Lord Hornbeam from behind me. "Leave her. She has a task, and will fulfil it."

"Yes, my Lord." There was a surprising amount of derision in his tone. Lord Hornbeam must really like him to allow him to speak to a Sidhe in that manner. Aspen gave me a mocking bow, turned his back and walked out. The floor shifted under my feet, and all the arrows slid to the back as though dragged by an invisible force, leaving the path to the door clear.

Bloody faerie magic.

"Thief," Lord Hornbeam said to Cedar. "Kindly escort her home."

Cedar moved to my side and we left the palace in silence. Fury buzzed through me. I didn't realise we were being followed until someone caught my arm—a young female half-faerie with medium brown skin and curly hair. "I'm Rose," she whispered. "Can you let Viola know I can't see her tomorrow?" She passed me a note.

"Sure," I told her, and then she was gone. *Those two are playing with fire.* And I thought I was pushing my luck with Lord Hornbeam.

Cedar raised his eyebrows at me, but didn't comment.

Once we'd passed by the crossbow-wielding guards at the palace gates, I stormed ahead into the forest.

"That's all it was?" I exploded. "A test? Lord Hornbeam's as bad as she was, and now he's as good as chained me to a vow."

As though I'd have more of a chance of finding information on my mother with a threat hanging over my head. It couldn't be more obvious that she hadn't wanted anyone to know how, and why, she'd died. Even her own daughter.

"He wouldn't have let Aspen kill you," said Cedar.

"I'd rather not take your word for it, thanks."

"I'm sorry," he said quietly.

I didn't answer. Incensed, I continued to walk at a swift pace, but he easily kept up with me. If not for a twist of fate, he'd have been amongst those archers, under orders to intimidate me. I had no idea why Lord Hornbeam had assigned him to watch me. It didn't seem a regular job for a thief. *Well, he's also a spy.*

Once we were safely out of sight of the palace, I turned to him. "So he wants to know why my mother died," I said. "He'll have to get in line, because I haven't a clue. But it makes no sense for him to be so interested. Sure, I'd like to know, but she was my mother. She's nothing to him."

Cedar walked alongside me, his hands in his pockets. "Like he said, she's the first Sidhe to die and not be reborn. I suspect he wishes to know why."

"Surely the Courts know," I said. "If anyone should, it's them."

"That's just it. I actually don't think they do," said Cedar. "If they did, they wouldn't want their own people to go extinct. Even the borderland Sidhe..."

"Extinct?" I echoed. "That's a little overdramatic, isn't it? Sidhe can have children. I think the number of half-bloods in the mortal realm proves that."

"Actually…" He paused. "I can't say I know for certain, but I think the chance of two pure Sidhe having a child is very low. Much lower than, say, a Sidhe and a mortal."

I twisted my head to look at him. "Damn. Really?"

"Everyone knows Lord Hornbeam was unfaithful to his wife, and she to him, but common gossip is that they were unable to have a pure-blood child."

"Oh." That explained why they'd had no pure faerie heir, when they'd both lived for over a thousand years. And—*oh.* Maybe Lady Hornbeam's desperation to find a way to stave off death wasn't so irrational after all. After all, if the only alternative was naming a half-blood as heir or someone from another family—it was understandable. Didn't mean she had to murder people, though.

"Exactly," said Cedar. "I don't know how many children there are in the Courts, but there can't be many. Half-bloods and quarter-blooded faeries don't seem to have the same issue, but pure-bloods—if it's true, and they can all die now, they might drive themselves to extinction."

"If the Sidhe keep murdering one another, it's their own fault." My footsteps crunched through fallen leaves as we reached the path I recognised as leading to the neutral territory where Gatherings took place. "Immortality sounds like a barrel of laughs. I don't understand why they want it so badly."

"You haven't lived it," said Cedar. "It's the natural order of things. If that order is broken—I'll bet that's why Lord Hornbeam didn't kill you. He needs you to find out the truth. Whether it was your mother's death that caused this change, or—"

"You think it's my mum's fault?" I asked. "Seriously? She just died. Without magic, unless she was hiding something else."

"It's just a theory," said Cedar. "I know less than you do. Certainly less than Lord Hornbeam does."

"So there's no pure-blooded heir at all?"

"Not currently, no." He glanced through the trees, and I spotted the place where I'd stood on a stage alone and faced down the leaders of the other families. Nobody had ordered another Gathering since the last one, but two of the Sidhe who'd been present there were no longer alive.

"Are you—wait, you're half-Sidhe. Are you a contender?" Aspen's cruel smile flashed before my eyes. He'd probably be as sadistic a ruler as his mother had been.

"Only if he dies," Cedar said. "Though, considering the rate at which the Sidhe are dropping like flies lately—"

"It's not funny, Cedar."

"No, it most certainly isn't," he said. "Aspen will most likely be chosen. He's made no secret of the fact that he dislikes me, so if Lord Hornbeam were to meet with a similar accident to his wife, I'm unlikely to be allowed to stay here."

My mouth fell open. "Are you seriously saying I'm considering arranging another 'accident'?"

"No, of course not. You didn't mean to kill her the first time."

Acid rose in my throat. "Maybe I did. She was evil incarnate. And you just wanted to use me to get information on my mother. Well, tough for both you and your Lord—I don't know anything. And now my life's on the line. Cheers."

"I didn't know he'd bring the *Court* into it. In any case, I can offer you my help. He never said I couldn't."

"You know, Cedar, that's not the most reassuring thing I've ever heard from you."

He fell silent, fiddling with his sleeve. I glanced at him. The greyish tint to his skin hadn't gone away. If anything, it'd got worse in the time since we'd been in the Court. I remembered his scars—and the band Robin had worn on his wrist.

I lunged and grabbed his arm, pushing up the sleeve. He tugged it down again, but not before I'd seen the thin, grey iron band.

He pulled his arm away from me. "We have to wear tags to show our loyalty."

I let my hand drop. "It's killing you."

"Not in a small amount. I thought you knew the Hornbeam family has a tradition of trying to reduce the effect of iron on us by ensuring every soldier carries iron weapons. This is no different."

"Of course it is," I said, unable to believe it. "Skin contact with iron—you *know* what that means. He's basically given you a death sentence."

He shook his head. "It hasn't killed me yet."

"Because this isn't the first time?" I asked. "She did it, too, right?" I looked him in the eyes, which were completely hazel —with no occasional hint of green Summer magic as I'd often seen in them before. No wonder he hadn't fought using his magic against the hellhounds.

"I'm fine. I don't have strong magic, so it has less effect on me."

"We're talking about iron. Our main weakness. You know, the thing they tell you not to touch as soon as you're old enough to understand it." I wanted to hit him in the back of the head, then rip the armband clean off. But touching it would poison me, too. "You can't seriously be telling me you enjoy being tortured on a daily basis? I saw your other scars. They were iron, too, right?"

He didn't answer. His body was taut, there was tension in every line of his features. "You don't understand the family's ways—"

"Yes, I do. Seems like a poor way to repay their loyal servants."

"Lady Hornbeam does not forgive mistakes."

"Did not," I said automatically.

"Did not," he echoed quietly.

Shit. Had part of him actually cared for her? I'd never known my mother, so I couldn't grieve her. But Lady Hornbeam—she was a monster.

Cedar grimaced. "Please don't talk to Lord Hornbeam about such things. What you said to him—if he didn't need your help, he'd have killed you for it."

"He doesn't scare me. Nor does the Court." A lie, but maybe if I said it enough times, it'd become the truth.

Cedar shook his head. "They should."

"I don't think it's productive to live in fear," I told him. "Just like it isn't productive to force your own soldiers to carry iron, of all things. Does he want there to be an heir left? Look, I live in the mortal realm. It's *covered* in iron. Doesn't make it less dangerous to us. You can't think this is right."

"In my family, there's no such thing as right or wrong," Cedar said, in a maddeningly calm tone. "Power rules, and those of us who aren't strong enough to prove our worth are punished with death. This is what I grew up with, Raine." He gestured around at the forest.

"You know it's fucked," I said. "I might not have lived here long, but what he's doing is out of line, and I'll bet the Courts wouldn't be happy to learn there's iron here in this realm at all."

"The Courts have no power over what one Sidhe does on their own territory."

"I gathered," I said. "Otherwise, Lady Hornbeam wouldn't have been allowed to get away with murder. Does nobody care that Lady Darkwater was killed, too?"

"Nobody is left on her territory," said Cedar. "Her allies were exiled, one at a time, for conspiring against the Unseelie Court."

"Exiled."

He nodded. "That is the price of your failure. I hope that neither of us will disappoint Lord Hornbeam."

And without preamble, he turned and walked away. I spun around. He'd left me right at the point where his territory met mine. Okay, then. Guess the investigation apparently wasn't urgent to him.

I crossed the boundary and waved a hand at the trees. Immediately, the path rearranged itself, leading up to the spiky gates in front of my palace. There, an eternal coating of white snow covered the ground. Viola and I had spent a few days building a colony of snow faeries, with wings made of bracken and crowns of thorn.

Viola opened the door before I reached it, Volt hovering over her head.

"Oh, thank the Sidhe. I was going to come after you."

"I wouldn't," I warned. "Lord Hornbeam and his chief dickhead aren't playing nice."

"What happened?" asked Viola. "He didn't contact the Court, did he?"

"Not exactly," I said. "Apparently he wants in on the investigation into how Lady Whitefall died. I'm supposed to keep him updated on our investigations, on pain of the Summer Court paying an unexpected visit."

"What in the name of the Sidhe does that have to do with him?" said Viola, as we went into the palace. Volt flew past, eying me worriedly. I wasn't sure if the sprite understood much of what was going on, but he belonged to Viola, and therefore to my family.

"I have no clue," I said. "He's dead set on me updating him on the investigation in three days. He got his archers to shoot arrows at me as an incentive."

Alarm flashed in her eyes. "Only three days? We'll have to figure something out before then. I don't know where exactly she died, but maybe you'll be able to find it. I know it was on one of the paths near the territory's edge…"

"I'll look for it. Oh yeah, and Rose gave me a note for you." I handed her the paper. "She also said she can't come over tomorrow."

"Hmm." She scanned the note. "Lord Hornbeam's taking a team out to the borderlands to deal with this Vale threat. Must be serious."

"That begs the question of why he's so set on me investigating a murder that has nothing to do with the Vale."

She folded the note up. "Maybe it does. She did die on the borderland path. We'd better hope there isn't anything there waiting for us."

"Very encouraging." She had a point, though. I made a mental note to check every shadow for Lord Hornbeam's arrow-firing soldiers. Or Cedar, come to that. To think I'd assumed Lord Hornbeam wouldn't be as harsh on him as his late wife was.

I shoved the thought out of mind. Some people couldn't be helped. My own sense of protectiveness towards Cedar after what we'd been through wouldn't stop him from hurling himself off a cliff if his Lord got bored. I hadn't figured out how to undo the vow binding Viola to my family, let alone undo another family's one. I'd deal with solving Lady Whitefall's murder first.

7

Before heading out again, I went into the kitchen to grab the breakfast I'd been on the way to find when Cedar had shown up. Where the food came from—whether it was real or made entirely of magic—I didn't particularly want to know. Viola had seemed confused by my explanation about how humans cooked things and had no idea what a microwave was. I shoved a piece of toast in my mouth and changed my clothes into plain, nondescript ones suitable for trekking through the woods. Viola did likewise, and we left the palace once again.

Outside the gates, I stopped. Pristine snowy forest surrounded us, with paths leading between the thick, leafless trees. Everything was coated in pure white snow you didn't see in the mortal realm. Faerie looked timeless, but it wasn't really. Not when you reached beneath the layer of magic sustaining everything. Even eternity was a lie.

"Take me to the place my mother died," I told the territory. Nothing moved, not so much as a snowflake.

"Hmm." Viola turned to examine our surroundings. "Apparently she died on the path leading out of the territory

—to the place where it ends. If we walk that way, we might find a clue."

She didn't sound particularly certain, but I shrugged and nodded. No time like the present, seeing as my life hung in the balance.

"Okay, take me to the territory's edge. The... edge of Faerie? Is the world completely flat?"

"Isn't the mortal realm?"

I stifled a laugh. "No. It's round, like a globe. You mean to say if you walk too far in Faerie, you fall off the end?"

"Not exactly," said Viola. "I found it by accident, actually, when I used the rift to come here. It's more like you keep walking one way and never reach the end. Faerie's magic stops you."

The territory did obey my command this time, the path reforming in front of us. Thick trees crowded on either side, and I hesitated before striding ahead. Faerie's creatures shouldn't attack me on my own territory, but these were the places whispered about in tales told to frighten children, tales of the thick and endless woods home to redcaps and wisps. The paths at the territory's edge linked up with Summer territory, too, and the areas where it was possible for the Sidhe to cross over into the mortal realm.

"Hang on," I said to Viola. "This part doesn't actually belong to anyone's territory, right?"

"No," she said. "The common knowledge is that it's the end of Faerie as we know it, but the paths never look exactly the same. Only three things remain constant—one end of the main path leads to Summer, one leads to Winter, and a third leads nowhere."

"That's the one you can't reach the end of?"

"We're near the path already. You brought us there."

While we'd been talking, smoke had crept around us, filling the gaps between the trees like ground-level clouds. I

walked on, frowning at the path beneath the fog. "She died…
here?"

"I can't find the exact spot, but the chimera's body ought
to have left a mark. It was a while ago, though."

I looked around. I'd expected—I didn't know what I'd
expected. Evidence that a body had lain right here, maybe.
Dried blood under the snow. Instead, only smoke remained,
swirling unnaturally. Faerie's weather was somewhat
predictable—sun and clear skies in Summer, snow or
freezing rain in Winter. Fog tended to signal some nasty
monster or other, but out here, it seemed to be the default
state. I crouched down on the path to better search, but time
would have washed away any traces, if there'd been any.
Straightening up, I damn near head-butted a man who'd
popped out of the fog. The Little Person jumped away
from me.

"Sorry," I said. "You surprised me."

"You are looking for answers," he said.

"Yeah." I gave Viola an uncertain look. She trusted the
Little People a lot more than I did. Generally, nameless,
ageless people who lurked in the fog around murder sites
didn't land on my top list of trustworthy people.

"You heard us?" she asked.

He bowed his head. "Yes. Such a tragedy that she was
taken from us all. It's a terrible thing to lose a Sidhe… let
alone several."

A chill broke out on my arms. "What are you saying?"

"I am saying that the answers you find might not be to
your liking."

"Does that mean you know?"

He shook his head. "No. I did not witness your mother's
death, but I felt the aftermath. Dark things crawled from the
shadows, whispers rose in the trees. The Little People cannot
die, no more than the Sidhe can. But if it's true, and we pass

into the place mortals go, never to return—then I would very much like to know why that is."

"That's… sort of what we're looking for," I said. "But we need to find out why my mother died in the first place. I know it happened here, but parts of the story don't make sense. Might the other Little People know? You all live somewhere out here, right? In the borderlands."

"No," he said. "Most of us live in the liminal spaces between this realm and the mortal realm, in the thin layers where whispers travel from the other side. However, it's possible one of them might have seen what transpired when your mother left this world behind."

"And can you take us there?"

"I can."

I waited. *Oh. Faeries take everything literally.* "Will you? I don't know this part of the forest."

"Nobody does," he said, setting off at a jog. I gave Viola a bewildered look, and she shrugged and followed him.

"The whispers say 'he rides no more'," the Little Person said over his shoulder. "I cannot say I know the meaning. But if it is what I suspect, we are all in more danger than any of you know."

"He's great at pep talks, isn't he?" I muttered to Viola.

We kept walking until fog reached our waists like thick, soupy water. The Little Person stopped abruptly outside a house nestled between two trees. There stood another Little Person—this one with a beard of moss. It was the same one who'd helped Cedar and me back to Faerie.

"Lady Whitefall," he said, bowing at me.

"Hi," I said. "Thanks for letting us through before."

Viola gave me a curious look. "I don't think we've met," she said to the Little Person.

"I am the Little Person of Hemlock Way, and I am here visiting the borderlands."

Heads popped up from behind the door, and for a moment, I was reminded of an old story my dad used to tell me. Something about seven little people... There *were* seven Little People. And every single one of them stared at me.

"What brings you here, two young mortals?" said one of them. Most were pretty much identical—short, red-skinned, and bearded, and apparently all male. Only Moss Beard had a distinctive appearance.

"Hi," I said. "My name is Raine Whitefall, and I'm here to ask if any of you witnessed the events of my mother's passing. She was killed in the borderlands, and I was told... you might... have more information." I trailed off as another of the Little People pushed past the others and lurched in my direction. His gaze was unfocused, his eyes bloodshot, and the smell of elf wine poured off him.

"You human scum," he hissed. "You shouldn't be here. We never allow mortals into our homes. You're all thieves and murderers."

Technically I *was* a thief, but bringing that up right now would not be wise. Worse, the Little Person who'd brought us here had vanished, leaving the moss-bearded one and his six companions. Three of them shuffled out behind the speaker—and they held weapons, crudely cut knives.

"Roast her!" shouted another of them.

"Skin her alive!"

I'm pretty sure this didn't happen in a human kids' story. "Guys, seriously!" I raised my hands. "I'm not going to harm anyone. I wanted to know if any of you witnessed my mother's death—"

A knife hurtled towards me. I raised my hands and magic answered my call, slicing the knife clean in half. Moss Beard shouted, "That's enough! She is an ally of mine, and you shall not attack her."

"You do have Lady Whitefall's magic," remarked the one who smelled of elf wine.

"Yeah, I do," I snapped. "Thanks for intervening *after* they threw a knife," I added to Moss Beard, as the others disappeared into the house.

"They wished to test you." He bowed his head. "Come with me."

I didn't want to follow him after the stunt his friends had pulled, but on the other hand, Cedar trusted him, and he'd saved my life last night. *Then again, I'm not sure I trust Cedar anymore.*

Moss Beard gestured ahead. The path was narrow and winding, and the thick fog obscured rotting ferns and tangled bracken.

"The person you're looking for is known as the memory-eater," he said, "and she's a formidable ancient faerie. Even the Sidhe might not dare approach her, though few know of her existence."

"I don't remember saying I was looking for anyone," I said. *Especially not your so-called allies.*

"The information you seek exists in the past, not the present. The memory-eater can read the memories of anyone who crosses her path, and she remembers every individual whose thoughts she has divined. If anyone has access to the truth about the day of your mother's death, it's her."

Damn. The alternative was kidnapping random faeries until I found someone who'd both witnessed my mother's death and was willing to tell the truth about it. Let's face it, someone who could read minds and couldn't lie was a safer bet—if I was willing to risk it.

"And she won't harm us?" I asked suspiciously. "You must know how many enemies I have."

"She might be independent of the Courts, but she respects the Sidhe, and your mother, most of all."

Moss Beard reached out and handed Viola a handful of dark red berries.

"What're they for?" I asked.

"You'll both need to eat those before you go to see the memory-eater. Her lair is in the clouds, where your mortal lungs will fail should you walk too high."

"Seriously?" I raised an eyebrow at Viola, who shrugged as though this was something she did every day.

"She does live up there," Viola said. "I wondered how people visited her."

"I'm not sure about this." Every human part of me that knew faerie tales screamed at me that this was a bad idea. "Is she really the only person who might know the truth? There must be someone else."

Moss Beard shook his head. "If even the Little People do not know, if nobody living does, either here or in the mortal realm, then she does. The past does not—cannot—lie. If anyone can find the truth, it's you, Lady Whitefall."

Hmm. Supposedly, the Sidhe didn't lie, either. And if anyone didn't want the truth found, it was my mother. But the alternative was letting my three days expire and facing torture at the hands of the Seelie Court, and leaving the fates of everyone I loved up in the air.

"Give me one reason why I should trust you," I said. "Considering what the others did."

"You are wiser than most who stray here. I mean you no harm, and you will not suffer any damage at my hands. But I would advise you not to speak to the others. They're a proud, dangerous people."

They're also my only way back into the mortal realm. Dad needed me. I had to get through this ridiculous mission if I wanted to see him again.

"All right," I said. "We'll go and speak to the memory-eater."

Viola tossed a berry into her mouth and handed me the other one.

"It's fine," she said. "I know these. They work."

And you can tell they're not poisoned? Though if she'd spent time in the Summer Court, she'd know. And the Little Person couldn't lie. Taking the berry, I shoved it into my mouth.

Juice exploded over my tongue. I grimaced at the odd taste, more like fruit-scented soap than anything. It'd taken a while to get over the usual warning given to mortals—"Don't eat anything in Faerie." As someone with a Sidhe's power, those rules didn't apply to me, usually. Still didn't mean it was a good idea to take the faeries' counsel. Moss Beard hadn't said the *memory-eater* meant us no harm.

The Little Person pointed ahead. "That way leads to her lair. Best of luck."

8

The path sloped upwards at such an angle I knew it shouldn't be possible to climb without falling. Gravity, however, had apparently decided to wander off, because when Viola and I walked vertically up the path, our feet remained as firmly in place as when it was flat.

"What weird trick is this?" I closed my eyes against the momentary vertigo.

"The magic of the person who owns this territory," said Viola. "So—this memory-eater, whoever it is."

Mist swirled between us, cloaking our bodies, and the ground became softer, less certain. Even knowing it wasn't possible to fall, I walked more slowly, then faster, just to get it over with. Finally, we halted on a level with the treetops, looking out into the sky. The clouds didn't look real, but maybe they didn't in the mortal realm either. White puffy shapes floated past, and the ground before us was solid cloud.

I stepped forward. My foot dipped and I withdrew it

quickly, my heart beating fast. Magic wouldn't save me. Here, a Sidhe could step off the edge and perish, maybe forever.

Viola's hand reached out for mine and squeezed it. "It's okay. Think of it as a combination of a magic trick and a glamour."

"You've been here before?"

"No, but a lot of the fey out here use glamours. Besides, we can't fall."

"Tell gravity that." I closed my eyes again to stave off the dizziness. Then I opened them and carried on walking. This time, the ground dipped but remained solid enough to stand on. Maybe I'd cope better if I'd ever climbed a mountain or flown in a plane, but I hadn't. The ground felt like walking on a giant sponge, and rocked alarmingly under each step. But neither of us fell, and despite the dizzying height, I could breathe normally.

The cloudy path halted at a larger bank of cloud, surrounded by a thin mist that was difficult to see through. I squinted, making out the shape of a house. Then the cloud dipped, and sank without warning.

I yelled in surprise, my voice thrown into the sky and back at me, hands scrambling for a ledge that wasn't there. The fall stopped a second later. The cloud had barely dipped. Viola gave me an amused look. I gave her a not-amused one back. Faerie had won this round.

"Hello?" Viola called to the misty shape of the house. "We're here to speak to the memory-eater."

A white-haired woman peered out of the house. "Who is it this time?"

"I'm Raine—" I cut off in a yelp when the cloud beneath Viola and me lurched downward. *Not again.*

"Give me one good reason," said the woman-creature in a silky voice. "One reason not to let you fall."

Her white hair was like a thousand strands of cloud,

braided with thorny branches. Her features had a distinctly greyish cast, and her limbs were longer than a human's, out of proportion with her relatively short torso. Rainbow-striped wings protruded from her back, a surprisingly childish contrast to her otherwise terrifying appearance.

"We're not here to harm you," said Viola, her voice high and shrill. If she was freaked out, then this *wasn't* supposed to happen.

"I'm Raine Whitefall." She wouldn't throw a family's leader to certain death, would she? Then again, it was pretty clear these borderland faeries didn't care about the Courts.

"Whitefall. Sidhe. You're half-blood."

"I'm the leader of the Whitefall Family," I told her.

"I know," she said. "I know everything, mortal. I know you're betraying your mortal father with every minute you spend in this realm. I know you're the only half-blood leading a family, and that deep down, you believe you do not deserve the position. I know you've had your heart broken into pieces before, and are well on the way to doing so again—"

"Stop that," I said, momentarily forgetting our precarious position. "Stop reading my mind—"

Her rainbow wings beat, and her eyes watched me with the depth of someone who'd lived a thousand years—or seen a thousand lives pass by. "You wished for me to do so, did you not?"

I shook my head. "No, I'm looking for someone else's memory. Someone who witnessed my mother's death."

"Nobody did, mortal," said the woman.

My heart sank. "Are you sure?" I asked. "Haven't—have you read my mother's mind, at all?"

"She never came here, so no, I didn't."

I swore under my breath. The memory-eater, having focused her attention on Viola, leaned forward. "Yours is a much more interesting mind than your companion's. Yet you waste too much of your time on guilt over betraying your parents and former family in leaving for another Court, for pursuing a love that can only end badly—"

"That is *enough*," said Viola, her face chalk white. "You can't invade our privacy like that."

She laughed, the sound like pebbles bouncing off glass. "Your thoughts enter my mind whether I will it or not. I've told you what you wanted to know."

"No, you haven't," I said. "I—look, I'm assuming you know I'm under threat from the Hornbeam Family to find out the truth about what happened to my mother. And you know neither of us are planning anything against you. You'd be able to tell if we were."

"I would," she said, "but I don't take kindly to people trespassing in my lair."

"Why do they call you the memory-eater, anyway?" I had a feeling she wouldn't object to a deal, but I needed to work up to it without antagonising her into throwing us off the cloud. "You consume memories?"

"I do, mortal." Her gaze flickered and I suppressed the instinct to step away. She was someone who'd seen too much, and had been driven to madness by it. But if Faerie's rules were anything to go by, I'd bet she had to continue to consume memories or she'd perish.

"Then I'll trade," I said. "One memory for another. You take one of mine, in exchange for a memory that gives me a clue about my mother's death."

"Very well," she said. "There are none who witnessed her death, mortal, but there is one person whose memories contain a hint of what you seek."

"And who's that?" I asked warily.

"Yourself."

My mouth fell open. "You—you can read my memories of when I was a child? The ones I can't remember?"

"A spell was put on you, but with my guidance, you may recall them again. If you wish to know the truth, I can show you."

"Okay," I said. "Show me."

She pointed a long, crooked finger, beckoning me closer. The world shattered into cloud-shaped fragments, and I plummeted down, down...

———

...I wanted to wear the blue dress, because it was my birthday. I'd begged and begged, following my mother around the palace's bright corridors.

"Please," I begged her. "I want to wear it for my birthday."

"Birthdays don't matter, sweet child," she said. "You're here forever, after all."

She was right. My dad told me tales of the world he'd come from, a terrible place of smog and dirt and violence and misery, where everyone died. Here, all was as endless as the snow that covered the palace, and never melted.

"Daddy says it's a special day. *My* special day."

"Every day is your special day. Go along now. I have business to attend to." She smiled, and it hurt to look at her face when she did that. Like staring into the sun on a day when it shone brighter than anything in the world, and turned the snow to glitter. In Daddy's world, the snow melted to sludge and disappeared in seconds. Not here.

She turned her back, breaking the spell. I looked down, playing with the edge of my sleeve. I knew what I'd do. She always left her room unlocked. I'd go inside and borrow the dress when she was out. Sometimes I asked why she never brought anyone here. She said Daddy and I were the only important people in her whole world. Nobody else would come and disturb us.

I went back to Daddy, who sat on the bright red sofa in the living room.

"We'll have a party for the two of us, won't we, Raine?" He smiled at me. She made him happy, and he didn't like it when she left, but we were lucky to have her at all. He told me so.

"Why won't she let me wear the dress? Is it because I don't look like her?"

"You're as beautiful as she is, princess," he said.

"Am I really a princess?"

"You live in a palace, don't you?"

"Yes..." Just for a second, images flooded my head—creeping hands around doorways, with claws instead of fingers. Screaming from outside. Horrifying blizzards in the middle of the night that racked the palace and made the walls bleed blue ink. *Magic,* was the word that floated around my head, the word whispered whenever I was out of the room. Magic gave me strange dreams, made me see things that weren't real.

When I was sure she'd gone, I slipped away from Daddy and went looking for her room. I didn't like the palace without her. Silence filled the empty corridors, and every sound echoed. My hand rested on the doorknob of her room. She'd left it unlocked.

The carpet inside was a vast plain, thick and pure white. Her furniture was gold fitted, too, towering over me and making me feel five inches tall. I walked over to the wardrobe—I'd seen her open it before, showing me the wondrous dresses I was forbidden to touch.

I opened the door.

Blackness yawned before me, like a giant mouth opening up to the centre of the earth.

I froze, staring. It must be a trick. I'd seen inside the wardrobe before, and it hadn't looked like this.

I stepped, tripping on the thick carpet. For a moment, I wobbled, then I tumbled down the tunnel, into a nightmare.

Cold stone brushed against my skin, damp and chilling. A foul stench made me gag. I slipped downhill, unable to see, unable to hear anything but a high-pitched echoing sound, and…

Music in my head, beautiful, eerie, haunting. I moved towards it as though under a spell, towards the light.

The light shone from a cabinet in an alcove at the corridor's side. The sword within the cabinet shone bright, etched with a lightning bolt symbol on its hilt. What was that awful smell?

I turned away from the cabinet and saw the first man. Then I screamed, high and loud. His hands were gone, torn away, leaving bloody stumps behind. He screamed back, gaps between his teeth, mouth covered in festering sores, kicking at the bars of the cage he'd been locked in.

He wasn't the only one. There were dozens of people in cages, all moaning, screaming, bleeding. Another man leaned out of the cage, hands seeking mine. A man with eyes like Dad's—

I whimpered and fell to my knees, reaching for the cage's door.

Pain shot up my hands instantly as though I'd stuck them in a leaping flame. I screamed so hard my throat burned as intensely as my hands. "Help!"

Out of the corner of my eye, a door opened wide and fog rushed in…

———

"Raine—Raine." Someone was shaking me. Viola. Icy sweat drenched my body and I looked up into the memory-eater's eyes.

"What was that for?" I croaked.

"You requested your memories, did you not?" The image of the dungeon flickered across her gaze again, threatening to pull me in. I looked away sharply, and climbed to my feet.

"I didn't need to know about my mother's collection of tormented mortals she kept in the dungeons. I was looking for information on what might have caused her death." My hands burned as though I really had placed them on iron bars, and goosebumps prickled my arms. "What happened after?"

"What else? Your mother found you, healed your hands, and regretfully deposited yourself and your father back in the mortal realm."

"So it was because of me, then."

No. It wasn't your fault. Eventually she wouldn't have been able to deny we were mortal, breakable, impermanent. She'd have locked Dad away with the other humans, and turned me into her servant. Not her heir. But why leave me in charge of her territory if that was the case?

Because Sidhe rarely had pure-blooded children...

"Did you take one of my memories?" I asked.

She looked away. "I did. And now, you leave."

The cloud disappeared under our feet, and Viola and I fell out of the sky. Too startled to scream, I grabbed for Viola's arm, but we both continued to fall. Below lay a blanket of trees. I directed my magic at the sharp branches, which twisted and warped into a net.

Branches snagged my hair, scratching my face sharply enough to draw blood. I fell, fell, then stopped, gasping, snagged in the net of branches. My heart beat frantically against my ribcage, my body still stuck in *I'm going to die* mode. Drawing in quick breaths, I disentangled one arm from the net.

Beside me, Viola lifted her head. "You saved our necks."

"I meant to turn it into a sofa." I looked down at the ground… a hundred feet below. "I also kind of hoped our landing would be closer to earth.

"We can get down from here." Viola climbed to her feet, lithely extricating herself from the nest of branches. I did likewise, thanking the years of being a thief for training me to move over precarious high surfaces. Even so, it seemed to take an age to descend through the branches, and ominous rustling followed our steps.

Then Viola stopped, staring at the nearest tree. Eyes stared back from inside a hole in the trunk, narrowed and white with no pupils.

"Oh, Sidhe's blood," she muttered. "Want to fight, or run?"

"Fight."

Spiny fingers protruded from another hole, extending to a spiky arm. I jumped down to the next branch, only for tiny grasping hands to latch onto my foot and attempt to pull me off the branch. I kicked the grasping hands—*damn tree imp*— and a fist shot out and punched it, sending the creature spiralling down into the gap between the trees.

"Hi," said Rose. "I thought you needed my help."

9

ose pushed her dark curly hair from her eyes, grinning at Viola. Leaves had been braided throughout her curls, gold and silver, and shimmered when she moved. She wore plain black clothes similar to the outfits the Hornbeam soldiers wore. But of course, Viola was a servant too, and she often dressed as though expecting to fight to the death.

"Hey," I said to Rose. "Nice to finally meet you properly face to face. I'm assuming you're on our side, seeing as you and Viola risked life and limb to meet one another."

She smiled. "Thanks for delivering my message."

"No worries. We'd better get out of this tree. What are you even doing here?"

"I saw you weren't at the palace and I remembered Viola saying you were investigating in the borderlands. Lord Hornbeam sent some of his soldiers along another path, and I tagged along hoping to find you."

"You shouldn't have," said Viola, hopping down to join her. "But I'm glad you did."

Viola and Rose carried on a whispered conversation

while we climbed down. My mind whirled with what I'd learned. *I can remember the years I missed. I can remember my mother.* And Dad… were those the memories that threatened to drive him to madness? Surely not. From what I'd seen, my mother had taken a liking to her pet human. For all I knew, she was putting on an act for me and Dad—the people she'd kept locked up were proof of her cruelty. But Dad hadn't acted like he was under a spell. He'd been happy. And so had I.

I shoved the thought away. The past wouldn't change, but as for my quest, I was back at the start. Nothing in my new memories had given me a clue about why she'd died. Except… the dungeon I'd found in the vision. I'd never been in her room—never found it, even. I hadn't been interested. But in the vision, the sword I'd seen in the cabinet had definitely looked like a talisman.

"What were you doing all the way out here in the first place?" Rose asked me. "The memory-eater isn't known for entertaining guests."

"I think I worked that much out for myself," I said. "We needed information that nobody else could give, but it didn't turn out to be much help."

"Viola tells me you're on a secret mission." She glanced over at her. "But you can't say what it is."

"I can," I said. "At this rate, everyone will know anyway. I need to find out how my mother died."

"Oh." Her brow crinkled. "I thought it was a wild chimera."

"That's the story," I said. "Your boss seems convinced there's more to it, but hell if I know what. Also, I need to find the Little Person who sent us up into those clouds and give him a piece of my mind."

"I vote we take someone else's advice next time," Viola put in. "I hope the memory she took from you wasn't important."

"Shit, I didn't even think about that."

I cast my mind around, but the influx of new memories made it impossible to pinpoint what might be missing.

"It should be okay, if she only took a single memory," said Rose. "I'm not an expert in that type of magic, but it's harder to erase more than one. Even for someone like her."

"There's more than one of her? Wait, you know what, don't tell me. One fall from the sky is enough, thanks."

Viola grinned at me, but Rose's expression turned serious. "I swear you're more reckless now you're out of the army," she said, picking a twig out of Viola's hair. "I don't think you should come onto the Hornbeams' territory anymore. Lord Hornbeam is being more vicious about kicking out potential intruders."

"I know all the ways in and out. It's fine." Viola waved off her concern. "Besides, the guards know me."

Rose's forehead wrinkled. "I know, but it's not safe. I was chasing a sluagh when I found your trail."

"Horrible creatures," said Viola. "The Whitefall palace's defences are up, don't worry. We'll head there now."

I stopped walking. "You know what, I think I might head home. I promised to see my Dad at Christmas, and besides, those memories—I don't know. I just got a bad feeling."

I'd be a fool to talk to him about anything in the memories that had nearly driven him mad, yet part of me wanted to know how much of the person I'd seen in the vision had really been her. Or him. Even me. I didn't recognise the girl who'd wanted so badly to wear a dress. I didn't even *like* dresses. The whole thing made no sense.

"Sure, but don't forget you have only three days to find evidence."

Rose looked from me to her, puzzled. So Viola hadn't told her Lord Hornbeam had been the one to order us on our quest. As Rose was also shackled to Lord Hornbeam, he could force her to spy on me if he found out about their relationship, or even punish both of them.

"I won't forget," I said. "Oh, yeah, it'd be great if you could find Lady Whitefall's private suite. It might be important."

Viola blinked. "I can look, but I haven't been able to find it since she died. Are you sure about leaving now?"

"Don't worry. Time passes slower here than in the mortal realm. I can be gone and back in half an hour."

"If you say so," said Viola.

I turned around and headed for the Little Person's cottage. I hadn't gone ten metres before a head popped up out of the bush, followed by a beard. "You're back," he said.

"No thanks to your friend." I couldn't tell for certain if he was the same Little Person who'd helped me, and not one of the ones who'd thrown a knife at me. "Do I owe you shoelaces?"

"You do."

I dug a hand in my pocket, relieved that they were still there. I'd got better at transforming my clothes without losing whatever was in the pockets—one perk of my magic.

He took the shoelaces from me. "Did I hear you say you need passage to the mortal realm?"

"Yeah, I do," I said. "What do you want as payment?"

"This time, I'd like you to bring me a single penny."

"Deal."

———

My hand fumbled the door key, my mind tripping over my rehearsed excuses. The potion would have made Dad groggy for a few days, and I hoped he'd been able to take care of himself in that time. I was the world's worst daughter, even if I hadn't a choice about going back to Faerie. Maybe I never would. There was always some reason, some excuse. The only friend I'd had in this realm was Denzel, and he didn't speak to me now I was a Lady of the Courts.

I'd gone back to town via the market to buy Dad a harmless present—skipping over the enchanted chocolates, charms and potions and going for a new scarf instead. He never remembered what day it was, so I didn't expect anything from him. Only for him to be safe. That was enough for me.

The living room, to my relief, was in the same tidy state it'd been in before. Cedar had done a decent job, though a new coating of dust had gathered in the time I'd been gone. Dad sat hunched in his usual armchair.

"Hey, Dad," I said brightly.

He looked at me blearily. "Where have you been?"

"I got a job."

He gave me a look that suggested he didn't believe me. I took in a breath and repeated my cover story—"I had an interview over the other side of town, so I stayed with a friend. I just found out I got it, so I'll be working long hours for my first week or two. I had to work long shifts because of the holiday rush. Don't you remember me telling you?"

He grunted. "You don't have time for me, do you?"

My heart sank. I should have known he'd think I was ignoring him. But I'd keep up with my alibi until I was certain that telling him I was going to Faerie wouldn't trigger the spell again.

"Of course I do. I got you a present."

I hadn't wrapped it, but he gave me a smile as he took the scarf from me. "Of course you didn't forget me."

"Obviously." I smiled back. "This new job is long hours. I'll try to make it home every night, but since it's so far away—"

"No," he said. "It's all right. I'm the one who should have

taken care of you, not the other way around. I'm a burden on you."

I shook my head. "It's not true. You're not a burden. It's not your fault…"

"Your mother gave you the job?"

I swallowed against my dry throat. "She's… busy."

"She always was. She always had time for us, though, sweetheart. Do you remember?"

He was lucid, but did he remember anything of what he'd been told about my mother's death? I'd guess not, but now I was here, I completely froze. There'd be nothing in his memories that wasn't in mine, but admittedly, I'd been scared half to death that the memories I'd seen had somehow found their way to him, too. I was being ridiculous, of course. I'd seen to it that Dad wouldn't recall his time in the Court unless someone decided to use magic on him again.

I forced a nod. "Yeah… I remember. But it's just the two of us now. It's better this way."

"That nice boy was here," he said.

"Who?" He must mean either Robin or Denzel, neither of whom qualified as 'nice' in the usual sense.

"Your dancer friend."

Robin. Maybe he *had* been the one to tell Dad the truth. "Where did he come from? Did he say why he was coming here?"

"He said something about not going back. I thought you'd gone back with *them.* I thought your mother…"

I held my breath, but no sign of the spell appeared.

"You're very lucky to have got to see her again."

I breathed out. *I did get to see her again. Just not in the way you think.* "I did. She's pretty… great. And scary. Did you ever find her scary?"

He looked at me as though I'd said something ridiculous.

"Of course not. She loved us both more than anything in the world."

"Er. Do you remember if she had a sword?"

"Sword? No. She hated violence."

Okay. There was such a thing as selective memory, but the job she'd done on him was creeping me the hell out. So she must have been careful not to show her evil side in front of him. Or he hadn't seen it, thanks to the spell she held him under.

"Anyway, I'm going out soon," he added. "I've actually been invited to a Christmas celebration at church."

"A human event?"

"What else?"

I shrugged. "I don't know. I'm glad you're making friends. You should… you should definitely go."

He nodded, holding the scarf like it was some beloved pet. "I miss you, Raine. I miss us."

He meant the three of us. I didn't know if I had it in me to keep lying to him. "I miss you, too, but I'm grown up now. It's okay. I'll get you another present on my next trip, all right? I've been invited to something, too."

Like a trip down memory lane.

It wasn't until I'd said goodbye and closed the flat door behind me that I remembered no buses would be running today. Resigning myself to a walk to find a rift, I turned around and nearly collided with Robin.

"Raine!" he yelped. "What are you doing here?"

"What?" I stepped away from him. "I live here. What are *you* doing here?"

Robin brushed a lock of fair hair off his forehead. He looked the same as always—silky hair, sharply angled features, dark hazel eyes, and a face as familiar as my own. Or, it had been. Now, he attempted to slide away from me without answering.

"Robin!" I snagged his sleeve with my hand, pulling him to a stop. He stared around, wild-eyed. "Is someone controlling you again?" Sidhe's blood, was the Hornbeam family behind the attack on Dad? I couldn't believe it hadn't crossed my mind before. But Lord Hornbeam would have told me, surely. He wanted answers badly enough to threaten my life.

"I'm being watched," he mumbled. "Please let go of me. I can't—you can't talk to me." He choked off, coughing uncontrollably. *Is he under a vow?*

"Robin, what the hell is wrong with you?"

He shook his head frantically and ran away.

I hesitated, then walked to the mercenary standing at the end of the road, one of Dad's guards. "If you see *him* again," I said to him, indicating Robin's retreating back, "throw iron in his face. Tell the other mercs the same."

Whatever Robin's motives, that he'd been so close to my flat raised all my suspicions. Maybe I should have never come back here at all. Dad didn't need any more upheavals in his life. Perhaps it was kinder to disappear. Like her.

———

I slowed my pace when I reached the hills outside the town. Tilting my head back to look for a rift, I scanned the horizon, walking as I did so. Within five minutes, I spotted a small bearded man vanishing into the fog. *Gotcha.*

I pelted after him, and a hellhound leaped out at me.

A branch lay nearby, and I grabbed it mid-stride. As the hellhound's jaws loomed overhead, I transformed the branch, sharpening it, and threw the improvised weapon at its mouth. The attack knocked out several teeth, and blue-tinged blood splattered the frosted grass. Wishing I had a more suitable weapon, I ducked its deadly bite, and the rift swallowed me up in a flash of light. I tumbled out onto thick undergrowth, which at least provided a soft landing. I pushed to my knees, my head spinning. The fog was so thick I couldn't see my hands in front of me, but my magic's comforting presence told me I was back in Faerie. Or rather, at the edge of Faerie. Was it my imagination, or was the fog worse than usual? It'd even been there in the mortal realm, in the liminal space where our realms met.

And where this realm met the land of the exiles...

The hellhound loomed over me. I rolled aside, grabbing another branch. Magic spread from my hands, spikes shot from the branch, and I rammed it into the hellhound's mouth. As it roared, trying to dislodge it, a blur of movement collided with the hellhound from the side. An arrow protruded from its flank, then another. My body instantly tensed, swivelling to face the new threat, but the Hornbeam soldier aimed his crossbow at the hellhound, not me. An arrow sank into its eye, and the beast collapsed onto its front.

Then he turned to me, and I stared at him. "Cedar."

My heart thudded against my ribcage. I'd known he was trained as a soldier along with the others in his family, but damn, he'd given me a scare.

He lowered the crossbow. "Raine? What are you doing out here?"

"Coming back from visiting home. What're *you* doing here? I thought he'd sent his soldiers after me."

Cedar took one step and stumbled, his face pale. Despite the swift way he'd taken down the hellhound, he moved slowly, not light on his feet like he usually did. Blood stained his clothes, but it didn't appear to be his.

"Viola told me. I was following you, in case you were attacked." His gaze skimmed my body, apparently checking for injuries.

"That thing followed me in from the liminal space. In the mortal realm."

His eyes widened and he cursed in the faerie tongue. "There may be more of them at large. I feared as much."

"Did you get attacked, too?" I moved in closer, eying his bloodstained clothes. "You know wearing iron slows down your healing ability, don't you?"

"I'll be fine. I just left my territory too soon after fighting a pack of hobgoblins."

"Sure you did." I rolled my eyes at him. "You might want to clean up that blood before a redcap tries to eat you. You *are* on Winter territory, remember."

"There's a way to combat that." He stopped at my side. "I could come back to the palace with you."

I glanced at him, perplexed. "I thought you weren't allowed in."

"Lord Hornbeam never forbade it." Cedar walked after me as I started away through the trees. "What were you doing in the mortal realm, anyway? Did you discover anything new?"

"My dad's memories are gone, so nope." He'd offered to help me, but I wasn't sure how much of recent events I could trust him with. I definitely didn't want to mention the sword, but the dungeon itself was the only clue I'd gleaned from the vision. "But there's apparently a secret tunnel underneath the palace neither Viola nor I have seen yet. We were going to search for it."

"I believe Viola left for my territory with Rose, to make sure she got home safely."

"Oh." Damn. Had she been able to find my mother's hidden bedroom? If she did, and the dungeon was there, would the sword still be there—if it was even a talisman at all? Maybe she'd had *that* one with her when she'd died, but if so, one of the other families would have stolen it.

"Where exactly is this tunnel? I could assist you."

"You mean Lord Hornbeam ordered you to." He'd already as good as said he was only working with me because he was under duress. But I really did need to get a look in that dungeon. I'd wasted too much time already.

"No. I didn't know your plan." He stopped when we reached the palace gates. "My offer is open."

"It must be bad if you'd rather explore a creepy dungeon with me than go home. Aren't you injured?"

"I'll be fine," Cedar said. "I rather think Lord Hornbeam will be quite irate with me for accompanying you here rather than returning to my own Court. But one of your three days is almost up."

"Let me guess," I said with a tinge of bitterness. "You get punished if I fail, too, right?"

His expression was grave. "What he might do to me is nothing compared to the pain of exile, Raine. I desire to spare us both that fate."

"If you say so." It couldn't hurt to bring someone else with me into the dungeon in case my mother had left a trap. And if he turned on me, there were a dozen cages down there I could lock him in.

I unlocked the palace and let us into the hall. After the vision, it seemed smaller, for some reason, but the frozen statues at the back were as creepy as ever. As were the tapestries depicting sinister imagery of brutal battles. Everything was ice-white with gold fittings, and our steps echoed off the high ceiling. A door lay open at the side. Viola must have left it there.

"Hmm…" I peered into an unfamiliar corridor. Its decorations were similar to the others, but the door slightly ajar on the right revealed a bedroom I hadn't seen before—except in the vision. The room was almost a mirror of my own, with honey-coloured fittings and soft golden light bathing the plush carpet.

"Raine?" Cedar leaned over my shoulder. "That's…"

"Her room. She hid the tunnel in there to the dungeon, in the back of the wardrobe." I walked that way.

Cedar followed. "And you're certain it leads to somewhere important?"

"It's the only clue I've got," I admitted. "When my mother wants to hide information, she doesn't do things by halves. Sure you want to come?"

I pulled the wardrobe door open, revealing an empty space where the back should be.

"I'm sure," Cedar said, closer behind me than I'd expected.

I took in a steadying breath. Even though years had passed since the vision, I knew better than to expect to find Wonderland waiting for me on the other side.

"Better hope there's a soft landing," I said, and climbed in.

10

The climb was short, if not quite as unpleasant as it'd been in the vision. Part of that was because I wasn't a toddler anymore, so I didn't have as far to fall. The other was that I landed on Cedar, and the two of us crashed into a heap.

"Cedar?" I squinted in the dark. "Are you okay?"

"Yes." He groaned as he sat up. It was too dark to see him, so when I straightened up, I hit my head on the ceiling and saw stars.

"Ow. I keep forgetting I was a little kid in the vision. There might be less space down here than I remember."

Cedar didn't answer. I scrambled around, conjuring magic to my hand to light the way. I should have snatched up one of those glowing firefly lights from the other dungeon. Cedar's breathing was harsh and he looked even worse in the bluish-tinged light.

"Cedar. Hell. There's iron in here. I shouldn't have brought you."

"I'm all right." He coughed.

"I won't take your word for it."

I raised a hand to the wall, aiming to open a door upstairs… and nothing happened.

"Something's wrong." I concentrated on my magic until my palm glowed blue, and still… nothing. "I don't know if it's the iron, but I can't open a way back upstairs."

"There'll be a way out," Cedar said confidently, stepping forwards, but he'd gone ashy pale and the presence of iron probably wasn't helping.

"Yeah, of course. But if this is part of the palace, my magic's supposed to work." I took in a deep breath. "Come on. Let's get this over with."

We didn't have to walk for long before the first cages appeared. Iron bars encased spaces hardly big enough for their human prisoners to move. So many… at least twenty. This whole tunnel was a prison just like the one in the Hornbeams' territory, but a separate one hidden beneath the beautiful palace. With splendour masking them from view, they'd died down here. Alone.

"She had the entrance to this place in her *bedroom?*" said Cedar. He'd grasped the nature of the setup without me having to tell him.

I swallowed. "Yeah. I know. She was sick. I mean, I hoped she'd turn out to be the exception, but all the Sidhe are the same."

"Not all of them," said Cedar. "Borderland Sidhe, perhaps, but the Courts would hardly permit a place like this to exist for someone who has done nothing to deserve punishment."

"They don't see humans as people," I snapped, letting some of my anger escape. "Nor us. If they find out the truth, I'm dead. And this place has *no* proof of anything useful. If there are answers in here about why one of the region's most powerful Sidhe lost her mind and left her magic behind before running outside to die, it'd be really helpful."

Echoes were the only response. Nothing living remained

down here. The cages' occupants had perished a long time ago. Not even skeletons were left behind. Just cold iron bars, damp stone floor, and the hint of magic long dead. We passed by cages until we came to the stretch of blank dark wall where I'd seen the sword I'd suspected was a talisman.

It wasn't here now.

Chills ran down my arms. This place was tainted with death, yet her kind, smiling face kept intruding. If she'd hated my father and me, she'd hidden it well.

Though I hadn't made a sound, Cedar's hand rested on my shoulder. "I don't want to alarm you," he said, "but there doesn't appear to be a way out."

I looked around. Behind the cages were blank walls and nothing else. "There must be."

Oh shit. I hadn't even considered the possibility. I'd seen a door, or something similar, in the vision, but it hadn't been within view. Now, I saw nothing at all.

"You have *got* to be kidding me." I kicked down the nearest iron door and went inside the cell, but what I'd thought was a door was only a shadow.

"Raine!" said Cedar. "The iron—"

I climbed out of the cage and marched over to him. "I know iron's poisonous. You're the one who apparently needs a reminder." My teeth chattered as though with cold. "We're trapped." He was already suffering the effects of iron poisoning. How long until it crept from the cages to us, and killed us both?

"Calm down," said Cedar, stepping closer to me. Under the sickening presence of the iron all around us, the steady buzz of his magic against me soothed me somewhat. But the spark of my anger refused to die.

"Would you be here with me if not for the vow?"

Why the hell had I *said* that? Apparently my filter between brain and mouth had totally evaporated.

Cedar looked at me for a moment. "No, I wouldn't. I wouldn't know you at all if I hadn't been ordered to go into the mortal realm and steal from you."

"You say the most pleasant things, Cedar."

"I didn't say I regretted it." He reached and touched my face, his hand unexpectedly warm considering how cold it was. His finger traced my cheekbone. I didn't move. His eyes were fever-bright. *He's not himself.* Maybe not, but the smell of him, scented candles and woodsmoke, wrapped around me like a warm embrace.

"Can you feel that?" The words slipped out before I could stop them.

"Feel what?"

"Your magic."

He closed the steps between us until our foreheads rested against one another, and quietly murmured, "I can only feel your magic, Raine."

When his lips pressed against mine, I didn't back away, nor when he deepened the kiss, his arms circling my back. He inhaled sharply and pulled away from me.

"I've wanted to do that for a long time." His breath came unevenly, as though he was in pain. Perhaps he was. "I wanted… Sidhe's blood, I've wanted to take you away from this place ever since I learned the price you'd pay for wielding the talisman."

"Cedar. What in the world has got into you?"

He shook his head, his breathing harsh and ragged. *The iron… it's killing him. He's confessing to me because he knows he's dying.*

"Cut it off," I found myself saying. "The iron. There *has* to be a way. Get a human to remove it. I'm sure there's someone who'll do it without asking questions."

"You don't understand—"

"*I* don't understand? You can't kiss me one second and

treat me like a clueless human the next. I *know* the Sidhe. Do you really think by now I'm not aware of what they're capable of?"

"I never said you weren't. But if you try to intervene, he won't give you three days' leeway anymore. He'll hand you over to the Erlking in person, and you'll be slaughtered."

"You sure know how to lighten the mood." I stepped back, then stared at the wall over his shoulder. "That wasn't there before."

A wooden door had appeared in the stone, a crack of light shining underneath.

Cedar placed a hand on my arm. "Raine. Don't open it."

"Cedar." I rolled my eyes at him. "There's a mysterious door in my mother's secret basement. Either you were the most boring child ever, or you're deluding yourself."

Maybe the door led back upstairs, maybe not, but there didn't appear to be any other way out of here at all. The door handle was icy to touch, sending a shock through my bones. I jerked back, and it swung open the rest of the way.

Grey smoke swirled into the room instantly, sweeping underneath our feet and rising to waist level like we'd walked into the memory-eater's cloud.

"Damn," I whispered. "I think this must be a secret exit, right next to the rift. Might come in handy."

"You can't go barging through every door you open here in Faerie."

His condescending tone made me bristle. "You know there's no other way out, right?"

"Right," he said through gritted teeth, "because you didn't bother to check if there *was* another way out before you dragged us down into the dark."

"I didn't drag you anywhere," I said. "You practically threw yourself after me. It's not my problem if you'd rather believe that than admit you're Lord Hornbeam's lapdog." The echoing chamber caught my words and threw them back at me, so they sounded like they came from someone else.

Cedar's mouth flattened, his jaw tensed, and the faintest trace of green Summer magic shone around his non-iron bound arm. "You don't know anything about me," he said quietly. "And you can be unbelievably dense sometimes."

Shame burned my face. Sidhe's blood, why was I so *angry?* The words were pouring out of some dark, unknown part of me, like someone had lifted the lid on all my impulses and I couldn't stop them, no matter how much damage they caused.

"Cedar, I…"

"Raine," he said. "There's something… a force in here somewhere, and it's affecting both of us, affecting our emotions. I think it's coming through that door, and it would be unwise to provoke it."

I looked away from him. *I knew I felt off for a reason.* The words I'd said—even our kiss—it wasn't us. Whatever force was screwing with our emotions had dragged words out of us that we'd never normally say.

A skittering noise sounded in the fog. Cedar moved, pushing the door's edge, but it didn't budge. "It's stuck."

"Dammit." I moved to his side and pushed the door, too, but instead of closing, it swung open wider as though it had a life of its own. Tendrils of smoke seeped out, turning black like living shadows.

Luckily, I'd encountered enough of this type of fae in the mortal realm not to be freaked out too much when the threads of fog wrapped around my legs like tentacles. Using iron would work better, but I could improvise. Magic shot from my palms at the ceiling, hitting the stone and causing the iron bars to loosen then fall directly into the path of the shadows. The threads of smoke let go of me, flailing, then fell still.

"Good job," said Cedar, pushing against the door. "We need to leave. There might be more of them."

"Yeah, slight problem. There's no door aside from that one."

He shoved the door again. "But you used magic to hit the ceiling. That means you might be able to open a way out."

"And bring the whole palace crashing down?"

Shadows engulfed Cedar, hauling him behind the door.

"Cedar!" I ran after him, magic flaring my palms, and into the fog.

Cedar struggled against a giant living shadow, which changed from a formless lump into a winged humanoid shape like the shadow of an angel gone horribly wrong. Skeletal wings protruded from its back, and its limbs were elongated and stick-thin. As the creature's arms locked around Cedar's neck, I lunged forwards, but Cedar had already drawn his iron knife and cut viciously at the creature's arm.

The iron should have incapacitated it. Instead, the weapon passed through the creature like it was a ghost. Even shadow creatures could be affected by iron. What the hell were we up against? A creature like a sluagh, part spirit and part solid?

I fired magic at the air, willing the fog to solidify. Shards of ice fell where my attack struck, piercing the creature from behind. It let go of Cedar, who sprung away. I shot a second icy spear through its chest. With an ear-splitting yell, the creature burst into shadowy pieces.

"Nasty thing. What's affected by magic but not iron?" I asked.

Cedar didn't answer but took a step back. "You just wounded it. It's not dead—"

A figure appeared at the end of the path. He turned to face me.

"Dad?" I said in disbelief.

I stepped forward, and Cedar caught my arm. He'd gone as pale as the spirit creature. "It's a shape-changer, trying to trick us."

"Raine," said Dad. "Raine, where am I?"

Cedar was right—this was the exact sort of trick a shapeshifting or illusionist faerie might use against me. But there was always that five percent margin of uncertainty. The faeries had come close to capturing my dad before, and someone had definitely spoken to him recently.

"Raine." His voice echoed back at me. I raised my palm, calling magic to me.

"Whatever you are, you're not my dad. Mind telling me how I can shut this door?"

A pause. Then he laughed. "You opened the door yourself, mortal."

Not-Dad grinned and turned on the spot, wreathed in blue light. The next second, Lady Hornbeam stood in his place.

Cedar didn't move. "Don't."

"As if I planned to." Annoyance rose within me—did he really think I was naïve enough to run after someone who was definitely dead? "Come and fight us, coward," I said. "You don't want my magic to hit you, do you? You're scared of me."

"You will pay for what you did to me, human," whispered Lady Hornbeam's voice.

I threw the magic at her. Fog froze into icy spears and she leaped, becoming smoke herself, flying right at us. Though I knew she wasn't entirely solid, I ducked to avoid her, and so did Cedar. He was breathing heavily.

"Mortals," crooned the creature, still using Lady Hornbeam's voice. "I will have your essence, mortals. Give me your fear, your anger, your pain. It sustains me. Give me it all."

"You're *really* starting to piss me off," I snarled.

I froze the nearest section of fog into ice, forming a spear-like shape, and hurled it at the shadowy-fog creature. It appeared to melt before my eyes, becoming part of the fog itself. My teeth chattered, and a wave of dread crashed over me, entirely disconnected from the fight. I couldn't seem to get enough air into my lungs. As angry as I'd been, fear had taken over, swamping all reason. My spear weapon broke, and my hands trembled. *What's happening to me?*

"Give me your essence, mortals, so that I may live and you may not."

The air trembled, the fog solidifying into a humanlike shape again. *It's alive... somehow, the fog is alive.* I'd injured it before, and it was clearly terrified of my magic, but I could hardly draw air into my lungs. Cedar collapsed against my side, gasping.

It's sucking the life out of us. I'd seen fae of that sort in the mortal realm, though I'd never faced one directly. And I'd heard stories of beasts that fed on dark emotions and used them to bleed you dry. I sent another spear of ice through the fog, but the creature had gone.

"Coward," I growled, limping forward. Cedar leaned on the wall to push himself upright and shot a handful of green light at the fog. How he'd managed to conjure any magic at all considering there was nothing living down here was beyond me.

"You were always such a disappointment to me," said Lady Hornbeam's voice. "You're both pathetic mortals."

"No." I shot blue energy wildly into the fog, momentarily illuminating the cracked stone ceiling, and turning droplets of moisture to ice that speared the air. But the creature must have hidden itself away. I'd never met a shapeshifter not made of anything solid before. Even sluaghs could be hit if you struck them in the right place.

"They're only good for one attack," Cedar hissed in my ear. "Divert it. I'll—" He stumbled against the wall, pushed aside when the creature appeared in a hiss of smoke, claws passing through me with a bone-chilling sensation that went right down into some primitive, terrified part of me. I backed up, magic springing to my hands, tasting ice on my lips. The air solidified at my touch and the creature did, too, screaming as it fell into the ice I'd conjured. Shoving it away from me, I braced my feet on the tunnel floor. Green light spread from Cedar's hands across the ground, latching onto the creature's indistinct silhouette. It let out a coughing scream, and exploded into shadowy fragments.

My anger and fear dissipated, and the light-headed sensation faded as feeling came back into my hands. I hadn't realised how cold I was—colder than any magic I'd sensed before.

"What the hell was that?"

"That," said Cedar grimly, "is known as a wraith. It's also what's been attacking my territory for the last week. It's immune to iron, so only magic works against it. As I'm sure you noticed, I'm running low at the moment."

"A *wraith?* You mean, ghost?"

"Sort of, but not a human one." He limped to the tunnel's side, leaning against the wall.

I brushed icy fragments from my hands. "That's what happens when a faerie dies?"

"No, but when a faerie dies somewhere their spirit can't move on."

What? "Since when did you know so much about it?"

"Since we came here." He pointed, and I realised the fog had cleared a little during the fight. We didn't stand in a tunnel but at the edge of a silvery path littered with leaves, flanked by tall ancient trees either side. It was Faerie... *or is it?* The world looked *wrong,* as though bleached in dye that turned it the wrong colour. Dark grey mist smothered everything, and a horrifying coldness blew in like a ghastly breeze. I choked and stumbled back, and Cedar caught me by the shoulders.

"Don't go any further. If you do... you won't be able to come back."

I stared, more out of horror than anything. The cold, empty place held no magic, and was still and silent as death. I'd thought being chained up in iron was bad. The forest ahead felt like it was drawing the life essence from me with every step.

"Is that—?"

"The Grey Vale," Cedar said.

11

I opened my mouth and closed it again. *The Grey Vale.* Sidhe's blood, no wonder it was so cold and foggy down here. This was the place where Faerie's magic ended, where nothing existed but the dead and the eternally condemned.

In unison, we backed away, into the dungeon.

"Why would my mother have a shortcut into the place where exiles hang out?" I asked, not expecting an answer. "Unless—exiles are sent out somehow, aren't they?"

"The Sidhe take exiles down the same path you use to leave this realm, but instead of using a rift to the mortal realm, they use one that sends you into—"

"The Vale." I swallowed. "Why is this here?"

"It's obvious," he said. "She was colluding with Vale outcasts. Maybe one of them killed her."

"I'd know if Vale beasts were creeping around under the palace," I said. "I've lived here for weeks. Viola would too."

"Have you considered the possibility that she's in on it?"

"No," I said shortly.

"But—"

"She's my friend, Cedar. She didn't know about this."

"Would you bet your life on it?"

Anger sparked. "Piss off, Cedar."

He blinked and stepped back, warily looking at the door. "Hang on. There might be another one."

"There's no wraith making me angry, Cedar. You are. Viola's more loyal than anyone else I've met here."

"Where I'm from, people are more likely to betray you than not. It's always my first assumption. I find it hard to believe that this place has existed without anyone knowing about it."

"Viola's only worked here for a few years. This dungeon might not have been in use for a while. The vision only showed when I was three—"

"Vision?"

"Cedar, don't take this personally, but I don't trust you not to pass on my secrets to your boss. Under duress or not."

"I can swear not to."

"I'm not being responsible for your death if Lord Hornbeam doesn't like that." But it didn't matter if Lord Hornbeam knew we'd spoken to the memory-eater, really. Besides, we still hadn't found a way out of this place. "All right. I got my memories back, of the first few years of my life I spent here. That's how I knew this place existed. When I was a kid, I fell in here, found a bunch of dying humans and nearly died of iron poisoning. I'm fairly certain that's when my mum gave up and kicked me out."

"And you didn't see this door?"

"No. Don't you think I'd have mentioned it?" I pushed against the side of the door, calling magic to my hands. This time, it moved. "Wait—I think I can use magic to close it. Maybe that's the key."

I walked around the edge, my hands flaring blue. At my touch, the door's edge came away from the wall. "Gotcha." I pushed harder, and the door swung shut as abruptly as it'd opened.

Cedar paced to the dungeon's other side. "There must be an exit. Maybe hidden near the entrance. I didn't get a good look around in the dark."

"There's nowhere else to look, so we might as well." No sign of the sword, either. I stopped beside the place where I'd seen it in the vision, hidden in an alcove in the wall. Nothing remained, not a trace. Though it *had* been over twenty mortal years since I'd last been in here…

"Raine," Cedar said. "I think we can climb back up. It's not far."

The tunnel was cramped and narrow, and covered in cobwebs, but I was just about tall enough to reach and pull myself back into it. "I suppose not."

"Want to go first?" he asked.

"Flip a coin. Who gets to climb into the creepy—" A spider landed on my head. "Ack."

"Let me get it off." Cedar reached and his fingers brushed my forehead.

I shuddered. "Get it away. Far away."

"You don't like spiders?" There was a laugh in his voice.

"I'm perfectly fine with anything with more than four legs, as long as there are several miles between me and them." I turned to the tunnel so he wouldn't see me blush. If that wraith had turned into a giant spider, I'd be screwed. "Stop laughing at me."

My elbows scraped the walls as I hauled myself up into the tunnel again. I cursed and shuffle-scrambled up the steep slope. Cedar swore in the faerie tongue behind me. "You okay back there?"

"Yes. I have the distinct impression your mother used the door to get out of here."

"You think?" I couldn't imagine her scrambling around in the dark.

Several metres and a bruised elbow later, I tumbled out of the wardrobe in a heap of dust. Cedar followed. His breathing was ragged again, and dust and cobwebs coated his usually immaculate shiny hair. He fell rather than climbed out of the tunnel, groaning.

I flopped onto my back. "I can't believe she didn't just install a lift."

Viola peered in from the corridor, Volt hovering over her head. "What happened to you two?"

"Long story. We found the dungeon." I mimed a half-hearted victory dance.

"I gathered. I was hoping you'd wait until I came back before you went in, but at least you had company." She eyed Cedar. "What's wrong with him?"

I mouthed *iron poisoning.* He must have stronger magic than I'd thought, if he was still able to use it.

Cedar lifted his head. "I should get back to Lord Hornbeam."

"Nope." I got to my knees. "You look like hell, Cedar, and if you show up covered in cobwebs and crap, Lord Hornbeam's going to ask questions."

"He'll ask questions anyway."

"Just stay an hour," I said. "I have a few questions about that wraith."

"About the what?" said Viola, eyes widening.

"I think you need to sit down for this part."

Ten minutes later, after both Cedar and I had showered and changed—well, at least I had, because Cedar refused to borrow any clothes, on the reasonable grounds that Lord Hornbeam would ask unwelcome questions—we gathered on the giant sofa in the living room. Unlike my battered couch at home, it was big enough to seat half a dozen people. I'd also conjured up dinner in the form of pizza which actually tasted like the real thing back in the mortal realm. Cedar gave it a sceptical look, but shrugged and accepted a slice from me.

"Wraiths," said Viola, with a shudder, licking sauce off her fingers. "Just when I thought the Vale couldn't get any more twisted..."

"Aren't you a little worried that it's right under our feet?" I asked.

"It hasn't bothered me for a year. If it's really that hard to get out of there, most monsters probably wouldn't bother."

"I think it's because the door was closed." A chill crawled up my spine. "I just opened it. I hope nothing got out."

Viola gave me the evil eye. "If we wake up with wraiths in the entrance hall tomorrow morning, it's your fault."

"Nothing did," Cedar said. "Except spiders." He flashed me a tired smile, which I countered with a warning look.

"I think we should find a more secure way to seal the door," I said. "I can handle most Vale creatures—they're pretty common in the mortal realm. But not wraiths. You just get standard ghosts over there."

"Dead faeries," said Viola. "Well, you won't get information on *them* out of the Courts. Might be some in the library, though."

"Never thought of that," I admitted. "I haven't found anything useful in there before, but she must have had a contingency plan for dealing with those monsters if she frequently went visiting them."

Viola put the last slice of pizza back in the box. "That's just it. I think she must have—the entrance is in her room, after all. She disappeared on errands a lot of the time. I never asked." Viola was under no illusions about my mother's nature as a Sidhe, but the Grey Vale part must be a blow. After all, she had more recent memories of my mother than I did.

"When you knew her," I said, "did she show any signs she might be working with outcasts? Because that's the only thing that makes sense here."

"Yeah, I know. But I didn't. She was secretive, and my role was predominantly to spy on the families and to run errands. She showed no signs of any allegiance with the outcasts." Her gaze went to Cedar, who'd fallen asleep on the sofa's side. "You might want to wake him up if he's to get back to Lord Hornbeam tonight."

"Honestly, I think he's better off staying here." I spoke in a low voice. Cedar lay sprawled inelegantly, one arm draped over the sofa's edge. I reached surreptitiously and pushed his sleeve up, revealing the iron band.

Viola raised her eyebrows, then climbed out of her seat when she saw what I was pointing at. "*That's* the iron poisoning?" she whispered.

I gave a small nod.

She cursed under her breath. "I suppose it doesn't come off."

I bent to examine it. The band was tightly fastened with a clasp. Touching it was out of the question, for both Viola and me. Only a human might be able to remove it, assuming Lord Hornbeam hadn't done something else to ensure it stayed on.

Viola shook her head. "Maybe slide something underneath it. I can make a potion for iron poisoning, but it won't work if he keeps the thing on long-term."

Cedar stirred. I quickly shifted back to my seat, but he didn't wake. I didn't blame him. The dungeon had wiped me out, and it was beyond me to figure out what to do now. With no clues or information to give Lord Hornbeam, I was further than ever from figuring out how to bargain—both for my life and Cedar's.

I didn't know at which point I'd decided to bring Cedar's freedom into it, only that I couldn't imagine handing the information over to Lord Hornbeam without at least trying to free Cedar from the vow he'd sworn. I doubted he'd done so of his own free will.

"Did the Hornbeams always do that to their soldiers?" I whispered to Viola.

"Only the most valuable ones. It seems counter-productive, but it did work. Their loyalty never came into doubt."

"Probably because they died," I said heatedly.

She looked at him again. "I'm amazed one thief lasted this long. He'd have been right in Lady Hornbeam's inner circle. I'd bet that's why Lord Hornbeam doesn't trust him."

"Ah." I hadn't even thought of that. Of course… as Lady Hornbeam's son, he'd be a contender for the heir. Was that why Lord Hornbeam wanted him out of the way? "Is there a way to take someone away from a vow without killing the caster?"

"Kill the person who has the vow put on them."

"Really not an option here."

Viola rolled her eyes. "Raine. Isn't one impossible task at a time enough for you? There's such a thing as picking your battles."

"I know. I am." Only Faerie would push me into deciding whether I liked someone I'd known for a few weeks enough to bargain for their life with a deranged faerie lord. But really, what choice did I have? Let him die?

"Honestly," said Viola. "I'm going to seal that door. Then I'll go and look in the library for books on those wraiths. And the Vale. And any one of our other hundred problems." Her sly smile came back. "Never a dull moment with you, is there?"

"I'll come join you in a minute." I yawned.

I meant to rest for moment, but my eyelids slid closed, and the next thing I knew, someone's hand brushed my cheek.

"Where am I?" Cedar's voice sounded close to my ear.

I opened my eyes, momentarily confused about how we'd ended up on the ridiculously over-sized sofa. "The palace. You fell asleep." Apparently I had, too.

He rubbed his eyes. "Sidhe's blood. How long was I out for?"

"No clue. You probably needed the rest."

Cedar sat up, running a hand through his silky dark hair. "Did you find anything useful? I remember one of you mentioning the library."

"I fell asleep, too." Had he heard my conversation with Viola? Did he know I planned to bargain for his life—and would he stop me out of some misguided effort to obey the laws of his family?

From the light streaming through the window, it was morning. Day Two of my allocated time to get useful information for Lord Hornbeam.

Cedar looked at me. "I should go, but before I do—I have to apologise for what I said to you in the dungeon."

"I know," I said quickly. "I didn't mean what I said, either." I meant the harsh words I'd spoken, but... maybe he meant his confession, and how he really felt about me. But the wraith's magic had brought out honest feelings, right?

Cedar turned in my direction. "What are you thinking?"

That I'm getting too attached to you for my own good.

"I'm thinking we need to check the next dungeon has an escape route."

His mouth tugged in a smile. "And no spiders."

"Very funny." I swatted at him, smiling despite myself. "No emotion-controlling menace of a ghost, either."

He caught my hand in his. His skin was warm to touch, roughly callused. No magic-induced haze covered his eyes, though the slightest hint of emerald crossed his irises. "What is it?" he asked. "You're looking at me strangely."

I half shrugged. "Thought you didn't mean what you said down there."

"You thought I meant I'm not interested in the fact that we're alone together?" His lips hovered over mine, his thumb tracing circles on my palm. Magic tingled up my wrist in response. "If you aren't convinced I was in my right mind in the dungeon, allow me."

My mouth parted under his, and the door handle turned.

"Raine?" called Viola.

Cedar sprang back without making a sound, and Volt flew over our heads, close enough to make my hair go static.

"Yeah?" I cursed the Sidhe for bad timing.

Viola stepped in. "I thought you ought to know Lord Hornbeam's people are patrolling the forest, and I'm getting the impression he's in a bad mood. Possibly because his thief disappeared last night."

Cedar was on his feet in a second. "I have to leave."

"Are you going to tell him?" Shit. For all that I was glad not to be alone down there, if Lord Hornbeam found out about the Vale…

"I'll tell him we're still working on the investigation," Cedar said, already heading for the door. "There's no need to mention our excursion. I highly doubt he's ever considered a secret dungeon leading into the realm of his enemies."

My heart sank. I didn't want to let Cedar go back to his territory, but at least I hadn't told him about the sword. Not that we'd found it anyway. I ran a hand through my hair, recalling the image of the sword I'd seen in the vision. It looked vaguely familiar, but that was the problem when you'd once made a living stealing valuable objects—they all merged together. I sure as hell would have remembered seeing it in the mortal realm, and I definitely hadn't handled a talisman before I came here. But I'd seen it in my dreams again last night, and the image had been a bit clearer. There'd been carvings on the hilt. A lightning bolt shape, glowing blue.

"Are you sure your family didn't work with the outcasts, too?" I asked Cedar. "Lord—or Lady Hornbeam?"

"I'd know if she did," he said. "As for Lord Hornbeam, a wraith nearly killed him the other day. He's not actively fighting them in case the next one finishes him off. Oh, and Aspen's disappeared."

The prince has gone? "Wait," I said. "Were you allowed to say that?"

"Yes," he said. "I haven't actually made a vow forbidding me to tell you anything this time."

I blinked. That was new. "Okay. Are you sure you're fine to walk back now? Because if they're still in the forest—"

"I'll be fine." He walked to the door into the entrance hall.

I followed close behind. "There's one thing I don't regret saying when that creature was messing with us," I told him. "That iron cuff needs to come off, asap, otherwise you're going to drop dead."

He didn't turn around. "I've been wearing iron in some form or other since I was a child."

"That's no excuse. You know you're dead if the skin breaks underneath it and the iron ends up in your bloodstream, right?"

"It won't break."

"Fine." I held out my own wrist, which glowed with magic, and tore off my sleeve end, using magic to turn it into a band of fabric, as thick as I could make it. "Stick this underneath. It won't affect the iron in the long term, but at least it won't be touching your bare skin."

He hesitated, but didn't pull back when I grabbed his hand. I gasped. The skin on his bound wrist had turned greyish, and had already begun to spread up his arm. "Cedar—"

He took the fabric from me and slid it onto his arm, pushing it underneath the iron band.

"You're going to be stuck like that forever if you don't get that thing off."

Cedar took in a breath. "Raine, you should be more concerned with yourself, and with gathering substantial evidence for Lord Hornbeam so neither of us suffer the consequences."

He crossed the entrance hall in the time it took to blink. I could have caught him up, but it wouldn't do any good. Keeping him from reporting to Lord Hornbeam would only make things harder on both of us.

"Whoa," said Viola. "What did he do?"

"He's wearing that iron band like it's a badge of honour. I swear the next time I see Lord Hornbeam—"

"You can't tell him about the door," she said.

"I don't have a death wish. But I wish I had some other evidence. Did you seal the wardrobe?"

"I did." She frowned. "I still don't understand. I knew she had her own private chambers, but what would she want with *that* part of Faerie?"

Knowing my mother, probably nothing nice. "So the Vale actually is part of Faerie? I'm confused."

"It used to be," said Viola. "It's stripped of all magic, and closed off so only the Sidhe can open passageways there, if they want to exile someone. You can't just walk in there."

"But we're at the edge of the territory. We're more or less on top of it." Not a comforting thought at all.

"I didn't know it was literally underneath us!" She paced around, biting her lip. "If the Courts find out, do you think they'll believe we weren't responsible?"

"Honestly, I hadn't got that far," I admitted. "Don't forget I'm already a murder suspect. I'm fairly sure that's worse in their eyes. Anyway, I failed. The dungeon was empty. In my memories, there was a sword in there. I'm sure it was a talisman from the way it glowed, but I couldn't find it."

"Another talisman?" She stared at me. "Are you sure?"

Even in the haze of memory, it'd been unmistakeable. I'd recognise another talisman from the opposite side of a room. "I know," I said. "But she might have lost it, or…"

"What did it look like? Can you describe it?"

"A sword, silver, covered in carved runes. There was a lightning bolt on the handle."

She swore quietly in the faerie tongue. "Didn't you see the Little People? They had one, in their house."

"No." I honestly hadn't paid any attention to their contraband whenever I'd been there, and whatever they'd taken from people as the price for using the rifts. "Are you sure it looked the same?"

"I'm not, but—they live right near the murder site."

I stared at her. "You're saying the *Little People* might be involved?"

"I don't even know." She sounded tired, and the dark circles under her eyes indicated she hadn't slept much. "Some of them did try to kill us."

"But why use my talisman? I mean, my mother's?" This just got more bizarre by the second. "The memory-eater would have told us if one of them knew about her death. And they're faeries. They *can't* lie."

Viola frowned. "You're right. Maybe they don't know it's a talisman."

"I doubt it. What did you do last night? Check the library?"

"Yeah. Grabbed everything I could on the wraith, the rifts, the Vale… not that I can read ancient faerie languages particularly well. I grew up with the more modern version." She shrugged. "But that's why I thought of the Little People. Apparently some of them can open passages between realms without using the rifts. They *created* them."

"And the Grey Vale? Have the Little People ever been there? I mean, it's sort of between realms, right?"

"I have *no* idea. I suppose they don't have magic in the usual sense, so technically they might be able to survive there. The liminal spaces—I think we'd know if they linked to the Grey Vale. If I had to guess, it's like Faerie itself—you can leave through the liminal spaces, but you can't come back without an invite. So the Little People... if they *can* get into the Vale, then they can bring anyone back with them. We need to warn..."

"The Courts?" I suggested.

"Not with a price on your head."

"But this is bigger than us," I said, though I wasn't exactly enamoured with the idea of going near either one of the Courts, even the one that didn't want me dead. "The exiles in the Vale want to destroy the Courts. That's what I heard. I mean, they were stripped of their magic and left to die. Wouldn't they want to destroy the Sidhe who did that to them? That's the whole reason they attacked the mortal realm."

Viola pressed a hand to her forehead. "Yeah. Using the Little People is a perfect strategy, because the main Courts hardly bother to check up on them. They're thought to be trustworthy. Maybe one of them got corrupted somehow."

"Perhaps," I said. "We should go and talk to them. I can't think of anything else."

"Nor me, but I don't know if it's worth antagonising them." She sighed. "Do you ever think someone's trying to divert your attention from solving her murder?"

"Frequently, but I think Lord Hornbeam wanted me to

fail. Unless I figure out why the Sidhe can die now, which is just as impossible…" I trailed off. "Wait. That wraith… it was a dead faerie. Maybe a Sidhe, originally. It had magic, and could shift forms. Cedar said it's what happens when a faerie dies somewhere its spirit can't move on from. So, the Grey Vale. What if that's the only place with answers?"

Viola grimaced. "I can't see how that's better than exile. Leaving for the Vale is treason."

"Fine," I said. "I'm going to invite Lord Hornbeam round, telling him I have the answers. Then I'll push him down into the dungeon. That's all our problems solved."

"Raine." Viola shook her head, but there was an amused slant to her mouth. "What possible excuse is there for making him look in Lady Whitefall's wardrobe?"

"I was getting to that part. Don't ruin my plan."

"Sorry." She grinned. "It's not a bad plan, actually, but I doubt Lord Hornbeam would be so easily persuaded."

I shrugged. "Probably not, but it's better to shove him out the way where he can't enslave any more of his people."

"Cedar." She didn't need to say more.

"He'll die if he stays." It'd hurt to watch that happen to anyone, but someone I knew… someone who might have been more than a friend, in another life… I wanted to run after him a damn sight more than I wanted to pursue the Little People on another pointless quest.

"Leaving the families is no joke," said Viola. "I don't know anyone who's done it."

"Neither do I." The image of Robin, dishevelled and terri-fied-looking, came to mind, and worry for Cedar roiled inside me. Something was seriously wrong on his territory, but I doubted interfering would win me any favours. "You don't have to come with me. Serving my family doesn't mean going along with all my weird schemes."

"No, but being your friend does," she said. "I figured you need someone on your side who isn't at the whims of an ancient, power-hungry Sidhe."

"There is that," I said. "Let's go and speak to the Little People."

12

"Where are they?" Viola asked, after we'd been walking in the forest for ten minutes. "We ought to have run into them by now."

"Guilty conscience, maybe," I muttered. "I can't believe Snow White's evil cousins stole my talisman."

"Who in the world is Snow White?"

"Human faerie tale. They're usually tamer than the real thing."

I was less than convinced leaving the palace was the best idea, though we'd sealed the entire corridor where the entrance to the dungeon was. But this foggy path looked a little too much like the empty awfulness of a realm which seemed to have no magic at all. The Sidhe's elaborate Courts sat upon a rotting foundation. Might other Families have similar skeletons in their closets? Would I dare to tell Lord Hornbeam, on the off chance that it might help clear my name? We clearly had a common enemy, but if my own mother was linked to them, he might blame me by default no matter what.

"I told you not to come back, mortals."

A bearded man sprang out of the nearest bush. I just about managed not to jump.

"We're here to ask a few questions," I told the Little Person. "Can you tell me where the sword is? The one Viola saw in the house?"

His expression stilled. "The sword."

"Yes. The one with the lightning bolt on it. It used to belong to my family."

"No," he said. "It once belonged to another. I picked it up on the forest path."

Shit. He was actually admitting he had it? Of course, he couldn't lie... but there was something downright fishy about how it'd ended up in their hands in the first place.

I sought to find the right words. "Did you happen to see my mother, in any shape or form, when you picked it up? Or anyone else?"

"A dead chimera lay elsewhere in the fog. Nobody else was present."

So it was in the same place as where she died...

"And where is it now?" asked Viola.

"Gone," said the Little Person. "Another one of us took it. We share everything. Besides, the sword won't solve your dilemma."

No. I bet it won't. I'd also bet several talismans he knew far more than he let on. Time to spring a surprise on him.

"I have another question," I said. "Have you ever been to the Grey Vale?"

Silence followed, and I half expected him to pull out a knife. Viola flashed me a warning look.

"You ask dangerous questions," he said softly.

"And you're evading. It means yes."

The Little Person's expression was grave. "I wouldn't trouble yourself with things which might get you killed, mortals."

"All right, then," I said. "Would you tell me where faeries go when they die?"

His expression didn't change, but he said, "Their souls are collected and taken into the death realm. It's not uncommon knowledge."

"So if I wanted to speak with someone who died…?"

Viola shook her head at me, eyes wide in a signal to be quiet. I shrugged one shoulder. I wanted answers, and I'd get them.

"That would depend upon who," he said.

"So it's possible? Do faeries go into… the spirit realm when they die? Like the humans' afterlife, but for this realm." I was thinking aloud, but it seemed clear that whatever had gone wrong had been in Death itself. Or here in Faerie, but if dead faeries had once been reborn, something must have screwed with the process. Speaking to someone dead was the realm of human necromancers, not the faeries—at least, I'd thought so. Up until that wraith appeared. And the dead lingered in the Grey Vale…

"I have never died," he said simply. "As for speaking to the dead, there is one person who knows all souls that pass beyond this realm. If you wish to converse with the dead, you need to speak with the Morrigan. She lives in the Kingdom of Death, in the Winter Court."

"Kingdom of Death?" I echoed. "Why does that exist when everyone's immortal?"

"Because immortality comes with a price, one the Morrigan provides. She is currently chained to the Winter Court, and will not harm you."

"Are you absolutely certain? Can you show us how to get there?"

"I can."

Bloody faeries. "*Will* you?"

"You take the path along there, and continue south. Do

not wander off the path. Dark creatures are slipping through the cracks, and as the Vale's attacks become more frequent, this is possibly a terrible time for you to go there."

He disappeared into the bushes without another word.

Viola grabbed my arm and pulled me aside. "I really wouldn't."

"You think he's lying?"

"No, he's telling the truth. Every Winter faerie I've spoken to has heard of the Morrigan, and the directions match up with what I've been told. Of course, that doesn't mean she isn't possibly the most dangerous Winter faerie there is, including most of the Sidhe—not that anyone says that in front of them."

I frowned. "I've heard she's a death faerie, and that's about it. Not like banshees, but to be honest, I've never met one of those, either." Banshees screamed when someone was about to die. If the Morrigan was worse, then I'd wager we were entering nightmare territory.

"She's dangerous," said Viola. "She makes most Sidhe look like harmless wood imps."

"But she might be connected to what went wrong," I said. "She's immortal, right?"

"Immortal, yes, but she has a connection to death no other faerie has."

"She's also chained to the Winter Court, if we believe him," I said. "Which considering he can't lie, is the closest we'll get to an answer."

"I think he's right. Something happened with the Morrigan—there was talk of her getting into a disagreement with the other Sidhe. But even the Unseelie rarely dare to speak of her."

"Hmm." I considered her words. "If anyone knows what went wrong with faeries' immortality, she would, wouldn't she? A year ago, my mother died, and wasn't reborn. Her spirit passed through this Death Kingdom. So the Morrigan must have seen her. If so, she might know what went wrong."

"I don't like it," Viola said. "But I think you're right. If the goddess of death doesn't know why immortality no longer functions, then nobody else will."

"Too true," I said, glancing around at the creeping fog. "Want to go there now? We don't have any more time to waste."

"Why not add a trip into Death to our list." She grinned. "Bring it on."

We walked along the fog-wreathed path. Now I knew it meant we were close to the death realm, it took on a whole new sinister meaning. We walked swiftly, and I kept my sceptre out as a warning to anyone who might cross us.

The path sloped downward, flanked by tall creeping trees. Entirely typical of Winter, but I felt the moment when the territory shifted. A bone-deep chill went through me, and I thought of that human phrase, *someone walked over my grave.* I'd never understood it before. I didn't like thinking about death, even as an inevitability, but I wasn't afraid of it like the Sidhe were.

On the other hand, the idea of being cursed to walk through this place forever gave me chills. Wraiths… this was the sort of place they'd live. Or ghosts, at least. I'd heard of the horrors human necromancers had to deal with, but Faerie had no equivalent. Apart from this Morrigan, apparently.

"Is anyone alive on this territory?" I asked Viola.

"Even most Winter faeries avoid this place," she whispered. "It's full of banshees and sluagh… basically, everything evil. Redcaps like hanging about here. Don't bleed on anything."

"I'll try not to." I stumbled when a thick bramble snagged

my ankle. The plants here were spiked and eerie-looking, unfamiliar.

A strong breeze blew towards us, carrying a smell like rotten meat. I gagged and covered my mouth, but carried on walking. Smudges of red appeared on the mud, which froze in places. Patches of snow lay ahead, and a sloping path led to the dark hulking shape of what looked like an enormous tent.

"The Kingdom of Death," I whispered. "Nice decor. Is that the Morrigan's lair?"

"I guess." Viola stood on tip-toe to get a better look at it. "I heard it was actually a palace, though. That looks like an aboveground cave."

"Hmm." I kept walking. The giant shape grew bigger with every step, and appeared to be surrounded by a moat. A moat filled with... *ugh.*

I stopped, swallowing bile. The moat was entirely comprised of dead bodies, rotting fae of all kinds heaped on top of one another. Thick blood swirled around the edges in a ghastly imitation of a river.

Viola gagged and turned her back. "Okay, that's vile."

"And she's *inside* the place? Is there even an entrance?"

I answered my own question when I looked past the river. A wooden bridge crossed over the river of corpses, leading to a wide pair of doors made of dark wood.

I wanted nothing more than to turn my back, not walk over the bridge. Sure, there was a soft landing if I fell, but an unpleasant one. The bodies seemed to be exclusively fae-kind, ranging from trolls to redcaps. Broken skeletons lay beneath the more recent dead. It was as though a backlog of several years' worth of bodies had been tossed outside and left to rot. I forced my gaze away, approaching the bridge.

A hulking figure appeared in front of the trench, green-skinned and at least ten feet tall. "Visitors," he growled. "Your name?"

If he spoke English, hopefully he could be reasoned with. When it came to ogres, you were more likely to get clubbed in the face than not.

"I'm Raine Whitefall." I kept the sceptre within clear view. "And this is my assistant, Viola. I'm here to speak with the Morrigan."

"Whitefall," grunted the ogre.

I held my breath as he leaned in closer to the sceptre, as though sniffing to see if the magic was genuine. Ogres didn't have magic, but he must have been convinced because he nodded and shuffled back.

Well, that was suspiciously easy.

The doors creaked open, allowing us to pass. Inside was a dark hall lit only by a handful of firefly fae in jars, floating along the high, dirty walls. It smelled of mould, but anything was better than the dead body stench. Dark shapes skittered along the floor. I shuddered, almost hoping they were spiders rather than anything more sinister. Our footsteps echoed on the bare stone floor. It was the sort of silence that made you dread to break it in case someone jumped out and grabbed you.

Nothing did, but rustling sounded overhead, growing louder when we passed through a second pair of doors into what appeared to be a giant cave. More floating lights illuminated birds swooping around the ceiling. Black shapes— ravens or crows. I vaguely remembering hearing that the Morrigan could shift into a giant bird, too.

The Morrigan, however, didn't look in any shape to be shifting. She was chained to a huge black chair, throne-sized but with no adornment save for a heavy-looking metal chain. Her appearance was like that of an old faerie with pointed ears, jet-black hair, and craggy features that suggested malice rather than kindliness. Black wings protruded from each shoulder blade. A bird flew to land on her shoulder as she raised her head to look at us.

I stopped walking. A shiver traced down my spine, an unnameable primeval terror that locked my limbs into place. Then she looked away, breaking the spell. *Whoa. That's some powerful magic.* But she was locked in chains, and now I looked closely, iron bands surrounded her throne. If she tried to escape, she'd run right into them. The presence of so much iron must sap her power.

"Mortals," she whispered. "I haven't seen you before."

"I'm Raine Whitefall," I said to her. "Lady Whitefall's heir. Why are you chained up?"

"Because the Courts don't trust me, but they can't kill me. I cannot die."

"Can't you?" Of course, if she really was a death goddess, as was rumoured, maybe she was exempt from whatever force had destroyed the Sidhe's ability to live forever. If so, maybe she knew why they could die now.

"Do they not speak of me in the Courts anymore, child?"

"I'm not a child. Yes, they call you a death goddess."

"You know nothing about me, do you?" She gave a cackling laugh. "I knew a human, once. Several of them. They're responsible for this monstrosity." She twitched one wing. "Fools, all of them—loyal fools who thought they could outwit death."

"I've no idea what you're talking about," I told her. "But I'm here for a reason. You know what happens when faeries die, right? Can you tell me why the Sidhe aren't immortal anymore?"

"Those humans." She grinned. "There was one who wanted to create his own personal army of immortals. The humans stopped him, and in doing so, destroyed the source of immortality."

Well, shit. *Humans did it?* "But… do the Sidhe know that?"

"The ones who signed the initial contract do. I imagine it's caused *quite* the strain between them and the mortals they claim to cooperate with now." She laughed. "They will all die in the end, and I will endure."

My blood went cold. Sure, I'd known *I* had a limited life-span, and I didn't personally know or like any of the Sidhe enough to particularly care that their lives could be cut short. But the notion of this monstrosity being the only immortal left in Faerie—in any realm, possibly—wasn't a pleasant thought.

"Is there a reason this concerns you?" she asked. "You're mortal. Some might say you're lucky."

"Someone I know died. I'm told you can tell me how."

"It depends how violent their death was." She grinned, her sharp teeth gleaming. "All pass through my Kingdom on the way to the place where even I cannot reach, chained as I am… who is this person you speak of?"

"Raine," Viola hissed urgently.

"Lady Whitefall. My mother."

"That's interesting," she mused. "I didn't know *she* had perished… the Unseelie Court are quite keen to restrict my access to information, for some inexplicable reason. However, I have not seen her pass through my territory."

I blinked. "You see *all* the dead?"

"Yes, for the most part. A soul like hers would have shone like a beacon, and I did not see it."

She didn't come through here. Why?

"Does every single person who dies pass through here?"

"I'd kindly ask you not to mock me, mortal. I've answered your question. Will you leave me alone now? Unless…" She leaned forward. "Unless you'd like to work with me, and free me from this prison."

"Nope," I said. "One last question—have you seen *any* Sidhe pass through here?"

She gave me a calculating look. "Whitefall. I *have* heard your name before. There was one who passed through here not long ago, cursing your name."

My blood turned to ice. *Lady Hornbeam.* "A… Sidhe?"

"A female Sidhe with very powerful magic. She was delicious."

I wanted to gag. "You *eat* the dead?"

"Souls are my sustenance, mortal." She reached out a claw, but the chains held her back. My heart beat frantically. *So Lady Hornbeam is dead for real… but what about my mother?*

Not for the first time, I was starting to get the distinct impression someone was playing an elaborate prank on me. The Morrigan, I was sure, couldn't lie. The most powerful faeries couldn't, and she belonged to the Court, besides. Didn't mean they trusted her—and I couldn't help being curious to know what she'd done to end up in chains—but what if she wasn't the liar, and my mother was? She'd colluded with Grey Vale outcasts, possibly right underneath the palace. She'd told a thousand lies without uttering a single falsehood.

"Where do the souls go to after they pass through your territory?" I asked. "The afterlife?"

"Would you like to join them?"

"No, thanks." So if my mother had died, her spirit *should* have passed through here. Unless she'd died in the Grey Vale. But witnesses had *seen* her consumed by her own magic. Maybe it had been faked, but that didn't explain where she'd disappeared to. Or why she hadn't come back.

It makes more sense that she died. But I don't trust anyone's word. Not the Little People, not the Morrigan.

"Pity. I could use some entertainment."

A raven dived at me. I jumped back, and she let out a loud cackle.

"The Huntsman rides no more, child!"

The raven shot past, its sharp beak snagging my sleeve. More followed, a thousand swooping wings rustling overhead.

Instinctively, I shot magic at them, blue light tearing through the cloud of birds. They scattered in a storm of feathers. *And that's my cue to leave.*

Viola grabbed my arm and we ran to the doors, not stopping until we'd left the sound of screaming birds behind.

13

We sprinted across the bridge. The ogre shouted after us, but neither of us dared turn back. Not until the forest had swallowed us up. I half-ran back the way we'd come, every scream of the dead and screech of a raven setting my nerves on edge. Viola caught up with me, clutching a stitch in her side.

"Why did you provoke her?" she gasped. "You're a fool."

"I lost my head, all right? Sorry."

"Sidhe's blood," Viola exploded. "Did you see those birds? They say she can shift into one herself, too."

"Well, we figured out one thing," I told her. "Either my mother hid herself really well when she passed into Death… or she isn't dead at all."

Viola gave an uncertain laugh. "Raine, her magic stopped working when she died. I *felt* it."

"Yeah, I know. This makes no sense. The Morrigan can't lie, right?"

"She's as pure a faerie as you can get."

I snorted. "There was nothing remotely pure about that

place. I can't believe she's the last immortal Sidhe. She looked more like a monster that belongs in the Grey Vale." She'd definitely had magic, though—a primal, terrifying type.

"Oh no, she's part of the Courts," said Viola. "The Death Kingdom might be isolated, but the Morrigan has some important role in relation to the Winter Court. Anyway, I guess she wasn't responsible for whatever happened to stop the pure faeries being reborn."

"It doesn't sound like my mother was involved at all," I said. "But I'm starting to think she died in the Vale, not here, if at all. Her spirit wouldn't have moved on. The wraith—I think that's what exiles who die end up turning into."

And that was my fate if I failed to give Lord Hornbeam the right information. Add in my suspicion that my scheming mother might have somehow skipped death entirely, and I'd be exiled within a day. Following my mother into the Grey Vale was a death sentence all on its own. Maybe my plan to throw Lord Hornbeam into the wardrobe instead had merit after all.

"I—" Viola stopped. "I just thought of something else. I know that when a Sidhe dies, their body is consumed, and their... soul, whatever makes up the real essence of them, is taken away. Then they return, within a day, the same as they ever were. But when they're taken... it must be through the Morrigan's territory. She said *The Huntsman rides no more.* The Huntsman... it rings a bell."

"It does." I frowned. "Wait a second. In the mortal realm— I'm sure the guy leading the army who attacked us last year was trying to make an army of immortals. But he was stopped. That's what the Morrigan was talking about. Whatever the humans did to stop him destroyed the source of immortality."

Her eyes rounded. "So the Morrigan must have been involved, because the Courts wouldn't punish one of their own without good reason. But—knowing that doesn't help us find out if your mother actually died, or—"

"Damn," I said. "My dad. Someone told him she's not dead. What if it's true?"

Maybe he hadn't been spouting nonsense. Perhaps someone had told him the truth. *Why,* I had no idea.

Viola stared at me. "Who?"

"Robin? Someone threatened him…"

I stopped walking as we reached the palace gates. A person waited outside, a tall someone with an unmistakeable demeanour. No way. My three days weren't up yet.

I pushed the gate open. "Lord Hornbeam."

It couldn't be anyone else. He was resplendent in green-and-gold armour, his waist-length hair tied back and tucked behind his pointed ears. His face made the bright snow look dull by comparison.

"Lady Whitefall."

Huh. He'd used my proper title this time. Not that I cared. "Did you come to speak to me? It hasn't been three days."

Also, he was trespassing. I hoped the palace would throw him out if he tried to break in, but why come here in the first place?

"I would very much like to know what you did with my thief last night."

Well, we nearly died in a dungeon, made out, then had an argument. "Nothing," I said. "He was injured in the fight and I figured it'd be easier to let him stay at the palace than to let him die out there in the forest. My mother used to have visitors."

He sniffed. "I can't recall her inviting a lowly thief to the palace, much less one belonging to the enemy Court."

Play it safe, Raine. "I'm part human. I'm told that makes me too empathetic."

"Check your tongue when you speak to me," he snarled.

"I did have an update, if you were interested."

He lifted a brow. "What have you discovered?"

I swallowed hard, my mind going blank. I should have prepared something, but how was I supposed to know he'd come to the palace in person, least of all two days early? "There are things I suspect, but can't prove," I said. "In my experience, people in your family have a tendency to overreact. I'd rather have evidence to put before you."

"That sounds awfully close to an insult, Miss *Warren.*"

He knew my mortal surname.

No. Has he spoken to—? Robin. Was Lord Hornbeam the one who'd threatened him?

"You spoke to Robin, didn't you?" I asked.

He tilted his head. "Is there a reason you're involved with so many members of my Court? What is it that appeals so much more than your own?"

I wanted to tell him it was none of his damn business, but I was still rattled from our encounter with the Morrigan. If he forced the truth out of me, I'd be in real trouble. So I had to tell him part of the truth, enough to divert his attention from the omitted details.

"I went into the Death Kingdom and spoke with the Morrigan," I told him.

"You did what?"

"I spoke to the goddess of death," I said. "I figured nobody else could give me a conclusive answer about my mother's murder, since there were so few witnesses. Her answer was that something's screwed up in death, but she didn't even see my mother's spirit. Apparently, either she didn't die, or her ghost got stuck somewhere like those wraiths."

"How do you know about wraiths?"

"Viola told me," I improvised. "They sometimes appear at the borders. Anyway, that's not the point. The goddess of death herself doesn't know what happened to my mother. If she doesn't, I'm pretty sure it's beyond me."

"That's not good enough."

"Then what is?" I asked desperately. "She left me no clues. I don't know if she didn't expect to die or if she just didn't care about warning me, but I have no clue why she died."

Or if she died.

"It's your task," he snarled, stepping back. "You have two more days to give me satisfactory evidence. I trust you'll think of something."

I didn't move out of his way. "I need to speak to Cedar."

"What business do you have with my thief?"

I kept my tone neutral. "He's supposed to be supervising me. I got the impression he'd take the brunt of the punishment if I disappointed you."

He shook his head at me. "You're the definition of a pathetic mortal. It's a wonder you've lasted this long. My thief is defending our territory, as is his duty."

"Just wondered." Mostly, I'd worried he'd been disciplined in some horrible way for staying here overnight and helping me out. It was bad enough that both of us faced potential exile for failing to solve an impossible mystery.

Lord Hornbeam swept away through the gates, leaving Viola and me alone.

———

I couldn't sleep that night. Small wonder after the day I'd had. When I finally drifted off, I fell into the memories the memory-eater had shown to me again. Dad, actually smiling. Dancing with me, like we were a normal family...

Nothing about my mother's death added up. With no body, the fact that she'd died at all was cast in doubt. After all, we were in the realm where glamours and illusions might fool even pure-blooded faeries. If she *had* faked her death, the only place she might have gone was the Grey Vale. It made as little sense for her to work with exiles as it did that she'd left her talisman behind, considering how much power it contained. And why not come back to the palace, to see her daughter? She must know I was here, if she lived.

I've cracked. Like Dad. Seeing things that aren't there. There might be some other explanation as to why her soul didn't pass into Death.

I got out of bed and paced the room, absently glancing at the dawn light shining through the curtains. Though there was hardly a sliver of light visible, my arms prickled like I was being watched, and the palace shivered as my magic responded to an intruder. I pushed the curtain back. A short figure stood below.

What the hell is one of the Little People doing here in the middle of the night? It was like my thoughts had conjured him up. Weird. I was wide awake and the sun had begun to rise already, turning the world an eerie grey colour. Using my magic, I switched out my pyjamas for practical clothes and then opened a door into the entrance hall in my bedroom wall. Stepping through, I approached the main door with trepidation. I had no way of knowing which Little Person had come to speak to me. Viola would be asleep. But he couldn't harm me on my own territory.

I opened the door. The Little Person stood on the doorstep, for all the world like I was answering a knock on the door. Not Moss Beard, but one of the red-skinned, white-bearded ones.

"What is it?" I asked.

"I've tracked down the person who took the sword," he said.

"Seriously?" I frowned at him. "You didn't have come here in the middle of the night."

I took one step forwards, and white light shone around his feet. "What the—?"

Like... a rift. He's opening a rift.

I raised my hands, wishing I had a weapon—but there wasn't a way to stop a rift, not if you'd already walked into it. Or rather, he'd opened it on top of my doorstep.

"How?" I gasped, but the ground opened up beneath us and smoke rushed in. I flailed and kicked, trying to find purchase, but kept falling. The Little Person's smiling face was the last thing I saw before the fog overcame my vision.

I hit the ground a second later, rolling onto my front. Usually passage into the rifts involved a flash of light. Not this time. A horrible empty feeling washed over me, colder than anything in Winter.

"You bastard!" I screamed at the air. It was hopeless. The Little Person was long gone, of course. He must have used the rifts and somehow opened a passage... into the Grey Vale.

I was in the realm of the exiles, alone.

Like behind the door in the dungeon, the forest was of a similar design—tall trees covered in silvery leaves, fog, and winding paths. No markers to indicate where I was, and no way back.

My magic. That was the empty sensation—the realm itself was as lifeless as the emptiness of death itself. Even in the mortal realm, I'd been able to sense the presence of magic, just on a lower level than Faerie. Here, it was as though the very essence of the world had been stripped away, leaving monochrome paths and eerie silence.

A howl ripped through the air. I shuddered. *Maybe not silence, then.* This place was the home of every faerie too cruel and bloodthirsty to have a home in the Courts, or those who'd accidentally wandered too far off Faerie's paths, and fallen through a rift. I'd suspected the rifts might link to the Grey Vale, but assumed it wasn't a permanent thing, because the mortal realm's representatives—Ivy Lane in particular—had fought hard to prevent another attack from the Vale outcasts.

But the Little People must have hijacked the rifts for their own, without the Courts knowing. They were the perfect spies. How many were working against us? For how long? They'd been present every time Viola or Cedar and I had been near their territory. They'd certainly know that Cedar and I were working together, and they might even know…

Did it matter if they knew I'd killed Lady Hornbeam, though? They were working against the Hornbeams anyway, set on some scheme of their own. *What*, I didn't know.

I also didn't have a clue how to get back to Faerie from here. I hadn't been stripped of my magic like the exiles, but I didn't have the ability to cross realms anyway. I didn't even have my talisman.

Calm down, Raine. People have been here before. Yeah—been *kidnapped.* The exiled Sidhe were possibly worse for torturing humans than the Sidhe in the main Courts, because it'd been the Grey Vale Sidhe who'd invaded the mortal realm. I sucked in a deep breath, trying not to panic. I'd never felt so utterly alone, not even when I'd been solely responsible for taking care of Dad as a kid. After all, we'd had each other. The only familiar person I was likely to run into here was my mother. Or her ghost.

With that cheery thought in mind, I began to walk. I'd encountered enough dark fae in the mortal realm to know that here, only the strongest and foulest creatures survived. Skin-eating beasts, monsters that sucked the very life out of you, and Sidhe who used corrupted magic to feast on the dead and living alike to fuel their power.

Come on. Take me somewhere that has a way out—

The path abruptly curved, moving before my eyes. I stopped walking. I'd used magic to rearrange the path, like I could on my own territory, somehow. *Oh.* It must be because the Grey Vale counted as neutral territory as far as Faerie's rules were concerned. Which meant I could rearrange it to my own ends.

All right. Take me somewhere I can get back to the faerie realm. Or the mortal realm. Either would do. Anywhere but this empty place. *Take me back.*

I walked. The path didn't change, but sloped uphill a little. I kept walking. Of course, I couldn't specifically say, *take me somewhere that won't kill me.* Magic wasn't that sophisticated. And it was clear this place *did* have magic, though muted. A reflection in a pond compared to the vibrancy of the true faerie realm.

The path kept going, and a wave of coldness rushed down my spine at the sight of a squat building nearby. I'd reached someone else's territory. *An exile. It has to be.* The fortress-like construction reminded me entirely too much of Lady Hornbeam's prison.

"Hello, half-blood," hissed a voice, and a giant hand closed around my throat.

The huge ogre hauled me off the ground. I struggled and kicked, but his grip threatened to snap my neck. Through blurred vision, I saw ogres and trolls gather around, laughing at me. My captor threw me into the air and caught me by the leg, dangling me upside-down.

"Let me go, you big ugly fucker."

"What is this?" asked a male voice.

My head spun with vertigo, but I recognised the speaker. A man with dark hair and impossibly bright green eyes... and that was all I could focus on as he advanced on me, grabbing me by the hair while the ogre continued to dangle me upside-down.

The man jabbed a finger at me, poking the crescent moon mark on my face. "I know that mark." He laughed. "She came to us. That saves us a lot of trouble, doesn't it?"

He was Lady Hornbeam's son, Aspen. Supposed heir to the Hornbeam family… and traitor.

14

His fingernail drove down my face, drawing blood, and I spat in his face.

Aspen cursed and stepped back. "Drop her," he told the ogre.

I threw out my arms to break my fall, but the impact slammed into my elbows. I got to my feet in a second, sprinting for my life.

I didn't make it ten feet before the giant hand caught me again, this time holding me the right way up.

"What are you doing here?" I asked Aspen, rotating in mid-air as the ogre dangled me above the ground. "Did your father kick you out?"

"You didn't think I'd consent to serve under a snivelling coward, did you?"

I shrugged, or tried to. "You tell me. You're a prick, so I guess it stands to reason you'd want your own castle. This place is pretty gloomy, though."

"Insolent human."

"I don't have any more human blood than you do."

"But I have more talismans than you."

So he took Lady Hornbeam's?

"Do you want a medal?" I said, to cover up my surprise. I guess if he'd defied his father, he'd have taken all the weapons he could. And if he'd got to the talismans first, then it was logical that one of them might have chosen him. After all, he was half-Sidhe, and… and the second half-blood to pick a talisman, after me. If he wasn't lying.

He grinned, his even white teeth gleaming in the eerie grey light. "You're being awfully quiet. Finally accepted your place?"

"Sure I have. Standing over your corpse."

"That sounded like a threat."

"You're obviously working against the Courts. What I don't understand is why. You were heir, right? So you're fighting your own father?"

"I'm fighting nobody," he said. "I don't want to lead any territory other than this one."

"But—you're not an exile." His eyes had the same bright green glow as a Sidhe at the height of their power. "You walked out of Faerie of your own accord."

"Of course I did," he said. "The fool thought to erase my mother's memory. And *you* are the one who took her from me."

Green light shone around him in a bright halo, and a vicious smile curled his mouth.

"Very scary," I told him.

"Oh, I am," he said softly. "Don't you want to know what this realm does to our magic?" He tilted his head. "On second thought, I'll save that for later. Get her."

He gestured not at the ogres, but at several half-blood soldiers wearing armour. They must have defected from Lord Hornbeam, too.

I got one punch in before an iron blade came inches from

stabbing me in the chest. I froze, caught between five weapons. Being this close, I couldn't draw on magic at all. They all wore too much iron for me to fight, and the sceptre wasn't much use as a combat weapon. I hadn't thought to grab anything else before I'd left the palace. *I'm going to kill that Little Person.*

Kicking all the way, I was dragged into the building with Aspen walking behind me. He barked out orders while they hauled me along a corridor. The building's interior was so dark, it was like being underground. *How long has this place been here?*

The soldiers threw me headfirst into a cell. Others huddled in cells alongside me, visible through the bars. Humans, and half-bloods, too. So Aspen was capturing mortals instead of ruling alongside his stepfather. All my shouted questions met with no answers, only echoes, and screams from my fellow prisoners.

It was several minutes before someone came up to my cell. Someone with fair hair and a despondent expression.

"Robin?" I whispered. "What are you doing here?"

"They caught me again," he whispered.

"But you're not in a cage."

"Only because I'm useful to them. Aspen is trying to get me to help capture mortals."

"How the hell did you even end up here?" I gave him a suspicious look. "He's the one who you were scared of before, right?"

"He caught us," said Robin. "Lord Hornbeam kicked us out, and his son swooped in."

"Stepson," I said. "Damn, that family's complicated. I don't suppose you've seen Cedar?"

"Who?"

I hope he's safely back in Faerie. Though 'safe' was a relative term. After all, he was doing battle with these very creatures on his stepfather's territory, without knowing part of his family had gone rogue.

"He's putting us under vows," he whispered. "He'll do the same to you. I can't say—" He broke off. "Someone's coming."

He moved swiftly away, leaving me in the dark.

Seconds later, Aspen appeared, flanked by two soldiers. "How are you liking your accommodation?"

"It's cosy. When are you planning to let me out?"

"Only after you swear yourself to me," he said. "I hoped I'd find a better use for you than bait, but your friend Robin is bound to me. I'm sure he'd be less than thrilled if I were to order him to carve pieces out of you while my servants watch. So I suggest you do as I say."

"You're a sick bastard, you know that?"

"We're all bastards here, you foolish child. That's what it is to be half-blood." His eyes glittered. "As for you, I wanted to thank you for showing me that anyone can claim power, even an ignorant and underpowered human."

I'm not underpowered. But the iron bars were immune to my magic, and having seen the monsters he employed as guards, my chances of escape had plummeted. If I got past the doors, though, I could make a run for it. If I made him think I was cooperating.

"What kind of vow are we talking about?" I asked.

"Swear you will serve me, Raine," he said, a delighted and malicious current to his voice. "Swear it."

That's it? Wait... as a half-blood, he wouldn't be as used to making vows or giving orders as a pure Sidhe. He'd given me a dozen openings, if I twisted the words to my own ends.

"I, Raine Whitefall, swear I will do as you tell me." *Until I cut your throat.*

He grinned and snapped his fingers. Something yanked me forward like an invisible rope attached to my chest. *Damn, that stings.* The trick was to twist the words of his vow, all the while knowing he could twist them himself whenever he liked. It came down to a battle of wills. I needed to get close to incapacitate him, then escape at the first opportunity. But already, alarm had begun to trickle through me. I'd never actually *been* under a vow before. I'd only witnessed their effect on other people. The horrible tugging sensation like part of me was physically attached to Aspen was a side effect I hadn't anticipated.

"Excellent," he said. "Let's just say my army needs some persuasion to stay in line. So I'm going to give them entertainment, and you'll be the central act. I'm told you make an unforgettable performance."

Icy dread rose in my chest as the sound of faerie music drifted in. He'd planned this. The music was low-pitched and eerie, but my blood stirred—not the faerie side of me, but the mortal one. He wanted to use us to ensnare mortals. As a performer, I knew our dance had a hypnotic effect, and made for a performance that couldn't be repeated elsewhere. Was that why he'd kidnapped Robin? Our act had been harmless, weaving a simple spell to rivet the audience's attention—not difficult, because we were damn good at what we did anyway. But Aspen had more sinister motives.

"Come," he said, and my knees buckled under the unexpected impact of the word. The vow had been vague enough that he could force me to do anything he liked, if his magic was stronger—and it was, because I was surrounded by iron. I needed to get away from the cells before I could summon up enough resistance to push him away.

Down the corridor, twin oak doors opened into a giant hall. There, humans and half-bloods sat in rows surrounding a raised stage, where an orchestra played. A human one. The players jerked like puppets on strings, bloodied fingers plucking at instruments. A sick taste rose in my throat.

"They are not all subdued yet," he said. "This is our

newest batch. We're hoping to make progress on all of them tonight. Half-bloods are a little trickier to persuade."

I looked past him, desperately, but the crowd blocked all possible exits, and armoured guards surrounded the captive audience.

Aspen held up a pair of pipes, and a tune began, adding to the orchestra.

The mortals followed, hypnotised, their heads moving up and down in synchronisation. I spotted Robin at the stage's side, but he wasn't looking at me.

"Dance," intoned Aspen, and my will disappeared as the spell consumed me, body and mind.

———

I'd danced all night. The hours had blurred together until I was nothing more than an empty shell, dormant until he woke me up and ordered me to move.

He woke me personally every morning, snapping his fingers in front of my cage. Half unconsciously, I obeyed, my body jumping to attention instantly. He sometimes remembered to feed me, sometimes not. Half-bloods could survive without food or water longer than humans could, provided our magic kept functioning. And mine did. He didn't try to take it away. Maybe he didn't know how, since it was no longer tied to my talisman. All I knew was that I was tired, and hurt everywhere, yet my feet kept moving, I kept dancing, every move was perfect, and there was nothing else...

Snap.

I jerked to my feet one morning, nearly falling into the bars. A strong hand steadied me. "Watch it," Aspen said, his mouth curling with amusement. "You don't want to touch the iron, do you?"

I shrugged one shoulder. It didn't seem to matter either way.

The cage opened, and I trailed after him. When he snapped his fingers again, I sped up, keeping pace with him. He'd snapped the questions out of me the first day. He thought of everything.

I had no will of my own, and I was his.

The others were terrified of him. They moved out of his way in the corridors, half-bloods and humans alike. As usual, I had to wait at the stage's side for the signal to begin the dance. Nearby stood Robin, and this time he looked at me.

Robin's brows rose, and he paled. I wondered what I looked like that terrified him so much.

The vow didn't affect him as badly as it did me, said a voice in my head.

What vow?

"Raine!" he hissed.

A hand slapped him from behind, sending him pitching forward. He seemed to be signalling with his eyes, but it was beyond me to tell what. *Look down.* Where? There wasn't anything but dirt and… *oh.* My feet had swollen up until they were unrecognisable, crusted with dirt and grime. I'd lost my shoes, or maybe worn through them, some time back.

How long had I been here?

I didn't even wear the same clothes, but a ridiculous sparkly outfit that clung to my body. Red marks on my arms indicated scars I didn't remember receiving.

Like… iron cuffs.

A scarred face flashed before my eyes. And a name. *Cedar.*

I faltered, and Aspen snapped his fingers again. Once more, I followed, my feet carrying me away from Robin.

Robin. I still knew him… he'd made me dance for him, once. No, I'd chosen to. The image of a different stage came to mind, one where mortals swayed beneath the beauty of our performance.

The dance I did here wasn't beautiful but terrifying, ensnaring, deadly. Blood was shed on the stage every night or day. Come to think of it, I didn't know what time it was. In here it was always dark, but outside, the sky remained light grey no matter the time of day. From another time, I remembered light shone from somewhere through gaps in the endless silver-leafed trees. Like another place I knew. The music muddled my thoughts and made it hard to focus. Aspen played the pipes, and the thoughts began to slide away.

The music is muddling my thoughts.

Where did that thought come from?

I raised my hands to my ears, momentarily muffling the noise, but it was everywhere, in the walls and the floor and *make it stop make it stop...*

A slap knocked my hand away from my ear. My hand stung, the first real sensation I'd felt in days. If not weeks.

Already the music carried my thoughts away, and all else faded.

———

I woke to a horrific scream. A human man lay on the floor in front of my cell, blood spilling from a wound in his chest. I reached for him instinctively, arms brushing against the iron. I recoiled, gasping in pain.

Iron. Iron hurt me, like the bars. Like…

Cedar.

That name kept coming back to me. For some reason, I associated it with the cage. With the horrible way the crowd swayed under Aspen's thrall.

I'd had a life before this one. Before the music.

I crouched, pressed my palms to my ears. Before the music, I'd… I'd been in a glass palace. No, ice. And then I'd left, following a bearded man, and I'd fallen… *dammit.* The music's spell was strong enough to hold me captive even when it wasn't playing. But I did remember. Enough to know I needed to break it.

My clothes were filthy and torn. I ripped part of my sleeve off, tore it in two, and stuffed each piece in my ears. The cloth hurt, but I didn't remove it. I kept very still, lying on my side. I normally only woke when Aspen snapped his fingers, but the human's scream had woken me early. He sobbed, but nobody came to get him. He fell still, his last breath stuttering out.

A jolt of disconnected rage went through me.

He's put you under a vow. You swore to serve him.

My plan came back to me, piece by piece, as rage began to spread through me.

Aspen's footsteps sounded. "Get this thing out of here," he snapped at someone. "Filth." His fingers snapped, and then my cage clicked open.

This time he grabbed me roughly, hauling me to my feet. I stumbled against him, and he snatched the cloth from my ear. "What is this?"

"I—there was a human screaming…"

"Yes," he said. "They're difficult, aren't they? Do come with me. We have unexpected company tonight. Someone you might know well. If we can catch her. It'll be a fun game."

Bile burned my throat. The key to my cell hung loosely in his hand. He hadn't expected me to break the spell.

I shoved the door before he'd pulled me out of it, angling myself so the iron bars caught him in the face. He roared in rage, but I was already past him, my bleeding feet skidding on the hard floor. A guard loomed in front of me and I jumped at him, fingernails digging into his eyes.

He screamed, the sound overwhelming the music's remaining echo in my head and further driving a nail into my skull. I climbed over him and kept running.

"Get her!"

Without the iron in the way, I could use magic. My fingers burned with cold as I conjured blue-white light and sent sharp icicle-like blades behind and in front of me, slicing through anyone who came near. The floor was slick with blood, and I kept running.

The body of a guard fell across my path as I careened around the corner. A curly-haired woman wielding an iron knife that looked like it belonged to one of the guards stopped dead at the sight of me.

"Viola," I gasped. "What in the world are you doing here?"

"I'll explain later." She turned and ran, veering into another corridor. I vaguely remembered being carried this way when they'd brought me in. Sidhe's blood, how much time had really passed? "They caught me and were going to make an example out of me. I only got away because I used magic to disguise myself as a guard and swiped their weapons."

I never thought of that. Aspen couldn't have more effectively shut off my magic if he'd stolen my talisman. Shame and anger burned in my chest as we ran through the door, past more slaughtered guards, and into the light. So much light, silvery and cold.

"I'm sorry," she added. "I saw you vanish when the Little Person was at the palace, and I confronted him. Then bribed him. I had to give away half the treasure in the palace, but I'm here."

"Damn." I stared at her. "You really did that for me?"

"Of course. Was it really Aspen?"

"Unfortunately." I stopped as a shadow crossed our path.

A Little Person—Moss Beard, to be precise—appeared, watching me with solemn eyes.

"Oh, no," I said. "I'm *not* going through the rift again."

"He's on our side," said Viola. "He heard what the others did. He was going to warn you."

A flare of light surrounded the three of us, and we disappeared. I stumbled into a patch of bracken, which scratched my bare legs. I still wore the ridiculous outfit from the stage —ragged, bright, and not warm enough for Winter territory. My teeth chattered. I shouldn't be cold at all, let alone on my own territory.

What the hell had they done to me?

The Little Person bowed. "I would not linger here," he said. "I might not be able to rescue you again, should one of my kin decide to oppose the Courts."

Right. The Little People were traitors. Thoughts and memories came back to me in an overwhelming rush. I'd been investigating my mother's murder for Lord Hornbeam… and the three days were definitely long gone.

"Shit," I said. "Has Lord Hornbeam been to the palace?"

"No," Viola said. "He thinks you're dead. The Summer Court hasn't come asking questions yet, but that's only because Lord Hornbeam hasn't told them."

"So he hasn't? I thought my deadline was up."

"His stepson betrayed him and he's fighting a war. I'd bet he has enough occupying his time."

Good point. "And has Cedar come asking after me?"

A pause. *That's a no, then.* I didn't know why I was so disappointed, considering I hadn't thought I had it in me to feel anything more than dull rage.

"Honestly, I haven't heard from him at all," said Viola quietly. "I went to look for him, you know—when I was visiting Rose. But I didn't see him."

"Oh no." Had he run? Or had Lord Hornbeam punished

him with a fate worse than iron for letting me slip away? That, or—or he'd given up on me. But wasn't his fate tied to mine? I was in no shape to rescue him. I could barely walk. My feet were numb and swollen. My knees nearly gave out when we passed the snow-people standing like guardian angels outside the palace. Once inside, I sat down heavily on the polished floor. "I fucking hate Aspen."

"He's the one in charge?" Viola asked. "He had a lot of allies. Way too many. Lord Hornbeam's lost half his council, at least."

"Apparently he wanted bigger things than being heir. Like hypnotising mortals." I winced. "I can't *believe* it. How many days was I gone?"

"Ten days."

Less than I'd thought, but Dad would think I'd abandoned him. And the Courts, now I knew just how powerful persuasive magic could be, would get the truth out of me immediately. They'd execute me as a traitor.

"Aspen…" She hesitated. "What exactly did he do?"

"He made me swear a vow to him. I did it because I figured I could work around it, but he had this music that made me forget everything. Who I was, how I got there. Hypnosis, of a sort, and powerful enough to work on half-bloods. This talisman was shaped like a set of pan pipes."

"He must have stolen them." Viola looked pale. "I killed a handful of his people—they were soldiers I used to work with, when I was with the Hornbeam family. I never thought they'd defect, even if they didn't like Lord Hornbeam. I can't believe they all left the *Court* as well as their family."

"I know, right?" I closed my eyes then opened them again. "What do I owe the Little People this time, anyway?"

She cleared her throat. "About that. There's something else I got. It cost me an arm and a leg, almost literally."

Viola reached for a sheath at her waist and pulled out the talisman sword.

15

The sword gleamed with elaborately carved glyphs, which ran up the blade to the hilt. A lightning bolt shone from the end, and blue light indicated its Winter magic. I didn't detect any power coming from it, but my own resources were burned to almost nothing. My hand dropped. "Honestly, I'm not sure it wouldn't kill me at the moment."

Viola nodded. "It's okay, you don't have to do it now. You need a rest and something to eat first. I think I have some cream to put on your feet somewhere."

"I'm okay." I wobbled to my feet, conjuring up a door to my room. At least I had that much of my magic left.

I avoided looking in the mirror until I'd scrubbed all the grime from my skin and rid my hair of all the dirt. Even after extensive scrubbing, the marks on my arms didn't disappear. My feet hurt like hell, and there was something wrong with my reflection in the steamed-up bathroom mirror. My eyes were no longer bright blue, but dull grey, like all the magic had been leached out of them. I could still sense it, so it couldn't have gone away completely, but the eyes staring out of my wasted face were a stranger's. I leaned closer to the mirror, and breathed out when a light blue spark passed through my eyes. *It's not gone yet.*

Only now could I really appreciate how lucky I'd been to survive. Boosting my magic in the mortal realm at the solstice had probably saved my life.

I moved back from the mirror, grimacing. My hair was still more grey-coloured than white. At least I'd probably scare the hell out of Lord Hornbeam—or if not him, the other faeries in his Court. Maybe they wouldn't shoot arrows at me this time. *Yeah, right.* He'd be pissed I had no answers, and the Sidhe alone knew what he'd do if he found out Aspen had been responsible for my capture.

I limped out of the bathroom and to my room, where I found Viola with a tray containing food and some unlabelled bottles.

"Super-strength healing cream. For your feet."

"Thanks." I flopped onto my bed. "Seriously. I can't believe you came into the Grey Vale. How did you know I was there?"

"The Little Person told me. I was rather forceful with my questioning. Then the Hemlock Way Little Person showed up and helped me. I gather he planned to punish the traitor in a memorable way."

"Lucky he got us out." I propped up on my elbows and picked up a sandwich. "Thanks. He wasn't great at remembering to feed me."

"Anytime." She paused. "I'm sorry I took so long to find you. I—you should probably know I traded a bunch of antiques from the palace for that sword."

"Are you kidding me?" I said between bites. "You saved my life. I meant it when I said I didn't want all of her antiques, anyway. The Little People will probably find a better use for them."

"Lady Whitefall would murder me if she knew."

I swallowed a mouthful of bread. "Better hope she's not still alive, then. Because I'll throttle her for getting me into this mess. If she *was* in the Vale, I sure as hell didn't see her."

"About that," Viola said. "I still think we need to warn the Courts. If there are Little People betraying both Faerie and the mortal realms, the Courts won't listen if the Little Person from Hemlock Way reports them. They might listen to us."

"Nobody bothers to check up on humans," I said. "I doubt the Courts would care. They *would* care that Aspen is building an army in the Grey Vale, but only if it's a direct threat to them. And if I admit I've been there, they might use it as an excuse to kick me out of Faerie for good. I mean, I still broke the rules, and I'll bet the Little People won't admit they tricked me."

"Damn," said Viola. "You're right. But I don't think we can fight Aspen alone, if at all."

"Then we'll handle Lord Hornbeam first. He must know his stepson's gone on a power trip in the Vale." Or maybe he didn't. After all, with the Little People opening rifts into the Vale, anyone from here might be working behind the Courts' backs.

I should feel more relieved than I did at the thought of the Courts intervening. I'd wanted someone to take this impossible mess off my hands all along, and I had little room in my head for much else other than revenge on Aspen for humiliating me. But I couldn't help wondering how many people were left on Lord Hornbeam's territory. Aspen must have offered a hell of an incentive to those he'd brought with him. But of course, if they'd left of their own free will without being exiled, they still had their magic and their iron armour. Lord Hornbeam might not even know the attack was coming.

"He'll pay for what he did," said Viola. "One way or another."

"Damn straight."

———

Early the following morning, I set out for Lord Hornbeam's territory.

"Are you sure you want to come?" I asked Viola. "I wouldn't ask you to risk your life again. If this goes wrong, I'll be exiled by the end of the day."

"I reckon you've a better chance than you did in the Vale," said Viola. "Also, I should be asking *you* if you're up for it. You look like you spent a fortnight living in a troll's nest."

"Thanks. And no, I've no idea if I'm up for it." Being back on my own territory had helped, but one glance in the mirror told me a decent night's sleep hadn't got rid of the circles under my eyes or their washed-out colour. "Also, I don't think you should come into the palace itself. Just in case he decides to punish us both."

"I'll be waiting in the forest on standby," she said.

I changed my clothes into the usual armoured coat, which helped me look a little more put together. What with my ragged hair and the sceptre, I didn't look like a queen, but a warrior returning scarred from a long war. *All right, I'll go with that.*

Enemy territory was suspiciously quiet. Viola led the way, since the forest paths had apparently rearranged themselves after my last visit. Otherwise, it looked pretty similar. Broad, leafy trees, crowding on either side. Thick undergrowth. Life thriving, unlike the eerie silver paths of the Vale.

Why would Aspen choose the Grey Vale over this realm? Not only had I fallen prisoner, I hadn't managed to get any useful information out of him in the process. What with his magic, and the music, I kept forgetting he was half-blood. He acted like a full-blooded Sidhe, with the arrogance to match.

Viola stopped walking when we drew nearer to the golden wire-like fence. The palace was the same golden monstrosity it'd been the last time I'd seen it, but no guards waited outside the open gates. *Weird.* Weirder still, the doors didn't automatically open, and when I pushed them, they gave a little. Okay, something was definitely off with their security.

Cedar. Where is he?

I heaved at the doors, earning nothing but a bruised elbow, but a loud clunk came from behind them, like a heavy object falling over. Then footsteps sounded.

"Get out, Vale scum," roared a voice, and two arrows shot down, landing either side of me.

I tilted my head to see two archers on the roof. "Do I look like a wraith?"

One of them nearly fell off the roof. "Lady Whitefall?"

"I'm here to speak to Lord Hornbeam." I held out my sceptre for emphasis. "What the hell is going on here?"

"He is indisposed."

"No, he isn't," growled a voice. The doors flew open, and Lord Hornbeam stood in the doorway, breathing heavily.

He was also covered in blood, including his face, which made it easier to focus on him. He didn't even look that special now the glamour wasn't turned up as high. Golden skin paled to ashy white, green eyes dulled of colour. *Oh. He got his magic drained.*

"Did Aspen get you, too?" I asked.

His hand shot out and grabbed my throat in answer, lifting me off the ground. You'd think losing that much blood should have made it hard for him to stay on his feet, but he lifted me to eye level and snarled in my face. "You traitorous bitch."

I tried to say, *I'm your equal, you massive wanker,* but only the last word came out.

"Lord Hornbeam!" The archers leaped down to land either side of him. "You shouldn't be overexerting your magic—"

"Would you like me to put a spear through your skull, Groves?"

"No, Lord Hornbeam, but that *is* Lady Whitefall. She has the talisman."

"I'm aware of who she is, you incompetent excuse for an archer. The other Sidhe must be in on this scheme, and her territory is practically on top of the Vale."

He has no idea how right he is. "I'm not—a traitor," I gasped. My vision went fuzzy around the edges as his grip tightened —then he let me go.

I dropped to my knees, fighting for breath.

"If she was with the Vale traitors, she'd have gone back with them when they'd cleared off," said the archer he'd called Groves. "She looks half dead, anyway. Want me to finish her off?"

"Hear me out first." I pushed to my feet and looked him in the eyes. "I need to talk to you alone. It's urgent. If not, I'm going to report in to the Courts one way or another. I know who's plotting against you."

"Fine," he snarled, moving back into the hall. "If you make one wrong move, you'll get an iron arrow through the skull."

Inside the palace, he gestured to the same side room as before, and I followed him in.

"You say you know who is leading the Vale forces?" he asked.

"I do," I said. "I was kidnapped by your son, Aspen. He's behind it, and he also has an army of half-bloods. Including some of your own soldiers."

"You're lying to gain my favour."

"What reason would I have? I know what he's doing. He's kidnapping humans and putting them under a spell to form some kind of army. Half-bloods, too. He intends to attack the Courts. I want to propose an allegiance."

He looked away. "You have no army. No resources. You have nothing whatsoever to offer me that I might find useful, in our battle with the Vale or otherwise."

"But I know where Aspen is hiding, and how he's building his army and sneaking in and out of the mortal realm. The Little People have been compromised. That's a matter for the Courts, and if they learn the truth, they'll send an army all of their own. If you say no, I'll be speaking to them one way or another. But they might listen to both of us."

"You're half-blood. You won't get within a mile of the Winter Court."

"Try me. I've already spoken to the Morrigan. You keep underestimating half-bloods, that's your problem. Look at Aspen. He's as strong as a Sidhe."

His eyes narrowed. "He'll get what he deserves when he comes to challenge me."

Looking at the state of him, I figured that was highly unlikely. "He has two talismans. Did you know?"

He scowled. "He's a foolish child."

I doubted he wanted to admit just how badly he'd fared in the fight against the Vale, let alone his own stepson. Faerie pride would do him in at this rate.

"If not an alliance, then I came to ask for something else," I said.

"What is it, mortal?"

"I want Cedar." Shit, that came out wrong. "Your thief. Where is he?"

"The thief? I locked the traitorous little worm up."

Oh, crap. "You locked him up? Why?"

"For betraying us to the Vale."

"Cedar isn't a traitor. He's not working for the Vale. How can he?"

"He was her spy, like Aspen was Lady Hornbeam's tool. I want none of her people working for me."

"Then can I—can he come with me?"

"If he's still alive, you're welcome to him. I should have known better than to employ my late wife's pets."

I stepped back. "Where—?"

"The jail. Get out."

Cedar.

I backed out of the room. To my relief, the palace door was open, and I all but sprinted out.

"Where are you going?" demanded the nearest archer.

"Home. Keep an eye on your boss," I warned them. "And watch out for Aspen. He's turning your fellow soldiers against you."

I hurried across the grounds past the deadly plants swaying over the fences, and slipped out the gates. Hurrying back into the forest, I found Viola waiting further down the path, hovering anxiously on tip-toe.

"Cedar's in jail," I said to her. "I have permission to get him out. Apparently Lord Hornbeam doesn't want anyone around who worked for his late wife."

"Are you sure?"

"I won't risk him dying." I took off at a fast pace, Viola easily taking the lead—I was still slower than usual from the beating my feet had taken. "Lord Hornbeam thought he was a traitor."

"Because he's Lady Hornbeam's son? Or an heir?"

"Shit. That'll be it. I mean, if Aspen's left, that removes one person between Cedar and being the head of the family."

Viola nodded. "He'll want to stop any chance of someone with her blood taking the position."

We reached the prison, which looked the same as before

—a squat building with iron built into its foundations. Unlike last time, there was nobody around, but guards weren't needed when you had iron bars.

"Yeah, well, he's losing this game," I said. "The Vale will have an open shot at the Courts then. Unless we stop them." I glanced around. It seemed awfully quiet.

"I'll watch out for traps," said Viola. "Either he lost more of his army than I thought, or they're all at the palace. There are supposed to be guards here."

"I'll be quick."

I sprinted to the jail doors, which were unlocked. My footsteps echoed in the gloomy corridor. No lights, and no guards either. Had all the prisoners been freed… or turned traitor? Most of the cages were empty. Except one.

Cedar lay slumped on the floor of his cage, one hand chained to the wall. The same one with the iron band on his wrist. His whole arm had turned the same grey as the stone and hung limply. He didn't seem to be breathing.

No. Please, no.

I kicked the door open. Cedar stirred. His head lifted, his eyes opening a fraction. His usually flawless face was streaked with mud, his hair was matted, and the cuff on his wrist had rubbed a layer of skin off which looked all the more painful because his magic should have healed it.

He blinked, eyes opening wider.

"Raine," he said. "I'm dead, aren't I?"

My throat closed up, relief choking me. "No."

"You look dead."

I forced a laugh. "How flattering. You don't exactly look amazing yourself."

He hissed in pain when he tried to stand, the chain holding him back.

"I need to get this off without touching it." Damn. I dug

my hands in my pockets, finding the gloves I'd put there before. I slid them on, fumbling the chain.

"Here." Viola handed me a lock pick. I took it in one hand and used it to free Cedar's wrist, then I turned his hand over, finding the band still clasped around his wrist. I wished I'd thought of using thick gloves before. He gasped a little as he was freed, slumping against the wall.

"We're in trouble," I said to Cedar. "Lord Hornbeam's lost the plot, and he's also lost half his guards to the Grey Vale. Aspen's building an army there. And some of the Little People are evil. I'll tell you the rest later," I added, as his gaze slid out of focus.

Drawing on what little strength I had left, I put my arm around him and helped him to his feet. He managed two steps towards the exit before leaning heavily on me.

"Come on," Viola said urgently. "We've pushed our luck already. I don't think all the guards were thrilled with our plan to let him go."

"No, I imagine not," Cedar managed through gritted teeth. "Where are we going?"

"My territory," I said. "You're lucky to be alive, you know that?"

He twisted to look at me. "What did you say about Aspen?"

"Let me explain when we're back at the palace."

16

Cedar didn't speak throughout my explanation, when we'd managed to get back to the living room in one piece. "Sidhe's blood," he finally growled. "I knew Aspen had fled the Courts. I assumed he'd gone to another family."

"Nope, he's started his own," I said. "Complete with creepy music, hypnosis, and a bunch of defecting soldiers."

"We killed several of them," Viola added.

"Oh, yeah." My flight from the prison seemed like a dream. Had I really run through the corridor in a mad panic, sending shears of icy magic after anyone who came near me?

"You didn't tell Lord Hornbeam?" Cedar looked horrified.

"No, of course not," I said. "Does it matter if we kill traitors?"

"I meant about the Vale," said Cedar.

"No." I hadn't yet told him what Aspen had made me do. I'd said I was a prisoner there, not the nature of the setup. The wounds were too raw. It'd take me a good while to wrap my head around the fact that Cedar wouldn't report every word I said to his boss. Keeping him here forever would be impossible, though, not with a murder charge still on my head. I just had to hope the war with the Vale outcasts would divert Lord Hornbeam's attention from our unfinished business.

Cedar closed his eyes. "Good."

"By the way," I said. "The Little People—some of them are traitors, too. So I wouldn't go back into the mortal realm for a bit."

One eye half-opened. "Did Lord Hornbeam ask you to bring me here?"

Viola and I exchanged glances. "No," I said. "He's lost his mind because Aspen went rogue."

Cedar swore in the faerie tongue. "If he knows I'm here—"

"He knows," I interrupted. "He let us come and get you out of jail. He thought you were a traitor, did you know?"

"He..." Cedar paled, apparently lost for words. Then he climbed to his feet. "I can't stay here."

"You sure as hell can't stay in jail, either." I folded my arms and looked at him. "You can stay here as long as you like. There are probably spare clothes in one of the rooms." I waved a hand and a door opened. "Take whichever room you —" I broke off when he strode into one of the rooms alone. *All right, then.*

I didn't have the energy to handle Cedar's situation, not now I knew exactly who was standing against the Courts. Because now I was away from Aspen's influence, parts of his plan had begun to come back to me. He'd subdued me in seconds using his hypnosis. What effect would that have on a pure Sidhe? If it worked... we were in a whole world of trouble.

Which left me with two choices: run back to the mortal

realm forever, or stoop to making an alliance with the one family in the borderlands with an army. I had none of my own. I was tired, worn down, and as much as I hated to admit it, I wasn't strong enough to face Aspen, not after he'd drained my magic dry.

But no matter who I had to ally with, I'd make him pay for what he'd done.

———

No word came from Lord Hornbeam the following day. Nor from Cedar. I went into the kitchen that morning to find Viola sitting alone, tossing an apple from one hand to the other.

"Our guest went for a walk," she informed me.

"He did remember that there'll be soldiers who are likely to shoot him on sight in the forest, right?" I shook my head and picked up a plate. "Why I ever bothered saving him. The ungrateful shit."

"You're both in a bad mood today," Viola remarked.

"I expected a little gratitude for risking my neck to get him out of jail, that's all." I tossed a grape into my mouth. "I'm not sending a rescue party after him again."

Viola shrugged. "He wants to go back to the mortal realm, but he has nothing to barter with. The Little People aren't letting anyone through."

"Why not lend him something to trade from the palace?"

"He won't take it. I already offered. He's got twice as much pride as a bloody Sidhe."

I picked up an apple and turned it over before biting into it. "I need to talk to him."

"He'll come around," Viola said. "It's a major shock to leave your family. I should know."

I dropped my gaze. "I know, but it's not like I forced him to. Unless he thinks he owes me a favour."

"I'm pretty sure that *is* exactly what he thinks."

I groaned. Sure, I was aware that we'd rescued him on less than ideal terms. There was no safe haven for him in Faerie, aside from here, and if the Seelie Court came after me for murder, he'd get caught up in it, too.

"What now, anyway?" Viola asked. "I mean—if you're feeling up to it, I still have that talisman sword."

"Hmm. I think I can do one better." I grinned. "How about you teach me how to fight with a sword, first?"

A delighted smile curved her mouth. "I thought you'd never ask."

———

Twenty minutes into the lesson and I wanted to throw the damn wooden practise sword out the window. Viola patiently corrected my grip for the fiftieth time, and I tried the basic forms again. My feet wouldn't move where they were supposed to, and my muscles weren't strong enough to hold the sword high enough to effectively stab anyone.

"Screw this." I threw the sword at the floor, but it bounced. At least it was only a practise sword. I hadn't tried to pick up the real thing yet.

She laughed. "You'll get used to it eventually. We learn fast. It's in our blood."

"Not fast enough," I said, prompting another laugh. Well, she was right. I'd regained some of the strength I'd lost as a prisoner already. But apparently it didn't extend to waving a sword around. "All right. I'm going to try to pick up the talisman."

I didn't technically need another one, but I was curious as to why my mother had locked it in a dungeon, and then somehow lost it in the forest. Its symbols were illegible to me, but suggested ancient power I couldn't comprehend, and the lightning bolt symbol on its hilt was so distinctive, I really should have recognised it for what it was when I'd last seen the Little Person's contraband in his cottage. It wasn't as bright as in the vision, but a thread of blue light shone in the silver.

"So she took it with her when she died?" I asked. "Did the Little Person give you any more clues about how it ended up in the forest?"

"No, but he kept saying *I picked it up.* That might imply he didn't actually pick it up from next to her. He might have found it somewhere else. They don't lie, but..."

"They mislead." I examined the blade without taking it. It was certainly well-made, forged from the ancient trees whose cores formed most faerie weapons. When I'd picked up the sceptre, I'd nearly been knocked off my feet with the force of its power, as it'd tested to see if I was worthy to wield it. The sword, however, looked more like an ordinary weapon, aside from the faint glow. "Maybe she took the magic out of it. Or someone else did."

A chill raced up my hand as though I'd pressed it to an ice-cold surface. *Winter magic. Okay, maybe not, then.* My hand buzzed with the contained power, and vibrated harder as I took it from Viola. My teeth rattled in my head, and the taste of metal rose on my tongue. The sword conjured images of echoing halls, and fear, and dark paths.

"You found another talisman?" Cedar leaned on the wall in the doorway. I hadn't even heard him come in.

"Yes." I didn't meet his eyes, the thief part of me not liking the way his gaze travelled over the lightning bolt carved into the hilt of the sword. He wouldn't do something drastic like steal the sword to take back to his boss and win Lord Horn-beam's favour, would he?

Why did I even think that? I almost expected to see a wraith hovering around, putting dark thoughts into my head, but the only presence I felt was the sword. It felt like the dungeon—cold, and marked with tortured screams of the humans trapped there.

It felt like her.

A chill raced up my back, as though I had the living essence of her magic in my hands. Maybe I did. The sword had been hers. *But what power does it have?*

"I won't report you to Lord Hornbeam," said Cedar.

"I should hope not." The words came out with more venom than I'd expected, laced with anger that didn't entirely feel like mine.

He blinked and didn't respond. His gaze was fixed on the talisman. *Oh hell. He can sense it, too.*

I stepped away from him, my hands firmly grasping the hilt. Viola looked between us, a bemused expression on her face. She hadn't picked up on its power—but she wasn't part Sidhe, even if she did have similar magic to me. Cedar had no talisman, but without any chains binding him—he *could* claim one. He'd always had that ability. Maybe that was why Lord Hornbeam had locked him up. A weird possessiveness took hold of me, like when I found something I really wanted to steal.

What's wrong with me? I'm not a talisman collector. I don't need another one.

Both of my hands locked around the sword's hilt. White light snaked up my arm, and I gasped aloud when pain burned where the light touched as though I'd stuck my arm into an open flame. Spots danced behind my eyes, my knees buckling, a searing trail of agony tearing at my arm.

It's testing me, and I'm losing.

Two voices shouted my name as I dropped with a cry,

trying desperately to break my grip on the sword as it burned its way up my arm.

Blue light engulfed the sword, prying it loose. My own magic. It swarmed the sword, breaking my grip.

Cedar's stricken expression was the last thing I saw before exhaustion hit me.

—

Green light shone behind my eyelids, and slowly, I opened my eyes. As I did, I became aware that I was lying on the sofa, that my hand didn't hurt anymore, and that Cedar was next to me. The agony that had spiked up my arm had disappeared, instead replaced with the pleasant buzzing sensation of Cedar's magic brushing against mine. It eased the tension in my body, the echo of the abuse it'd taken recently. I was fairly sure I'd failed to take the talisman, and if not for my own magic, I'd be dead.

I stood abruptly, and Cedar jerked upright, blinking at me. "Good. You're awake. How do you feel?"

"I'm fine." I sat back down. "You just startled me. Where's Viola?"

"Asleep. It's midnight." He handed me a bottle. "She told me to give you this, for your hand."

I flipped my hand over. The sword had left an interesting raised white mark across my palm and halfway up my arm. "Yay. More scars."

Cedar stiffened, catching sight of the other pinkish marks. "Iron?"

"You know, I can't actually remember."

He swore in the faerie tongue. "Aspen?"

"Yep. Or one of his people, maybe." I tipped the white powder from the bottle onto my hand.

"I apologise," he said quietly. "I've been ungrateful

towards your generous offer of shelter. I was concerned the Seelie Court would make trouble for us, since I'm on Unseelie territory."

"I doubt they care," I said. "You could have left if you wanted to."

I'd left him an opening. If he took it, I understood. He didn't belong in Winter, there was the slight matter of the murder charges against me, and the whole of this territory might be engulfed in war any day now. Also, he'd been drained of most of his power, though he looked a damn sight healthier now that cuff was gone.

Cedar spoke again. "In the eyes of the Courts, I'm a deserter. There is no place for me in Faerie, but as long as the Little People forbid travel to the mortal realm, I can't leave. Besides, I had to stay to make sure you didn't get yourself into trouble. That talisman contained some viciously powerful magic. I asked Viola to seal it in the dungeons."

"Yeah, it was nasty." I shuddered. "Did it feel like there was someone else in the room, pushing at us to steal it? Or like—like the *sword* was?"

"I don't know, but it's ancient and dangerous. I've never seen a talisman like it before."

"Nor me," I said. "Oh, well. It's not like I needed another one."

"How did you find the sword in the first place? Viola mentioned the Little People..."

"One of them apparently picked it up off the path after she died." I shrugged. "Also, some of them are traitors, so I expect that sort of behaviour from them by now."

"Aspen must have offered them an incentive," said Cedar. "The Little People have a special agreement to use the rifts. Breaking that agreement is grounds for exile. There's nothing they could gain from the Vale, so I don't understand why they'd betray the Courts. But their position explains how the Vale faeries have managed to stay hidden."

"Aspen probably bribed them. It might have been going on for ages. Since her death, anyway."

Cedar nodded slowly. "Lady Hornbeam spent an awful lot of time talking about her plans for expanding the territory and surpassing all the other families. It's possible her son didn't see Lord Hornbeam as competent enough to fulfil those plans."

"But that makes no sense. I mean, yeah, I get that he probably disagreed with Lord Hornbeam, but he didn't ask about my magic, or the sceptre, the whole time I was captive."

"He didn't?" Cedar frowned. "What exactly did he have you do? You must have been useful to him in some way."

"Dance." The word stuck in my throat. He still didn't know what a critical part of my life it'd been—almost a crutch to compensate for having no magic like other half-bloods did. On the stage had been the only time I'd felt like one of them. What we'd done was harmless—a little manipulative, but the humans had come to the show knowing they were getting a faerie performance. The victims of Aspen's antics never chose to come to Faerie at all.

Cedar blinked, not understanding. Then his hand closed over mine, his magic caressed me, a soothing presence, and I whispered the words, telling him it all.

"Sidhe's blood, I had no idea he even had that power." His voice was low. "So his plan hinged on using your magic to hypnotise mortals."

"My magic wasn't involved. He shut it down." Robin had presumably told him my history, but Aspen didn't know me personally, aside from as his mother's murderer. Which would be grounds enough for revenge, but now I thought about it... how did he know I'd be able to contribute to the spell his music held the crowd under? Anyone could dance. What I'd done was different.

He'd planned the act around me. He'd been waiting for me.

"Raine," said Cedar. "He knew what your magic did."

"My magic had nothing to do with it," I said quietly. "I was a professional performer for four years, and I didn't have magic at all."

Then how did you and Robin work so well? Because you were compatible. Because your magic complemented each other.

But... it wasn't her magic. I didn't have it. Had I inherited a version of her magic that didn't manifest in the usual way? It was unlikely. I mean, I couldn't even use glamour.

And the spell you put the crowds under?

"No," I said. "My transforming ability—he never asked me to use it. I didn't even have the talisman with me."

"But you were part of his act. Not in the audience, but the act itself. Right?"

His words twisted in my chest like a wrench. Because he was right. Sure, Aspen had wiped my mind, but I'd been in control of my thoughts ever since I'd come back and yet I'd never thought...

I stared at the carpet. Robin had *known.* He knew my magic better than I knew myself. He'd played me as much as Aspen had.

"Do you want me to leave?" Cedar asked.

"Yes."

He left swiftly and silently. The instant he'd gone, I buried my head in my hands.

Robin's own magic would have told him ours were compatible from the get-go. And what had I done? Told him I didn't have magic, the second time we'd met. I'd just lost my job, and he'd suggested I join him in his new business venture. I'd said yes because I had nothing to lose. He'd complimented my dancing before, because we'd first met at one of the few parties I'd been to in half-blood territory...

But of course he'd known. My magic, whatever it was, gave me the ability to manipulate people through dance—maybe through other ways. I didn't know. Because instead of telling me, he'd hijacked my talents and used them to make money from hapless mortals. And now I understood why he hadn't made any effort to escape Aspen. He got high off it.

Aspen had just moved to second place on my revenge list.

I'll make him sorry for it.

17

When Viola knocked on my door, I sent her away, not trusting myself to be around people until I got my head together.

I'd laughed at all those stories I'd grown up with, the ones where clueless mortals end up with a magical destiny. They should *know*, I'd thought. But not only had I not known about my own magic, I didn't even know how it worked. *Hypnosis.* There were some species of faerie, like sirens, who could sing mortals into total obedience, but dance was a less obvious way to go about it. And Lady Hornbeam, if she'd known, hadn't mentioned it. Any half-blood raised human would have difficulty sensing an invisible magic. That I'd spent so much time onstage and hadn't noticed, though, was a testament to how wrong-headed I'd been to let Robin's compliments convince me I'd charmed the crowds on talent alone. I'd put hundreds—thousands—of people under a Sidhe-style spell, and I hadn't noticed. At all.

And it apparently worked on half-bloods, too. Not Aspen, though now I thought about it, he hadn't directly been watching me when I'd danced. He'd stood on the side lines.

So had Robin, though I'd felt his magic supporting me. Of course, our magic was compatible, but perhaps that gave him some degree of immunity to the effects. Maybe I could work with that.

That night, I dreamed of revenge, of dancing shoes stained with blood, and woke up early the following morning with a new resolve to figure out how the hypnosis worked. My memories of the last couple of weeks might be jumbled, but I had four years of memories of dancing for Robin and still knew the steps of every routine backwards. I'd always rehearsed alone at Robin's request. *But of course he did.* He hadn't wanted me to hypnotise the other performers—or, more likely, he hadn't wanted me to figure out what I could do.

Of course, there was only one sure-fire way to know if my theories were right: I needed a test subject.

I left my room and wandered the corridors in search of Volt. Viola's pet sprite didn't sleep much, though hell if I knew if the hypnosis would even work on him the same way it did on humans or half-bloods. I didn't have a better idea, though. Viola was probably sleeping, and Cedar… I'd rather figure out if he was actually right before I spoke to him again.

The sprite was in the weapons room, flitting about like a giant moth. The room looked different to before, like someone had moved everything around. The talisman sword had gone, at least. Creepy thing.

"Hey, Volt." I waved at the sprite, feeling vaguely ridiculous. "I need your help. Can you come with me?"

I opened a path back into an empty hallway, and the sprite followed me.

"Sorry," I whispered. "I didn't want to wake Viola. I need to practise something—magic, and I need someone to test it on. I promise it won't hurt."

The sprite crossed his arms and gave me a questioning look.

"Have you ever seen me dance?" I couldn't remember if he'd been at the party when I'd been up on the table—wait, of course he had.

The sprite nodded enthusiastically. *Now we're getting somewhere.* "I need a test audience for a new performance piece," I told him.

More nodding. He probably only understood half of it, but I was pretty sure my magic wouldn't affect a sprite as much as a human or half-blood. He was pure faerie, too, but with little magic. *Okay, then.*

I imagined I was onstage, before the curtains rose, and tried to conjure up the feeling of nervous excitement, of a long-held breath desperate to be released. I fell into the movement as easily as breathing, feet tracing well-trodden paths. Robin hadn't taught me the moves. They'd come naturally. I stopped, staring at the floor. Blue light shone where I'd moved, and I'd been so focused on my movements that I hadn't noticed I'd left a trail behind me. A trail of magic, not just from my feet, but from my whole body.

The sprite hovered dead-still in mid-air, his eyes glazed and fixed on me.

"Oops." I waved a hand in front of his face. The sprite followed the movement. Ah. How was I supposed to undo... wait. It must wear off over time. The audience got a few hours of entertainment, and were back to normal by morning, nursing raging hangovers.

But if my steps alone hypnotised people, though, then why did it only happen when I was onstage? Fighting was a kind of dance, if you stretched the definition, but I'd never hypnotised anyone while fighting, or in any other circumstances. Maybe because I hadn't been aware of what I could do. If I could turn the dance into a deadly weapon...

"Raine!" Viola yelled from the corridor's end. "What are you doing in here? Is that Volt?"

I turned around. "Couldn't sleep."

"And you're avoiding Cedar. Speaking of whom, he's driving me out of my mind. Did you see what he did to the weapons room?"

"That was him?"

"He decided we needed to rearrange every weapon in order of size." She tugged a hand through her hair. "I've turfed him out of every room, and he keeps trying to *clean* everything. Anyway, what in the world is Volt doing?"

The sprite sat on my head. "Er, it's a long story."

Her brow furrowed. "Did I miss something?"

"No, I did. Something pretty big. It's Robin's fault, not Cedar's. He's an addict. Hypnotising humans is his drug of choice."

I told her. I also mentioned what I'd been up to all morning. Her expression turned from shocked to angry to confused and then settled on a mildly accusing expression.

"You hypnotised my sprite."

"Accidentally on purpose. It'll wear off," I said. "The humans—damn, now I know why so many of them asked me to marry them after the performance."

Viola snorted. "Sorry. This isn't funny. But you decided to practise on Volt?"

"I did ask his permission first."

"Because Cedar wouldn't appreciate it? Actually, he's already in love with you, so it probably wouldn't work."

My face heated. "I don't think so, Viola."

"I'm teasing you."

"Sure." I shook my head. "You don't find it creepy? Apparently I'm just as much of an evil seductress of mortals as my mother was, only I had no clue, because it was second nature."

"Only when your magic was linked with Robin's."

"It was *all the time.* For four years. It's a good job my dad never came to my performances." I exhaled heavily. "Robin stole my magic from me. And there's no excuse whatsoever for not telling me."

"Absolutely." She swore under her breath, pacing to the other end of the corridor. "That Robin… I almost want to say he should have been arrested, but it's not like he broke any laws."

"Oh, no. The mortals were more than happy to be hypnotised." I rolled my eyes. "All he did wrong was not tell me about my own magic, which I ought to have noticed anyway. I thought I was good at what I did, but apparently I got caught in my own spell."

"No, you are good. I know I was drunk the last time I saw you do it, but the point still stands. Anyway, all the blame lies on him. And you think he told Aspen…"

"And Aspen figured out we were compatible. No wonder he wanted us to stay near one another all the time. He had others, too—that music had a similar effect. It's like a hypnotic orchestra."

She nodded. "I didn't guess you had that sort of magic, either, by the way, not even after seeing you dance. Cedar told me he didn't guess until you mentioned Aspen made you dance, either."

"No, I guess he didn't. So you spoke to him?"

"More like grabbed him and demanded he tell me what he said to upset you." She smiled wryly.

"He didn't," I said. "I mean, I was angry, but not with him. I can't believe he noticed and I didn't, though. It's *my* magic."

"And you've figured out how to use it?"

"Kinda. Not enough. I'm pretty sure twelve-year-olds are faster learners. It's not like learning to use a talisman. I've had this magic… ten years or more. I don't know."

"I reckon you've probably used it more often than you know," Viola said. "It's instinctive for most of us. But it's not like you grew up here. The Hornbeam family tests all their half-bloods every six months from their tenth birthdays. Of course, they usually know what type of magic to expect. You didn't."

"Honestly, I'm glad I never met Lady Whitefall if she could hypnotise people," I admitted. "I inherited a toned-down version of her natural magic, right? So the sceptre's magic is something different entirely. The sword, too. Neither are the magic she was born with."

"You're right," said Viola. "I never saw her use hypnosis, though. She only ever used the sceptre."

"Maybe she secretly hypnotised her Court," I said. "Hmm. That explains the statues in the entrance hall. Anyway, we have a new weapon against the Vale now. Have you heard anything new about what's happening over on Hornbeam territory?"

"No." She bit her lip. "Rose was supposed to come here the next chance possible. If it's true that the Vale army is coming, we need to be ready."

"Yeah, we do." I wanted to take out Aspen, but I needed more than magic to bring down an army.

Bringing down the Little People, though… I could handle that much.

"All right, I'm going to check our security again," said Viola, waving Volt over to her. "You should speak to Cedar, too."

"I will." Eventually. My plan came first, and a chance to really put my new magic into action.

When Viola had gone, I opened a shortcut to the weapons room and retrieved two knives, not iron, but made of some kind of hollow metal. I changed my clothes into armour, and left the palace before I could change my mind.

They knew I was coming. I heard rustling in the bushes and spotted a bearded figure fleeing through the trees on the path leading to the house. I ran after him, not quite as fast as before, but quickly enough.

As he glanced over his shoulder, I took my first step. Then the next, deliberately but fast, each step calculated for impact. I didn't need to be dancing. I might even be able to use magic when fighting—and what better way to find out than to corner the bastards who'd trapped me in the Vale?

I kept walking, aware for the first time of the blue light trailing my steps and flaring around my whole body like a light. The Little Person froze, one foot on the doorstep, staring at me with mesmerised eyes.

His traitorous companion appeared in the doorway. "What is this—?"

Have fun being my test audience.

The magic swirled from my feet to my hands, trailing light as it surrounded them in a net of wavering lines. My whole body glowed with it.

The Little Person remained in place. Two more heads popped up, falling under the same spell. I snapped my fingers in imitation of Aspen, beckoning them outside.

"You're going to come with me," I said softly, dropping my voice in the creepy way the Sidhe did when they were about to inflict mortal damage on someone. I didn't expect it to work on a genuine faerie, but something about me apparently convinced them. All eyes locked onto me, and the guy on the doorstep moved down, allowing the others to come after him.

I faced four unmoving Little People, all wearing the same glazed expression. "Tell me," I said to them. "Are you all working with the faeries in the Grey Vale? Those of you who are, stand in front of me. Those who aren't, bring me the other traitors."

They did. Two stayed, and two scattered into the trees, moving swiftly. I didn't know exactly how long the spell would last, but it'd be long enough for what I'd planned.

In the end, I had five Little People held captive in front of me, while several others looked on from the sides.

"Is someone giving you orders?" I asked them. "Aspen?"

"I serve only the Queen," intoned the one on the end. "The Queen of the Grey Vale."

Shit. So there *was* someone else in charge.

"Does she have a name?"

"We are not worthy to speak it," said two of them in unison.

The Queen… whoever it was, she was clearly pulling the strings in the Vale. But she must have left Aspen at the wheel. Which meant killing him wouldn't stop the army.

Luckily, I had several captives willing to confess to the Courts.

"Come with me."

Five sets of footsteps followed mine. Rather than heading to the palace, I skirted around the back of my territory, aiming for the path that led to the area where the half-bloods were brought into Faerie, where I was most likely to find a messenger.

We walked in absolute silence. My sense of direction didn't fail me for once—apparently I'd absorbed more knowledge of this realm than I'd thought. That, or I was more attuned to it now. Considering I had *two* different kinds of faerie magic, it wasn't a surprise. I didn't even recognise my reflection in the stream that flowed alongside the path, a white-haired faerie woman leading a group of bearded men who wore glazed, worshipful expressions.

Then I stopped. I couldn't walk any further without going into Summer's territory, and choosing one of the other paths into Winter's woods would take me onto another family's property. Since the attacks on the mortal realm directly through this path, it was one of the most heavily guarded areas of Faerie. It wouldn't be long before someone spotted me.

Sure enough, the bushes rustled, and the shadowy outline of a man appeared.

"What," said a silky voice, "are so many Little People doing here with a half-blood such as yourself?"

18

A man melted out of the bushes, tall and beautiful in the manner of all the Sidhe. There was something eerie about his pitch-dark eyes, where the pupils and irises were the same colour, unlike the typical bright blue of other Winter Sidhe. But his form glimmered with magic, and his pale features glowed bright. His black and silver finery pointed him out as a member of the Unseelie Court—and I actually knew his name, Lord Lyle. He'd come to the mortal realm before and scared the hell out of everyone by turning into a giant wolf.

"I'm requesting to speak to an official of the Unseelie Court," I said. "I'm Raine Whitefall."

He gave me a dismissive look. "I heard the Whitefall clan had fallen to a half-blood. The Unseelie Queen is too busy to be concerned with the likes of you."

I ignored the jibe—I'd expected worse. "Aren't you aware of the Grey Vale attacking borderland territory?"

He tilted his head. "The Unseelie Queen is aware there is a threat beyond our borders. It need not concern you. What are those Little People doing?"

"Turning themselves in." I gave him a smile. "They helped the enemy use the rifts to steal mortals into the Grey Vale and help outcasts attack the borderland families. I'm sure they're willing to testify to the Unseelie Queen."

His gaze sharpened, appearing to focus on me for the first time. Not that it made his cold beauty any easier to look at. "You brought them here yourself?"

"I gave them a little encouragement." I kept my smile in place though my face ached, and part of me screamed that I was betraying my very nature in pretending to be one of them. I didn't recognise the cold, lightly melodic voice that came from my mouth. But Lord Lyle's brow furrowed and he looked from me to them with an expression which I might have labelled concern or worry on anyone else.

"The Unseelie Queen *might* be interested to meet you, but it would take a great deal of persuasion to convince her to speak to a half-blood, whatever the occasion."

"They're traitors," I said. "Whatever I am, they're breaking the rules of the Courts."

"Then they will present themselves to the Courts as such, at our next trial before the Queen."

"Which is…?"

"Whenever she sees fit."

Crap. I'd heard of some faerie petitions in the Courts taking years. "We don't have time to wait. They can help you stop the Grey Vale's army. They've told me enough already. They're kidnapping mortals."

His gaze moved from them to me again. "Little half-blood… you're barely a child, aren't you? When you've come to spend more time in our realm, you will realise that it's less than easy to police our own kind when it's in their nature to fool and beguile. If hapless mortals fall victim to their pranks, it's not the fault of the Sidhe."

"You're blaming humans for the faeries kidnapping

them?" I'd known that argument forever, but to have it thrown in my face as though nothing made more logical sense made me want to hit Lord Lyle in the face. The worst part was that if I hit him, I'd get a worse punishment than the Little People, assuming they actually got a trial. They were pure faeries, so anyone would believe them over me, even though they'd betrayed the Courts. That was faerie justice for you.

Rage spiked, tinged with desperation—this was my only shot to convince the Courts that Aspen presented a genuine threat, yet *I* was the one most likely to be treated as a criminal.

"It's not the fault of anyone else if you can't have fun tormenting people without repercussions anymore," I told him. "You fought alongside humans in the war against the Vale, right? They saved your lives. Show some respect."

He moved forwards, and I raised my sceptre, my throat dry and my heart pounding.

"Respect is a quality you are apparently lacking," he said. "Leave."

I jerked my head at the Little People. "And do what with them? You're willing to let traitors run away free?"

"All are innocent until proven guilty."

"Except humans, of course."

He opened his mouth to speak, and one of the Little People lunged at me. I kicked out and knocked him flat before he made contact. Two of the others had stepped back, too, the glazed look in their eyes disappearing. Apparently my spell had a shorter time limit than I'd realised.

The Little Person was on his feet in seconds, his hands locking around my ankles. At the same time, two of the others sprinted for the trees. I kicked, trying to loosen the Little Person's hold, but he held on tenaciously. I freed one foot and kicked him in the face, feeling bone crunch beneath the toe of my boot. His grip slipped, and I trod on his hand before he could grab me again, hauling him up by the scruff of his neck. He headbutted me in the face, which probably hurt him more than it did me. My head throbbed and blood from his broken nose splattered me all over. I yanked one of the knives I'd brought out of my pocket and pressed it to his neck. "Don't you dare move."

Lord Lyle ran forward, jabbing a finger at the bushes and shouting in the faerie tongue. Trees trembled, shedding their coating of snow as a giant ogre rumbled into view, grabbing a fleeing Little Person by the throat with a horrible snapping noise.

"You're not supposed to kill them!" I yelled at Lord Lyle.

He gave me a cold look. "They don't all have to be alive for the trial, do they?"

Yeah, if they're supposed to confess. "Do you believe me?"

"I think it's in your interests to leave, mortal," he said.

"I'm not letting him go until you promise to hear him out," I said, indicating the Little Person in my grip.

Lord Lyle bent to speak to him. "Are you a traitor to the Court?"

"Yes, curse your bloodline. I spit at the feet of the Unseelie Queen."

"She will see to it that every foul word is tortured out of you," hissed Lord Lyle. "You will pay. Whom do you serve?"

"The true Queen, may it please you to know. Your time is soon to expire, Sidhe."

He lunged forward, right into my blade. The skin of his throat gave way and blood poured onto the leafy path. I let go, dropping his limp body.

"Was that evidence enough for your Queen?" I asked.

Lord Lyle gave me an unfathomable look. "Leave."

Another Little Person dropped to the ground from the ogre's hands, his sightless eyes staring at me. Suppressing the instinct to shudder, I backed away. "You'll need to keep at least one alive if you want to find out exactly what his boss is planning. The Grey Vale is coming. They'll wipe out all the borderland families and then come for you. If you can't summon up any sympathy for mortals, then consider what he just said. He wants the Courts gone."

"I'm aware," he said, his voice deathly quiet. "It's up to the Unseelie Queen to act, if she chooses."

"As long as you tell her." He couldn't lie, but it wasn't in his interests to start a war, not when the main Court hadn't been attacked yet. The borderlands didn't count. Unless he believed the Vale was enough of a threat to set his usual prejudices about half-faeries aside.

He gave me a cold look and swept away into the trees, leaving me alone with the ogres. They might be loyal to the Court, but I'd just watched them kill several Little People, so I walked away from them into the trees. There was nothing I could do here. If the Courts took too long to come to a decision, there'd be a massacre. Going to Summer was out of the question. Which left one option.

I walked quickly back through the woods. I'd meant to head for my own territory, but found myself veering in the direction of Lord Hornbeam's instead. The annoying shit had an army ready and waiting, but he hated me too much to be my ally. I couldn't believe I was even considering working with him, but nobody else knew how big a threat the Vale outcasts presented to the Courts.

"Raine." Cedar stepped onto the path in front of me. "Whose blood is that?" He eyed my boots, which were splattered with the Little Person's blood.

"The Little People. I handed the traitors over to the Winter Court."

"You did *what?*"

"What I said. Hopefully at least one of them will survive

long enough to tell the Unseelie Queen what exactly Aspen has planned. I wouldn't hold my breath, though. She probably won't help us." I looked at him. "You know who might."

His mouth tightened. "He won't. He's paranoid, locking up the territory, but if Aspen's as powerful as you said…"

I dropped my arms to my sides. "We can't just wait for them to show up and trample us. We need a plan."

"I don't doubt that, but Lord Hornbeam has doomed himself. He'll get no assistance from me."

"He can't order you to fight for him… right?"

"No. When the iron band broke, my vow did, too."

"So you're…" *Free.* I didn't dare speak the word aloud. I'd been so wound up over the sheer upheaval of the last few days, I hadn't spared a thought for the notion that I'd got at least one thing right. I'd freed Cedar. True, Lord Hornbeam had wanted rid of him anyway, but he was no longer bound to the Hornbeam family. Without the cuff, he practically glowed with magic. Just how powerful was he, anyway?

"A fugitive," Cedar said. "Or outcast. I never swore a vow to serve the Summer Court, you know. Lady Hornbeam didn't want us obliged to fight for the Court over our family."

"I didn't know there was a difference. I mean, between swearing a vow to a family and one to a Court."

"Normally, Sidhe are bound to their Court at birth," Cedar explained. "But most half-bloods aren't born in this realm and swear no such vow. The binding words mean that any Sidhe is obligated to fight if their Court is under threat. It also means that if any of the Court's rules are violated, then they're subject to punishment."

"Lady Hornbeam should have been," I said. "For murdering Lady Darkwater, amongst other things. My mother, too, for keeping a door into the Vale under the palace. I wonder if the Courts ever suspected."

"I doubt it," Cedar said. "But the point I was making—

we're not bound to the Courts. We can leave, for the mortal realm, if you'd prefer. I don't think it's safe for either of us to stay."

He stepped closer to me, his magic brushing against my bare hands. It should be an easy decision. My dad was in the mortal realm, and now I'd removed the traitorous Little People, we could escape safely. Leave the Sidhe to reap what they'd sown, and fall at the hands of the outcasts. But it seemed to me that there was a big piece missing from the whole setup. Who was Aspen serving?

"Raine?" Cedar looked at me expectantly. His hazel eyes were brighter than usual, alive with magic again. I'd saved his life once. Dragging him into an unknown battle again would be a selfish act. The old me would never have got involved in the first place.

The old me wouldn't be here now, with Cedar, on his own territory. What would happen if we did just—leave? Ran away to where the Courts couldn't catch us?

"You don't mind staying in the palace, then?" I asked. "I got the impression you're making Viola's life difficult."

"If you mean the appalling state of the weapons room, I saw to it."

I laughed. "You're bored out of your mind, aren't you? Guess you led a structured life."

"Not necessarily," he said. "I was often left to my own devices. In the mortal realm, especially."

"Like when you took me to the ball. Though that was part of your job, right?"

He shook his head. "Yes—to some extent. But my motives were entirely selfish. I would rather have taken you somewhere alone."

"What are you saying?"

"Hmm?" A smile curled his lips. "Do you want me to spell it out, as the humans do?"

"You aren't the most straightforward person, Cedar. I never know if you're acting on your own volition or not. And I guess I could say I don't know who you really are."

"You know who I am," he said. "I've told you every time my oaths have coerced me into spending time with you. The rest was my choice alone."

My pulse sped up. "I thought you might be angry with me for forcing you to become an outcast."

"I was never angry with you. Only with myself, for failing to realise what Aspen was planning, and to prevent him from taking you captive."

"You couldn't have known. Even Lord Hornbeam didn't. Did it ever occur to you he might be afraid of you?"

He blinked. "What?"

"Look, he knows—and the other Sidhe are realising, too— that we have the potential to be just as powerful as they are. He failed to claim his wife's talismans, and he's hanging onto power by a thread. One of her sons already betrayed him. Don't you have a reputation in your family as an unpredictable thief who can sneak up on you and cut your throat without you even hearing them?"

Cedar shook his head. "I highly doubt it. He saw me as an asset at first, but not a threat. The Sidhe need not fear us."

"But they do." I smiled. "They do fear us. Lady Hornbeam turned one of her sons into a weapon against him. His best soldier stole *his* talismans, and won their allegiance."

"Yes, there's one part I don't understand," said Cedar. "You said Aspen was serving someone else? A Sidhe?"

"The Little People called her the Queen of the Grey Vale."

There it was again—a suspicion, a prickling on the back of my neck. I'd pinpoint it as understandable paranoia, but knowing the way my luck was turning lately... I had a horrible suspicion about who it was. I wouldn't voice it aloud. Not until I had proof.

A sudden thumping sound came from ahead, followed by screaming. Cedar drew his blade, stepping forward.

I did likewise. "Tell me that's not what I think it is."

"Vale beasts," he said. "They're heading for Lord Hornbeam's palace."

19

Redcaps sprinted through the trees with gleeful, bloodthirsty cries, while sluaghs swamped anything living they came across, suffocating them into silence. The limp body of a soldier dropped from a sluagh's gaping mouth. This one had transformed itself into a monkey-like shape, like a baboon the size of a small troll, made up of a horrifying meld of flesh and shadows. It spotted us, dropped the soldier, and ran right into Cedar's blade. Cedar withdrew the knife—not iron, but one he must have taken from the palace—and faced his opponent, dealing vicious strikes that brought the beast crashing to its knees. As I caught up, he sank the blade into the back of its head.

His eyes were bright, blood splattering his face. "They're here. We're less than half a mile from the palace. They must be attacking Lord Hornbeam by now, and his defences are down."

Indecision split his features, and I almost saw the effort it took for him to move in the opposite direction, torn between serving the family he'd sworn his life to and getting both of us out of harm's way.

A large ogre lumbered ahead, its skin bleached the colour of bone. One of its horns had been torn off, leaving a bloody scar. Though ogres didn't have magic, the Vale had altered it, making it sharper, more brutal and unforgiving in appearance. It was massive, too, at least ten feet tall and wider than most of the trees it passed—or tore out of the ground, leaving destruction in its wake.

In fact, the distinction between Winter and Vale beasts was obvious. The beasts of the Courts were restrained, while Vale ones were destruction incarnate. The ogre trampled everything in its path with abandon, not seeming to care if it hit any of its allies. It roared loud enough to make the roots quake and the ground tremble. Leaves poured down from the ruined trees, masking the view ahead.

"Damn, that's one nasty beast," I muttered, hovering behind to get a clear shot.

Cedar's mouth pressed into a thin line. He clearly didn't want to watch his former territory stormed by the enemy, even if Lord Hornbeam deserved it. There were a lot of innocent faeries here, like Rose, who'd be collateral damage if the palace fell.

I could run off alone, get back to the Vale, and punish Aspen, but that wouldn't stop them from destroying the palace. Besides, the half-faeries who'd stayed here were loyal to the Courts, not the Vale. Like Rose. Like Viola's former fellow soldiers.

I'd better not regret this.

I conjured magic to my hands, alerting the enemy to my presence. Cedar spun around, shock flashing across his face. "Raine—"

"I'm not letting them attack the other half-bloods here."

I didn't wait for his response, throwing a handful of magic at the nearest bramble patch right in front of a group of redcaps. They screeched as the brambles encased them, locking them in place. Grabbing a knife from my pocket, I ran in their direction. Their sharp knives stabbed the brambles, but my magic held it together. I cut their throats and turned back to find Cedar approaching the ogre from behind.

Green light suffused his palms and his brow furrowed in concentration. As he advanced after the ogre, a redcap jumped at his back. I kicked it aside, causing it to drop its weapon, and stabbed it in the chest. Cedar gave me a nod of thanks and continued on. I moved behind him, deflecting any enemy which came near. The green light disappeared in a sound like a thunderclap, and the trees on either side of the ogre bent without warning, their huge branches curving to trap the ogre in place. It struck out, its tremendous strength tearing the trees apart, but they kept moving, fuelled by Cedar's magic. Branches stabbed the ogre all over, and it screamed as they tore through its thick skin and pierced the vulnerable flesh beneath.

The beast gave one final flailing shudder, and went still.

Cedar dropped his hands, his shoulders bowed, then he straightened up and carried on walking, skirting around the fallen ogre. I followed, watching for any ambushes. This territory favoured its own inhabitants—quiet Summer faeries who could hide in the gaps between trees to strike at any ambushers—but its thick maze-like winding paths could as easily work against them. The way the thick trees muffled any sound prevented us from hearing anyone being attacked. The occasional cry of pain rang through the forest, but it was beyond me to tell where it came from.

Cedar broke into a run, drawing the crossbow he must have borrowed from the palace. He fired before I saw his target—a vicious oversized goblin wearing armour, who fell with a cry as Cedar's arrow pierced its back. He didn't break stride, angling towards the shape of the palace visible through the trees. The gold wire fence surrounding it didn't appear to have been breached, but the sounds of fighting came from nearby. Screams and cries of tormented faeries split the air. Cedar stopped, holding out an arm. He didn't need to tell me why he'd stopped me. The exterior of the fence had mobilised, turning into thick spiky vines, stabbing at anyone who came close.

I raised an eyebrow. "That's the palace's security?"

He gave a grim nod. "It might not recognise me as the enemy, but it'll certainly attack you."

"All right. Then I'll—"

Another horrible scream came from behind us. A sluagh shaped like a long-limbed man with bark-like skin had wrapped its arms around the neck of an armoured faerie soldier. His body jerked as he fought against its grip.

Cedar fired at the same time as I directed my own magic at the air, sending a shard of ice piercing the creature's arm. It let go, and the soldier fell, fighting for breath. He was only a kid, sixteen or so, with silvery eyes and jet-black hair. I ran over as the sluagh recovered and stabbed it with my knife, piercing its heart.

"Why—did you save me?" the soldier wheezed, his eyes on me rather than Cedar. Like the others, he wore plated armour and carried an iron knife in his hand.

"Throw that away," I advised him, indicating the iron knife. "It'll only come back to hit you in the end."

I gave him one of my own knives and turned my back before he could gasp out a bewildered thanks. A commotion drew my attention to the gate nearby. A group of three armed soldiers on horseback rode into the grounds, carrying iron knives.

"We want to make a deal," said one of them, leering at the nearest guard, who was bleeding heavily from a wound to his face. "Get Lord Hornbeam to come and surrender in person. I know he's hiding somewhere in there."

The guard choked as the knight's spear caught him in the chest, pinning him to the ground. He fell still, blood streaming from the corner of his mouth.

I might not respect Lord Hornbeam, given his under-handed methods to secure loyalty, but his half-blood guards didn't deserve to be slaughtered defending him. I readied my weapon, warily. Their horses shifted, hooves stirring up dust, but they looked… odd. All were jet black in colour, and shimmered in the weird way part-spirit creatures like the sluagh did. Were they spirit faeries? Was that why the secu-rity had let them into the grounds?

"Traitors are not welcome here," snarled another guard. "Leave now, or—"

He choked, a spear jutting from his chest, thrown by one of the riders.

Cedar appeared beside me without warning. An arrow soared at the warrior, a shot that should have pierced the back of his neck. At the last second, he wheeled the horse around. The arrow snapped past, missing by inches.

"And who might you be?" asked the warrior. His two companions turned to face Cedar—and by extension, me.

"Your enemy," said Cedar, and fired again. The soldier shouldn't have been able to dodge, but he did, the horse dipping its head in a fluid movement more like smoke than anything solid. They weren't regular horses, even faerie ones. Vale beasts, maybe. Their riders, though, were unmistakably half-blood. Aspen's allies.

Even if Aspen hadn't been in charge, I'd rather have Lord Hornbeam ruling the borderlands than the Vale rogues. The Grey Vale was the antithesis of everything that made Faerie what it was, a magic-free wasteland that sucked the life out of its inhabitants. If the Vale beasts won the war, they'd turn the borderlands into the same, and the rest of Faerie would follow.

Not if I can help it.

Cedar fired two arrows in quick succession, his rapid-fire reflexes more than making up for the time it took to notch an arrow to the bow. But the horses moved too quickly. If we were to win, we needed to take out their steeds.

I used magic, conjuring a shard of ice, and threw it at the nearest rider. He dodged the ice shard, but his attention momentarily slipped onto me, and Cedar took his chance to fire. The arrow caught him in the arm, and he snarled in rage.

"Winter faeries?" he spat. "Lord Hornbeam needs the assistance of his enemies to defend his own territory? How pathetic."

"I'm here on my own account," I said, and conjured icy shards to both hands, leaping to engage the rider in battle.

The horse reared up, moving forward like a waterfall of shadow. I sprung out the way on sheer reflex. *Holy hell, that thing moves fast.* I needed to get the rider off the horse, but the shadowy steed moved quicker than anything I'd met before—and in Faerie, at that. My knives, no matter how quickly they slashed, whipped through thin air, as did my magical attacks. The creature must be solid enough to strike if it could support the weight of its rider, but it was too damn quick. I kept backing away, dodging the blunt strikes from its hooves, striking at the rider's legs. Every time I came close to making contact, the horse would rear up and strike at my face. A hoof caught my ear, drawing blood, and I stumbled. It was impossible to try my hypnosis trick here in the forest, where the ground was choked with undergrowth. But I had one trick left.

I backed up and sprang, high, landing on top of the rider. Pain shot up both my knees where they collided with his armour, but the horse fell forward. The rider cursed and twisted, trying to stab me with his spear, but I caught his weapon hand in time. He didn't move half as fast as the horse did. I directed my magic at his spear and it collapsed, turning into powder.

He swore and struggled upright, further unbalancing the horse, and aimed a clumsy punch at me. I caught his wrist and leaned into him, and both of us tumbled off the horse into the bush.

"You—" He spluttered in rage, light brown eyes narrowed. A Summer half-blood, and not one who had the slightest clue about physical combat. "Get off me, Winter scum."

"You're lucky," I growled. "Tell me who's leading your army."

He moved suddenly, a knife in his hand, but I dodged the stab, punching him in the jaw. His eyes rolled back in his skull and his grip slipped. I knocked the weapon from his hands and twisted his wrists together, directing magic at his armoured sleeves. At once they fused together, effectively handcuffing him.

"Tell me. Is it Aspen? Where is he?"

"Here, of course... he's here."

A rustling behind me warned me of movement, and I rolled off him as the horse tried to kick me in the head. It really was a magnificent beast, if you got past its creepy, half-transparent nature. I rolled to the side, leaping to my feet, and easily climbed onto its back.

"You can't steal my horse!" yelled the soldier.

"Tough," I said over my shoulder, and left him in the bushes. The horse broke into a trot. "Take me to Aspen," I told it.

The horse shook itself in answer, nearly bucking me off. All my practise climbing roofs and performing dangerous stunts paid off in the blurred five seconds it took to drag me through the trees, hanging on by sheer reflex.

"Wait!" I yelled. "Stop—"

The horse stopped so abruptly, I flew forwards a good ten feet, flipping over in the air. Only the number of times I'd practised landings stopped me from face-planting and breaking something. I landed on my feet, and whirled around to glare at the horse. "You little shit."

"That's not a friendly way to speak to a horse of the Death Kingdom."

Aspen sat astride another horse, smiling a wide smile. "I knew I'd find my best performer here somewhere."

Hatred burned in my blood. "You."

"Me." He held up the pipes. "Ready to play a song?"

Raising a hand, I aimed my first attack at the air, freezing it into a solid wall that collided with his arm, knocking his grip on the pipes. I drew my blade and conjured magic in the other hand, throwing it at him in shards of ice that diverted his attention and prevented him from pausing long enough to play a single note. I needed to get the talisman away from him, *now.*

Aspen drew a thin blade, no longer smirking. So he did have a proper weapon. Slashing at me with surprising speed, he circled me, dealing strikes that took all my effort to block and dodge. His fighting method was familiar. He and Cedar were brothers, after all, but they couldn't be more different. While Cedar moved quietly and underplayed his real strengths, Aspen was brash confidence and open cruelty. He fought dirty, and wanted to humiliate me and turn me into a slave. *Now you'll be sorry.*

The trees rustled, and two half-bloods riding horses appeared.

"It's done," said one half-blood. He was bleeding from one

arm, but sat up straight. "The palace has fallen. The traitors are dead."

No. He can't be dead. Cedar can't be dead.

Aspen smiled. "Just in time. And now… our master is here. Look upon the true Queen of Faerie, Raine Whitefall."

The world turned white. Everyone turned around, transfixed, as the edges of my vision began to blur.

The last thing I saw was the outline of an impossibly beautiful white-haired woman smiling at me, shining with iridescent light.

20

I expected to wake up in the cell, surrounded by iron. Instead, music woke me, but not pipes. The twang of a harp, pulled by inexpert fingers, jerked me awake. I lay on a bed, not particularly soft, but not the floor, either. My room was hardly bigger than a cupboard, but still an improvement on the cell.

The Vale announced its presence with a sense of emptiness that filled my bones, but there was no iron, and magic sprang to my fingertips at my call.

Okay, then. If I wasn't a prisoner, where in the hell was I? Unless I'd been upgraded to the deluxe prisoner suite. The room looked more like it was in a castle. The stone walls and slitted window suggested as much. I tugged at my clothes. I *thought* they were the ones I'd been wearing before, but my own memory felt… weird.

Like I was missing a crucial puzzle piece.

Oh. My talisman had gone. Someone had taken the sceptre. And my knives. But had Aspen been responsible for the spell which had left a big question mark in my memory? I hadn't seen him do anything.

The door opened. I froze, not ready to fight, but unwilling to do anything else. *You're dead this time, Aspen.*

My mother stood in the doorway, framed in curtains of bright light.

Just like in the vision, her face gleamed, more transparent than solid, like an angelic being not part of this world. Her eyes were the sort of bright shade of blue that accompanied an agonisingly bright sky on a day too pretty to be real. All of her was the same—too much for this world, for any world. She didn't wear a dress like in the vision, but armour, black edged with silver like the other soldiers. She looked more like a conqueror than a queen from the humans' story books. The sort of person who'd trample the bodies of her enemies into dust.

That last realisation shocked me out of my trance.

"Mother," I whispered. I couldn't move. I could hardly breathe. *This isn't happening. This can't be happening.*

"Daughter," she said. "You've led me on quite the chase."

I stared at her for a good twenty seconds. "You... you're alive."

Possibly, I was supposed to feel thrilled that the mother I thought was dead was standing right in front of me. Except she'd led me to believe she'd been murdered, instead hiding in a castle in the *Grey Vale.* No way could this mean anything good. She wasn't an illusion or glamour. You couldn't fake absolute perfection.

She reached out and touched me, stroking the mark on my face. I flinched. "This is our family's mark, the one I put on you after you left me. So you'd know to whom you really belong."

What?

I nearly recoiled, but held still, not willing to break the image and show her how much we'd both changed since the memories I'd only recently regained. But for one ridiculous second, I hoped she'd smile at me like she did then. Her beautiful face was blank of emotion, as distant as any Sidhe. Even to me.

"Why are you here?" was the first question to come out of my mouth.

She tilted her head. "Because I wished to see my daughter."

Faeries. Even she was as literal-minded as the rest of them. "I meant, why are you alive? Why'd you fake your death?"

"Because there were those who sought to remove me from this world. I made their jobs a little easier."

"Like who?"

"These things don't concern you."

She didn't add the word *mortal* to the end, but I heard it all the same.

"They do," I said, "because I was called to Faerie to pick up my inheritance on account of you being *dead.* I've had more people try to kill me for it than I can count. You left me to clean up your mess, and it turns out you were hiding in the home of exiles and traitors."

She raised a hand. "As I said, you are incapable of understanding—"

"I'm perfectly capable of understanding a weapon aimed at me, *mother.*" I spat the word. "Why did you bring me here?"

"Because you were about to meet your end at the hands of my assistant."

I arched a brow. "Aspen? I thought you had more class than that."

"You've changed. You were such a sweet child."

"Sorry to disappoint you." I met her stare. Maybe it was because we were related, but I found it easier to focus on her features than the other Sidhe. Or perhaps because I understood exactly what was going through her mind. I didn't look like the daughter she'd expected to find. I was too old, and however pretty I'd been before, Aspen's torture had wrought enough of a change in my appearance that we hardly looked related to one another. Aside from the white hair, soft as powdered snow. Mine was hand cut—I didn't like to keep it too long. Hers swept past her shoulders in a magnificent curtain. She had a regal air, I slouched like a human.

Mostly, she expected the world to lie down at her feet and worship her. And I wouldn't do it. I'd never beg her for anything again. I was years too late for faerie tale endings. I knew enough of both worlds to be certain they didn't exist.

The mother who'd loved the child version of me had been as much of a lie as her death.

I stepped back. "I don't appreciate being held against my will. I'd like to know where the door is so I can get back home."

"Home," she repeated. "You call the palace home?"

"Yes." No way in hell was I letting her know about Dad. "Since you aren't using it any longer. I don't suppose you'd like to explain *why* you left?"

"Because the Sidhe refused to see the threat in front of them."

"What threat? The Vale? You left a year ago, right, so just after the second failed invasion of the mortal realm...?"

And right after the Sidhe had lost their immortality. Had she known, somehow? She'd certainly known that everyone would accept her death without question, even if no Sidhe had died before.

"A year by mortal reckoning, perhaps."

"But... *why* did you do it? Why leave the sceptre behind?"

"So you claimed its magic as your own after all." She paused. "This is a complication, my daughter. As long as you possess part of my magic, I cannot let you go."

"Er... what?" I scanned her for the talisman, but she didn't appear to have it. No other visible weapons, either. "It's not your magic, it's mine. You knew the risks when you left it behind."

"The sceptre wasn't supposed to choose another. I left it because its magic is incompatible with this realm. It requires power that is not inherent in the place where magic never lives and never dies."

"Never lives and never dies? You're not making any sense."

"You've spent too much time amongst mortals. I was aware you'd claimed the talisman after rumours reached me here, but not that you resided in the palace. It wasn't until you trespassed here in the Vale that I realised I needed to have you close by, to ensure you don't stand in my way."

"In your way?" I rolled my eyes to cover up my shock. "You seriously think—okay, first off, you left the talisman there, so the mistake is on you. Secondly, you knew you had kids you'd abandoned in the mortal realm. More than one."

She gave a dismissive wave of the hand. "You were never supposed to learn your heritage," she said. "I assumed you'd have perished by now, as mortals do."

Her words struck somewhere deep and cold, like an icy knife between the ribs.

"You're mortal," I said. "You all are. Half-blood, Sidhe, whatever. You're deluding yourself if you think otherwise."

She shook her head. "It's clear the mortal realm has poisoned you against your own kind."

"You are not my kind. You already told me that. I'm not staying with you, mother, because I'm not responsible for your mistakes. Also, this place is dead. I don't know what the attraction is."

"Enough." The word was quiet, but clearly an order. It kindled my anger into a furious blaze. "You will obey me, daughter."

Magic pressed her words, driving into me like a force of nature. Her eyes were twin glass storms of swirling blue, transfixing me to the spot. I stumbled back, unable to look away.

She was pulling the same trick on me as Aspen had, but with her own magic. My body swayed against my will, but my mind was my own.

Had she really expected her magic to work against someone who shared her blood?

I prepared to push right back, and behind her, two guards walked past, accompanied by Aspen—and Cedar.

So he wasn't dead. Relief flooded me, along with fear for him. She must have captured everyone who'd survived the attack on the Hornbeam palace.

"Don't resist me, child," she said quietly. "You don't want to forget our time together, do you?"

A threat. She'd wipe my mind clean the way she'd erased my memories, and she wouldn't be careful about it. I'd lose everything, and Cedar would die here.

I kept staring into her eyes, not speaking, letting her think she had me. If I couldn't fight her with a weapon, I'd fight her with words. She didn't rule me. She might be my blood mother, but she would never be my queen.

"Good," she said. "Stay here."

I bit back sharp words, instead saying, "Can't I come with you? If I'm your heir, I'd like to be involved in your plan."

For a second, I thought it hadn't worked. But she was already looking past me, at Aspen. "I suppose it cannot hurt to have you learn the way of things here. Walk with me, and do not leave my side." Magic pressed her words into me, similarly to a vow, but not quite. If she did force a vow on me, I'd be in trouble, but her hypnosis was enough. I could *see* her magic as she used it, threads of blue creeping across the ground and surrounding me. It wasn't solid, but was definitely there, and she didn't need to make a performance to use it.

I made a mental note of *that* for later, nodded meekly, and followed.

Dangerous games. Unlike Aspen, I had to trust that she, at least, wouldn't torture me for acting against her will. Or would she? She sure as hell wasn't the mother from my memory, but she wasn't Lady Hornbeam, either. She believed I *belonged* to her. And if pretending to be on her side got me close enough to cut Aspen's throat after humiliating him for what he did to me, so be it.

I followed her down a stone corridor, towards the sound of a harp being plucked. The source lay behind a half-open door revealing an entire room of humans. Some painted, some played instruments, and all looked half-starved and wore glazed expressions. Everyone was utterly under her thrall. Her magic hovered around bloodied fingers plucking at strings and daubing paint. I stopped for a second to stare in sick fascination.

"Coming, daughter?"

I suppressed a shudder. "Yes. What are those humans doing here?"

"I brought them for my entertainment. They don't make good soldiers, but half-bloods make adequate ones. You, however, will have a special position at my side. We'll teach them their place."

Goosebumps sprang up along my skin. I wouldn't be able to keep up the act if she asked me to torture a human or half-blood. Though the half-bloods had mostly chosen to be here of their own free will, if Aspen was any indication.

"Where are you recruiting them from?"

"Here and there. The mortal realm's outcasts, those not chosen by a family or who resent their fate… I like to think I can offer a better option."

"And you're going to war with the Courts?"

She gave a tinkling laugh that raised the hairs on the back of my neck. "Not war. Invasion. War assumes one has the chance to fight back. The mortals certainly don't."

"And the Sidhe? They have armies."

"As do I. The borderlands are already mine, and the rest will follow."

My throat closed up. Viola, and the rest of the Hornbeams' Court, were there. I couldn't let them hurt Cedar, but if the others were gone… I needed to find them. Viola still technically belonged to my mother, since her vow bound her to my entire family. What if she realised, and stole my closest friend from my side?

"Is something wrong?" she asked, with a smile so false I could have reached out and peeled it off.

"No." I faked a smile back. "I was just confused, because the last thing I remember before I woke up here was the fight with Lord Hornbeam's soldiers. If you won, where is he?"

"Why, he's here, of course, along with the survivors."

Survivors.

Rose. Losing her would crush Viola—assuming she hadn't been caught up in the fighting, too.

We reached a large hall with a high ceiling, full of half-bloods and other faeries. Lord Hornbeam stood in the middle, his clothes torn, chains binding his feet and ankles. Other soldiers surrounded him, all of whom were also in chains. Not in iron, as I'd originally thought, but thick vines scored with thorns. They stood and stared, blankly, not looking away from my mother's face when she walked in. Blue light surrounded them above the chains.

Oh. She'd used her mind power on them. Was Lord Hornbeam's own magic really that pathetic? Or hers that strong? Either might be true. No wonder my mother had been willing to leave her talismans behind to go into the Grey

Vale, where even the most powerful Sidhe would slowly wither and die.

"It's time for the show," Aspen whispered in my ear.

21

My body stiffened. Slowly, Aspen circled me from behind. Smirking, he walked to join the other soldiers surrounding the Hornbeam captives. My heart tugged to look at Cedar, who stood upright and calm even surrounded by enemies. She hadn't touched him with her magic yet.

"This one," Aspen said, indicating Cedar, "attempted to follow you."

My heart sank. *Cedar, what are you doing?*

Lady Whitefall strode forward. My breath caught in my throat. *Please, please don't hurt him.*

"Traitors," she said. "Now… *kneel.*"

Her words rang through the room, and my knees buckled of their own accord as her power tore the air like a ferocious storm contained in a single word. She hadn't spoken in English but some other alien, terrifying language that I somehow understood anyway. Whatever language she used carried echoes of another age, where words commanded power, and those without were forced to obey.

The echoes drifted away. Lord Hornbeam knelt before

her, frozen in position. The rest of the court was, too, including Cedar and even her own courtiers. Aspen had got down on his knees at her command, too. Silence reigned, so potent I was seized with the wild urge to shout before the terror drove me out of my mind.

My mother broke the silence first, striding up to Lord Hornbeam and grabbing him by the throat. "The only crime you've committed is being a nuisance, but I heard your soldiers are wilful, especially that one." She gestured at Cedar, whose eyes were on the floor, his posture stiff.

She lifted Lord Hornbeam bodily off the ground, her other hand reaching out as though to pull off an invisible coat. Green light surrounded him, and surged towards her hand. He gasped and choked, not just because her grip was squeezing his neck but because her other hand had latched onto the magic that made up his very soul—and yanked it free.

There was a moment of resistance where the whole room shook with the power struggle—Lady Whitefall froze, her body hardly betraying the strain of fighting the force which bound Lord Hornbeam's magic to him. Several people screamed, others fell over as the ground heaved and the walls trembled and my own magic switched on like a live wire. Blue light flooded my body, and similar starbursts of blue and green light shone throughout the room. Then there was a horrible crack more like a sensation than a sound, and the green light surrounding Lord Hornbeam rushed over to Lady Whitefall. Her grip on his throat relaxed and he fell onto his face, presumably unconscious. Or even dead. Ripping someone's magic out was a fate *worse* than death.

Why hadn't she just killed him?

I'd forgotten my plan. My mind blanked out. I'd just witnessed my own mother tear out someone's soul—but he was still alive. Agonisingly slowly, he glanced up, his green eyes no longer glowing. The spark had gone out.

"That's better," she said. "I need your assistance, Tariel. You'll be my spy, travelling into the mortal realm and into Faerie whenever I require it. The Little People, are, unfortunately, no longer reliable."

What does that mean? Have Winter come to take them over? More to the point—she'd literally enslaved Lord Hornbeam to use his Sidhe abilities to cross realms and spy on the Courts. Stealing his magic apparently hadn't taken those abilities away. And because she'd never been exiled, she could cross realms herself whenever she felt like it.

All my plans had been for nothing. Who could stand up to her now?

"Now," she said to the crowd. "It's time to celebrate our victory over the borderlands."

The hall exploded with noise. Music struck up, and I instinctively raised my hands to press them to my ears then lowered them again as the crowd erupted into delighted celebration. It wasn't hypnosis—but Aspen and his pipes were in the crowd somewhere. Guards blocked all the exits, and I couldn't slip away while pretending to be under my mother's spell.

Lady Whitefall glanced at me as though she'd only just remembered I was there. "Do you want to take part in the celebrations?"

"I'm tired," I told her. "I want to go back to bed."

"Well, of course," she said. "The celebrations will go on for some time. I'll escort you to your room… we can't have anyone taking advantage of you, since they all know who you are."

Yet another threat lay beneath her words. I barely noted it. *She just ripped Lord Hornbeam's magic straight out of him.* But I'd hoped to get away alone. Maybe she didn't quite trust me after all. I needed to know what her plans were, but even if Winter did send help along, they'd never be able to find us. The Vale's magic was unknowable, and if anyone could rearrange the paths however they liked, it wasn't hard to imagine the person who owned this territory masking it from view.

"So," I said to her as we walked into the corridor again. "Aspen helped you all along?"

"The prince? He's useful to have around. He's helped train a large number of undecided humans, half-bloods… even some pure-blooded fae-kind. It's hard to inspire loyalty to exiles who have no love of the Courts."

"Wouldn't just using a vow take care of it? Or that—whatever you did when you told everyone to kneel?"

"That?" She gave a false laugh. "That was an Invocation, daughter. The language of the gods is only gifted to the very best of us. The Courts rarely use those words—they're afraid of the power. I don't share their fear. I believe in using every weapon available to us."

Language of the gods? Plainly, I didn't know nearly as much about the Sidhe as I thought.

"Which gods?"

She didn't speak again until we'd reached the door to my room. "I think it's about time you stopped trying to fool me, child."

Damn.

"Though I'm curious as to why my magic didn't work on you," she said. "Of course, I forgot you shared my blood. You look so very human, yet you have too much of the fey in you to be trustworthy."

"Speak for yourself. You're breaking about every rule of the Courts, not to mention enslaving people. For what reason? You *had* a kingdom, and it'd have been yours until someone killed you."

"Not quite," she said. "The Courts were exiling anyone who didn't fall within their parameters."

"You mean, anyone who was collaborating with the Grey Vale. You had an entrance right underneath your palace. Why, exactly?"

"Why else? It's a haven of untapped resources."

"It's a hellhole." But… that meant she'd been working with the Vale far longer than a year. No wonder she'd been prepared for the moment she left her kingdom behind.

I'd heard the Darkwater Sidhe had been exiled, but had forgotten it would have taken place around the same time as my mother's supposed death. Were there others she'd allied with? She'd built a Court all of her own, and was willing to drench Faerie in blood to achieve her aims.

"I wish you'd make things easier for me, Raine. You and I might have ruled this kingdom together."

"Like you planned that. You already said you never wanted me to find the talisman at all."

"That is true," said Lady Whitefall. "I don't particularly want to kill you, but you're proving more of a hindrance than I anticipated. Are you not open to an allegiance? You can't tell me you *liked* living amongst those filthy mortals for your whole life? They treated you well?"

Images flashed through my mind—humans laughing at me, throwing fragments of iron in my face, signs in windows saying *faeries not allowed.*

Her tone was so persuasive, so beautifully pitched…

No. I'm not under her spell.

"You want to know why I have a problem with you?" I said. "It's not because I care about humans. You *abandoned* me there with them, and I'll never forgive you for that. And for every human who hated me, another helped me. I'm *half* of one, and that's the only part of my life I remember, thanks to your magic."

Her mouth parted in surprise. "You claim you're allied with those fools?"

I'd actually convinced her. Now to press my advantage.

"As for *this* place," I said. "You can't convince me it's better than the Courts. It's literally draining the magic out of all of us the longer we spend here. I can't fathom why anyone would want that when they could have the real faerie realm."

"As I said, it's not permanent. My own magic is strong enough to resist the drain of this realm."

"Well, mine isn't," I snapped. "For your information, I have been here before. Aspen and the Little People kidnapped and tortured me less than a week ago, and it turns out they were acting on *your* orders. So don't pretend to have my best interests at heart, mother. Whatever you say. I'm not that little girl you could bend to your will. You saw to that."

I'd kept my tone even, convincing, the truth in my words masking the lie beneath them. My magic might not be as strong here, but I wasn't completely powerless. The trick was convincing her that I was, despite her hypnosis not working on me.

"I wasn't aware you were the captive. I did hear of a new prisoner with similar magic to mine…"

"It's gone, thanks to him," I whispered. "It's too late—you can't convince me to join you. Unless…"

She raised one eyebrow. "Yes?"

"Let me fight Aspen."

Her pretty eyes blinked. "That's it? You aren't going to bargain to free your friends?"

Unfortunately, no. If I gave away my relationship with Cedar, and that Rose and Viola were involved with one another, I wouldn't put it past her to make examples out of us. The other three weren't immune to her magic. I was. I needed to divert her attention and then free my friends later, so her focus would be on me instead of them.

"Aspen deserves to die for what he did," I said. "Give me the stage, make a performance out of it. I want him to suffer, and I want everyone to see it."

"You are not to kill him," said Lady Whitefall. "I still need him. But he does need to learn some humility. Tomorrow, we march on the Courts. You can have your match before we leave. My servants will guard your room tonight."

Message received. If I tried to run, she'd retaliate. I walked into the box-sized room, and she closed the door. I'd be in real trouble if she elected not to keep her word and let me fight Aspen, instead leaving me locked up in here while she took her army into Faerie itself.

I didn't sleep that night, instead rehearsing my plan the best I could, trying not to let panic overtake me. I was playing a dangerous game, and revenge on Aspen should have been the last thing on my mind. But if I could create a diversion—lock the crowd's attention on something other than my mother—I might have a chance in hell of breaking her control and making everyone see her for the monster she truly was.

A knock on my door came at dawn. I sat up, my heart beating fast, as a key turned in the lock.

Viola came into my room, and smiled. "Hey, Raine. I figured you needed an ally."

22

I gasped. "She's making you be her servant again?"

"Not quite." She grinned. "She doesn't know that I'm bound to you as much as to her. She also underestimated your boyfriend."

"What—Cedar?"

Seconds later, he came into the room behind her.

"What are you doing?" I hissed.

"Escaping." He gave me a smile. His eyes were shadowed, but didn't betray the glazed look of one under her spell. "What Lady Whitefall failed to grasp is that I'm a thief, and she forgot to forbid me to wander the castle of my own accord. I think she assumed her magic sufficed, but she's holding too many people captive at once."

"Wow. So what did you do?"

"I stole the keys to the humans' cells. But I couldn't steal Lord Hornbeam's. She took him with her."

He knew I'd want to free the humans. "Thanks," I whispered. "All right. How are we going to do this? I'm not sure I can defeat her in combat or in magic, and even if I could, we're outnumbered here. Not to mention, I'm not a hundred percent certain of her plan. Or Aspen's. It involved hypnotising and enslaving people. I've managed to bargain with her and I get a one-on-one duel with Aspen this morning."

"You did what?"

"It's all I could think of. She has you locked into a vow, and we all know what happened the last time."

Cedar gave me a strange smile. "No, she doesn't," he said. "You broke my vow when you cut the iron band off me. She didn't check the exact wording, because she assumed that the vow was tied to his magic. It wasn't. And she already ordered the other soldiers' bonds to be removed, at Rose's suggestion, to avoid the iron poisoning."

I stared at him. "You mean they're all free?"

"Not all of them. Some are still under her spell, and others are working for her. And none of us can walk out of this realm without a Sidhe or Little Person."

Damn. "Lord Hornbeam and Lady Whitefall can do that. No one else."

"Did she tell you anything last night?" asked Viola.

"She's planning to march on the Courts today."

Cedar swore. "That means she'll likely use Lord Hornbeam in some way first. Maybe send him with the first army. The Courts will be on the lookout for trouble, but they don't know he's no longer a Sidhe with functioning magic."

"Damn," I said. "That sounds like her, actually. She'll avoid showing up in person until she wants to. I've no idea how she plans to involve *me* in this, considering I've already shown her up. I think Aspen and I are the entertainment."

"She did mention entertainment," said Viola. "I'm supposed to attend. I—I saw Rose, and she's safe for now, but I wasn't able to get her away. Once the celebrations are over, I planned to use my servant status to speak to everyone I know isn't affected by any vow."

"If I free the humans now, they'll probably get killed

trying to escape," Cedar said. "We need Lord Hornbeam as leverage. He can still walk between realms, as far as I know."

"Get him to take the humans with him." I nodded. "So he can pave the way for the rest of us and stop her from taking hostages. And—and the soldiers who weren't affected by the vow?"

"I'll talk to them, but they're likely still under her thrall. I can't break her spell."

I'm not sure even I can. But I had to try. A half-blood could kill a Sidhe. I was living proof.

And a half-blood army might topple the Courts.

A knock on the door. "Who's in there?" said my mother's sharp voice.

Cedar moved in a blur, disappearing out the window, seconds before the door opened.

"What's this?" Lady Whitefall looked from me to Viola with narrowed eyes.

"My servant was updating me on what happened after you unceremoniously yanked us from our homes," I said, not missing a beat.

"I think you'll find she's my servant, daughter."

"I inherited her along with the talisman. Her vow binds her to the family, which includes me."

She didn't even blink. "Walk at my side," she commanded. "Servants aren't much use in the war... but you were once a soldier, correct?" She addressed Viola, a knowing glint in her eye.

"I was," Viola said quietly.

"And then I stole you from under Lady Hornbeam's nose." She smiled as though recalling a fond memory, then glanced at me. "Speaking of Lady Hornbeam."

A pronounced silence filled the room, daring me to break it and deny what she already knew. Of course Aspen would have told her everything.

"You see why I don't believe you're not scheming, Raine," she said. "I doubt you're powerful enough to have killed her on purpose, but you certainly have an unpredictable streak."

"What makes you think I didn't?" I asked coldly. "You Sidhe have a habit of underestimating us. For the record, I reported you directly to the Unseelie Court, and the Little People who worked with you are dead."

"You still don't understand, child, do you? You might have inherited a little of my power, but your fragile humanity doesn't stand up to our true strength."

Agony sliced open my back as though a whip had struck me. I bent forward, gasping, expecting to feel blood slide down my skin, but none came. A second whip-strike brought me to my knees. I bit back a cry of pain. Of course she had other Sidhe's magic. Like all exiles, she'd stolen the magic of others. And she'd been here for a year, in human years at least. Not to mention she thought of the sceptre—a talisman the borderland families had fought bitterly to the death over—as nothing more than a small fraction of her power.

"Oh, Raine, what have they done to you." She cupped my chin, lifted my head, and stroked my hair in a familiar gesture which made me want to gag. "I have no love for the mortal realm, but only our world could have made you into this cold-hearted creature."

"You don't know me," I said.

She gave me a smile—the same one I remembered from the vision. "I understand that this world is too much for you. I can make you forget... walk out of here and never look back. As I did before. You were happier not knowing, weren't you?"

Objectively—yes. Sort of. Life had been a damn sight less complicated when I'd lived as a human, taking care of Dad and screwing around with Denzel when I wasn't thieving.

But now I had Viola, and Cedar, and didn't have to steal to survive. I had a family.

As though I'd ever consider abandoning everyone here.

I shook my head. "I don't know what you're playing at this time, but you promised me a match with Aspen, and I'm hoping you'll deliver on it."

"I suppose I did," she said. "I'd prefer not to lose one of my soldiers, though, so you are to fight with no weapons aside from magic. That sceptre of yours will remain with me."

I opened my mouth to say it made no difference, then remembered she didn't know I'd pulled the magic out of the sceptre and into myself. Which meant she had no idea I could use it at all. It was a good job I hadn't done anything fancy with my clothes, otherwise she might have guessed. *Looks like I've got an advantage after all.*

I gave her a bland smile. "Sure. We humans are used to fighting dirty. I'll win, and then I'll go home. To the mortal realm."

She laughed. "Your friends will have special seats to watch the show. I've arranged it. That includes the girl… Rose, was it?"

Ice slid down my spine. *Damn her.* I hoped Viola had more of a plan than I did. And Cedar, who had a shot to escape freely for the first time in his life, yet had chosen to help free the humans here instead.

We walked down the corridor to the main hall, which looked much like it had the night before—in fact, more like the celebrations hadn't ended at all. The crowd stood in groups, mingling, but there was a stiffness to their interactions I hadn't picked up on yesterday. It was too controlled. Faerie gatherings were where the fae-kind went to let off steam. Here, she was in control of their every move even if she hadn't directly used her magic on them. Nobody raised their voice too loud or stepped out of line, and an aura of fear hung over the place.

In the middle of the crowd was a stage. And as my mother had said, the front row of seats was already occupied. Viola sat at the end, face carefully expressionless. At her side was Robin, between her and Rose.

Cedar was nowhere in sight. That was my one consolation. But on the other side of the stage, Aspen waited for me, his mouth twisted in a smile. The crowd cleared at Lady Whitefall's command, and we approached the stage. He carried a sword, and I didn't. In his other hand were the pan pipes. Smiling, he lifted them to his mouth.

No.

I made to leap forwards and snatch them from his hand, but magic lashed me around the ankle, sending me toppling to my knees.

She was cheating, holding me in position with her magic. Her power whispered in my ears, telling me I needed only to say the word and she'd take me away from here, spare me from ever fighting, if I'd give in—give up my magic and my memories…

You won't take this from me.

I raised my hands, conjuring up a handful of icy shards. There wasn't much else in the room to transform—aside from the people, which my magic didn't work on. She'd told me that the transformation magic didn't work in this realm, but she'd also thought it was tied to the sceptre. If she was wrong… Aspen was in for a world of pain.

He dodged my ice attack, blocking with the side of his blade, but I sent another one at him, lunging forwards to meet him in battle.

Aspen and I circled one another carefully. His blade cut at my knees and I jumped over it, using my speed to my advantage. His pipes were as deadly a weapon as the sword, but he couldn't use both at once. This realm sapped my power, so I'd probably run out of steam first. But my mother's frown spurred me on. She hadn't expected me to be able to use magic at all.

And nobody knew what was coming.

He lost patience, slicing at me. I took the hit, blood welling from a shallow cut on my arm, and locked my arm around his wrist, yanking him close to me in a similar manner to the way he'd once pulled me into the closed iron door of a cell. Transferring my grip to the wrist that held the pipes, I froze the air around them. Then I let go. He stumbled back, grinning at the blood seeping down my sleeve. It stung, but wouldn't incapacitate me.

Then he saw what I'd done to the pipes. If they hadn't been a talisman, I'd have transformed the pipes and fused them to his hand. As it was, he stiffened in surprise upon finding them entirely covered in ice, then tossed them aside. His eyes narrowed and he stalked forwards, no longer playing games. He raised his sword.

I was faster. I grabbed the pipes and flung them at him. They were heavier than they looked, and smacked into his hand hard enough to make him loosen his grip on the sword. I tackled him and kicked his legs out from underneath him, headbutting him hard in the face. Cartilage gave way beneath my forehead as pain blossomed from my skull, but damn, that felt good. I caught my mother's eye. Shock marred her features for a split second, quickly enough for me to notice. She'd expected me to lose. That, and she was probably stunned to see the perfect daughter from her memories brawling like a human.

Aspen groaned and tried to elbow me, but I twisted his arm, hard. Then his broken nose began to shift before my eyes—to heal. I should have figured he and Cedar had the same healing power.

I struck his ribs with sharp jabs, too quick for him to heal in time for the next one. Doubled over, he failed to block a sharp kick to his leg which brought him down onto his back. I threw myself on him, punching every inch I could reach. "That's for humiliating me, you sick fuck."

He began to laugh, coughing through broken teeth, and brought his knee up into my chest, flipping me over so he was on top of me instead. From his clumsy movements, he clearly had no clue how to brawl, but he had the advantage of healing as quickly as I wounded him. I needed a second to catch my breath, and he used the opening to thrust the blade at my chest.

I knocked into his sword arm, unbalancing him, and the blade hit the floor instead of me. Hooking my legs around his, I pushed him off me, onto his back. He sprang to his feet, spitting out blood. He couldn't replenish his magic here, because there was none at all. If I injured him seriously, he'd take longer to heal. But that wasn't my plan.

He was so intent on my face, he wasn't looking where my feet were moving. The steps came as easily as breathing, even as I adapted my movements to dodge his attempts to strike me.

An exclamation came from the audience, abruptly cut off. It sounded like Robin.

I hope you get caught in the spell, too, you lying bastard.

It'd taken mere seconds, but Aspen's gaze was locked on me, his body still. No longer fighting. The audience, too, remained silent as my spell spun its effect over the crowd. My mother wouldn't be affected, but it'd be seconds before she realised. I'd inherited this gift from her, after all.

The dance captured him, lured him in. Aspen's eyes began to glaze over, his grip on the sword slackening.

"Attack your queen," I told him. "Kill her."

Aspen raised his weapon and leaped at Lady Whitefall, who beat him aside with a furious snarl. The crowd gasped and stared at me. I'd caught them, too. But how to keep their attention? Lady Whitefall wasn't captive, and she could easily overpower her servant.

"Trip her!" I yelled at the two guards at the side of the stage. "Block her path. You, too."

Blue light shone around my feet, around the crowd, as clear and bright as any magic I'd seen, but the spell worked even though I was no longer moving.

And I knew why, now. The reason my magic had only ever worked when I danced was because it was the one time I felt like I had magic, like the others. Both human and faerie worlds had spurned me, but onstage, I was in another world entirely, where none of that could touch me. That's why my magic had worked. And why I'd been so susceptible to Robin's influence. Now the power was in my hands alone.

The audience held still.

The world held its breath.

"Those of you who hold no vows to any Sidhe," I said, "act as you would if you were free, and turn on the traitor who wants to take your Court from you."

Before I'd got the words out, the crowd broke apart, soldiers brawling with one another. Whoa. Not only had I affected the captured soldiers, I'd affected the ones bound to serve her, too. Pandemonium rippled through the crowd. The soldiers not bound to her weren't under her thrall any longer, and they recognised that traitors from their own family had brought them here to die. Even with Lady White-fall so close, her power so absolute, they defended their Court, their family. I could almost respect that.

Rose and Viola had disappeared in the chaos. Leaving Aspen staring blankly, I jumped down from the stage—and a blade sank into my side. One of her soldiers loomed over me, his eyes blank. Still under her thrall.

Blood wet my lips and I staggered, desperately trying not to let go of the threads of magic keeping the crowd in place.

"The games are over," said Lady Whitefall. "Now—"

"Attack her!" I yelled hoarsely at the nearest soldiers, her personal guards I recognised as other half-bloods who'd taunted me as Aspen's prisoner. There was no way to tell how many of the others were here of their own volition or not, but the ones she'd kept close were the most loyal. Including… *there he is.* Lord Hornbeam stumbled away from the brawling crowd, still wearing chains.

"Come with me!" I yelled at Lord Hornbeam. "I command you to take my friends and me to the mortal—"

A blade protruded from his chest. He gasped and slumped forwards, lifeless.

Now my own mother was the only way out of this godforsaken realm.

Her eyes met mine, and narrowed in rage. "If you don't release my soldiers, child, all of your friends will die."

She can't undo my spell. But of course—we had the same magic. Hers couldn't affect mine. Even Aspen remained under my control.

"Try it and you'll be next," I told her. Blood soaked my side, and the way my vision flickered told me I was in serious danger of bleeding to death.

"Fine," she said, in a low voice. "I didn't want to use my true talisman on my daughter, but you've given me no choice in the matter."

She held out a dagger, which gleamed silver under the low lights.

"There will be other, more worthy heirs. Hand your magic over to me and I won't rip it from you as you cry for mercy."

Whatever magic she had, it must be worse than what she'd shown me already. I looked her defiantly in the eyes, refusing to beg.

"Bring it on," I croaked.

She raised the dagger and brought it down.

23

The dagger ripped through the air, but nothing happened. No magic, no special effects. The world remained frozen—half under my spell, half under hers.

Lady Whitefall lowered her talisman, turning it over, then threw it to the ground.

"Who stole it?" she whispered. "Who stole my talisman?"

I stared uncomprehending for a moment, the dizziness of blood loss slowing my thoughts. Her talisman hadn't worked... because it was a fake.

Cedar. It couldn't be anyone else.

Lady Whitefall turned to the crowd, and shouted. A ripple went through the air as her power bent all our knees. If she told us to die, we would—but she'd used the exact same word as before. *Kneel.* One word with the strength of a thousand.

"Right," she snarled. "My ridiculous daughter's magic will wear off soon. When it does, you'll all do exactly as I say. Robin, get over here."

I knew she'd singled him out. She knew he wasn't affected by her magic.

"You're going to search the crowd for anyone not affected by her spell. She's disgustingly loyal, so anyone unaffected is either her ally or mine. She and I are not so different in our manipulation of mortals."

I wanted to argue, but from the whiteness creeping into my vision and the bluish tint the world had acquired, I'd pass out at any second. I'd die, surrounded by people whose lives I held in my hands. Some hero I was.

Viola screamed as she was yanked out of the crowd. Robin held her off the ground, his face a mask of torment.

"I—" She gasped. "Mistress, you gave me your magic yourself. How can it affect me?"

Her gaze darted towards me, terrified, but she was trying to protect both of us. And she spoke the truth, even if she carefully omitted the part where it wasn't the hypnosis my mother had given her.

Lady Whitefall frowned. "You're right," she said. "Of course. Viola, you're to stay with me while we root out the rest of the vermin."

My vision swam again, her words blurring together. Then a bright green light flashed in front of me. My breath came slowly, but the pain didn't get worse. Instead, it faded.

Someone had healed me. The green light was a healing magic transfer—from a Summer faerie. It came with the scent of candles and woodsmoke. Cedar. I'd hoped he'd run while he had the chance. What had he done with her talisman?

My vision cleared and I managed to roll to my side. Good job, because the audience had begun to calm, and their glazed expressions were disappearing. Subtly, I tugged on the magic holding them in place, making sure my mother couldn't step in and hypnotise them, too. But I couldn't see Rose *or* Cedar, and Viola was stuck at Lady Whitefall's side pretending to be her ally while she prowled along the crowd. I rolled over, closer to the nearest soldiers.

One of them turned to me, but didn't speak. *An ally.* Or close enough. In fact, he was one of the assassins who'd shot at me from Lord Hornbeam's balcony. So were some of the others. But they were under my control now, or they had been.

"If you're loyal to the Courts," I whispered. "Take her down. We outnumber her."

They exchanged glances, then one of them said, aloud, "I'm not under her spell."

"Nor me," said another, his voice ringing across the hall. "I'm on her side."

"So am I."

"Stop that," snarled my mother, but a dozen voices drowned her out. More than half the crowd declared themselves as allies, looking at her defiantly.

Lady Whitefall whirled around to face me. "I thought you were dead already?"

"No," I whispered, still pretending to be mortally wounded. If she thought I was about to die, she might spare some of the others. Wherever Cedar hid, it must be close. It was a wonder he hadn't been caught already.

"I've had enough of this game." She cut a path through the crowd to me, pushing the half-bloods viciously aside. "Get in there and root out the traitors. All of you."

"Don't obey her," I told them. "If you're truly on the side of the Courts, stop the traitors before they invade your realm, or you'll be exiled to this place forever."

For the second time, the crowd broke apart in chaos. They were trained soldiers and loyal to their family. The half-blood soldiers fighting against Lady Whitefall's soldiers were braver than most Sidhe I'd met. And they'd turned on her, outnumbering the soldiers Lady Whitefall truly had under her spell. The crowd surged, trapping her in place, but she blasted them aside with magic, striking me with another wave of energy that sent me flying a good ten feet into the air. I flipped and landed in a forward roll which took some of the impact off, but revealed my injury was gone.

"You can't heal yourself," she said. "Who is your ally?"

"We are," shouted a voice, and the doors were thrown wide as a group of Little People ran in, followed by…

"Winter?" I gasped in disbelief. Three Winter Sidhe led the chase, accompanied by other smaller faeries.

"You call this an army?" she screamed. "Kill them."

The Hornbeam soldiers continued to fight, slaying the traitor soldiers with unrelenting strikes despite most of them having been unarmed. Our army might be small, but thanks to my magic, more than half of hers was no longer under her control. Even the Little People had come to join us, wielding sharp knives.

"We're taking you back to the Courts," one of them said. "All of you. She will stand trial in the Unseelie Court."

Damn right she will. Apparently my message had actually got through.

Lady Whitefall let out a furious shout, but the crowd hemmed her in. I took the opportunity to back out of range, running to the nearest Little Person. "There are humans here."

"I know. I helped them back to the mortal realm on the way here."

"Thank you." I released a breath. "There are others in the hall. We need to get the innocents caught up in her game out of here, now. And her—take her to the Courts."

The Little Person nodded, moving aside as the Winter Sidhe swarmed in. Lord Lyle led one contingent, turning into a giant wolf before our eyes and tearing into her soldiers.

Lady Whitefall screamed in rage. "You won't beat me here, you fools."

"Then we'll beat you on our own territory," said another Sidhe.

Grey smoke blurred my vision, followed by a flash of light. Magic surged through my veins—Winter magic, flooding my body in a dizzying rush. Fog smothered the trees which had appeared around me, but I recognised the path as being near the Little People's place. The sound of a thousand hoof-beats echoed. Winter's army.

Lady Whitefall appeared in front of me, a blade in her hand. Not a talisman. I called magic to my hands, and the trees bowed beneath the power. Blood pulsed in my ears, a reminder that even with the wound sealed, I was in serious danger of passing out from blood loss. But I wouldn't rest until I had her brought to the Court for her crimes.

She moved, her arm blurring as she cut down the branches. Magic arced from my hands, striking branches, forming a cage in the air. She raised a hand and swatted it aside, a bitter smile on her face. "You'd really attack your own mother."

"Don't pull that one on me." Magic flowed from my hands, hitting every solid object in my way. "You've lost."

A shower of icy shards rained down on her, but turned to rain before they broke on her skin. My vision blurred, my legs like dead weights. Even the rush of magic from Winter didn't quite make up for the draining effect of having been in the Vale. *Keep fighting. She must have a limit.*

Lady Whitefall raised a hand, and a current of Winter energy struck me in the chest, slamming me into a tree. Struggling for breath, I pushed upright. The sound of hooves echoed louder. *Come on. Get her.*

She cast a look to the side, as though she heard. I stumbled forwards, already too late. With one final glance at me

—half furious, half sad—she vanished in a flash of white light.

Damn. She'd gone back to the Vale.

My knees hit the ground, the world blurring. *No. I have to catch her. I have to...*

The next thing I knew, green healing light enveloped me, strengthening me. I sucked in a breath, my heartbeat stronger, blood pumping through my veins.

"When did you plan to tell me you could do that?" I mumbled to Cedar. My head rested on his knees.

"When you decided to stop nearly bleeding to death." He brushed a strand of hair from my forehead, his touch painfully gentle.

"Ha." The world came back into focus. "Crap. I didn't kill her."

"You did your best." He moved back to let me sit up. "She lost her army."

"The Vale will have another one." I climbed to my feet, wincing. "She'll be back. She wants the palace. Are Viola and Rose...?"

"They're fine." He pointed through the trees. "They're helping the Hornbeam soldiers who escaped. The ones who didn't turn traitor, that is. I think this has proved just where our loyalties lie."

"That's one way of putting it." With their leader dead... what would become of the Hornbeam family now?

Lord Lyle cantered up to us, showing no signs of the giant furred monster he'd turned into before. "Where did she go?" he demanded.

"She went back into the Vale." I indicated the place where she'd vanished. "Don't look at me like that. You know Sidhe can cross realms, including you. She was never exiled, so she has all the abilities she had when she was a Lady of the Court."

Fury suffused his expression. "Can anyone confirm it? Are there any pure faeries amongst you?"

"You think I'm lying?"

He steadied his horse, which snarled, as though it wanted to take a bite out of me. "I refuse to take my people into unknown territory on a whim. The Vale is a vast and unpredictable place."

"Yeah, I know that," I snapped. "So you're not going to chase her? You think she's given up?"

"It's not our job to police all rogues, but if she is spotted in our territory again, she will be executed."

Bloody stubborn Sidhe. I opened my mouth to say something along those lines, but Cedar spoke first.

"We have her talisman," he said.

Oh. He kept it?

"Who might you be?" asked Lord Lyle.

"Cedar Hornbeam, your lordship, of the Seelie Court." He inclined his head.

"Seelie," said Lord Lyle. "Is there any reason you ended up involved?"

"Lord Hornbeam is dead," we both said at the same time.

"She captured my entire family," Cedar added. "Some of us weren't affected by her spells to the same degree, so we were able to escape."

"Oh?" said Lord Lyle. "Hornbeam... the Summer Court wanted to speak with Lady Whitefall about her death, as it happens."

My heart sank. "You mean my mother?"

But I knew he didn't. My time had come. I was so screwed.

"Whatever Summer does is none of our business," he said. "We have done more than enough for you, Whitefall."

And he turned and rode away.

"Prick," I muttered, as soon as he was out of sight. "Great.

She's not dead, and he's pretty much said nobody will come and help if she attacks us again."

"It'll be okay," Cedar murmured. "The Unseelie Queen herself must know, I imagine."

"Hmm." I turned to him. I'd almost forgotten—he was free from the vow. However much of a mess our lives were in, we had that one small victory.

"What is it?" he asked.

"Nothing." I couldn't help smiling. "I—I don't even know where we go from here. But first, I need to make sure she hasn't sneaked back into the palace through the secret passageway."

"Of course."

If she had, I'd take her down this time. It'd always been clear the Winter Court put its own interests first, and I wasn't one of them. So be it. I'd been making my own rules here from the start.

I waved a hand and the path moved, shifting from fog-wreathed trees to the wider path leading up to the palace gates. Two horsemen waited at the gates. I stiffened. *Hornbeam soldiers?*

No. I took one step backwards, and both horses wheeled around. Their riders wore green and gold finery. Not iron armour, but fancy clothes decorated with embellishments.

"Raine Whitefall," one of them said. "You're under arrest for the murder of Lady Hornbeam of the Seelie Court."

24

For a second, I froze. So did Cedar.

"I didn't murder her," I said to them.

"Lies," said the one on the right. "We have evidence that you did, and eyewitness testimony. You have committed a crime in the eyes of the Courts."

"Look," I said. "Can we do this later? It might have escaped your attention that someone just brought an army from the Grey Vale with the intent of invading Faerie. She's still out there—"

Magic warped the air in a current of Summer energy, turning into sharp vines aimed at me. I raised my arms, and the vines froze in their paths. I was in no shape to take on two Sidhe at once, especially with the might of the Summer Court behind them.

Roots erupted from the ground. Magic broke against mine, shattering any defence I could conjure. The roots caught my feet, trapping me in place—Cedar stopped, cursing, and directed his own magic at the roots to make them let go. I nodded my thanks, climbing free—and right into the path of Moss Beard.

"Come quickly!" he said. "You're not safe here."

"I can't run away!"

Too late. Cedar's hand locked onto mine as white light enveloped both of us.

We landed on the hillside in the mortal realm, on cold, damp grass. I sucked in a breath, the world spinning. "How?"

"I have the ability to create rifts anywhere a liminal space overlaps with the mortal realm," Moss Beard said in explanation.

"They won't chase us here, will they?" I got to my feet and looked down at myself. Blood soaked my clothes, and had left red smears on the grass. "Wait, don't answer that. Of course they will."

"I will lead them astray," said the Little Person. "Do not go near half-blood territory."

He disappeared in another flash of white light.

I swore under my breath. Then I transformed my clothes into a plain top and jeans I kept at home, hiding the blood.

They know the truth. Nowhere is safe now.

"The mortal realm might not be their first assumption," said Cedar. "They don't know how many half-bloods use the rifts."

"Yeah, but they'll figure it out eventually. And then…"

"We'll go," said Cedar. "Somewhere far away from here."

"There's nowhere to go," I said. "Faerie and the mortal realm are tied too closely together to properly escape it. Besides, Viola and Rose are back in Winter, and they don't know where I am. I don't want them to be punished for my mistakes."

"It wasn't your mistake," said Cedar. "You couldn't beat her—I've never seen a Sidhe as powerful as she is, and I grew up in the Hornbeams' palace."

"I meant killing Lady Hornbeam." I sighed. "If I hadn't

done that, I wouldn't have set the wrath of the Courts on me."

"And at least one of us would be dead."

"Maybe." I shook my head. "I had no choice. If I were a Sidhe, I might be able to argue my case, but as I am now? No way. Not to mention if they find out my mother's the self-proclaimed Queen of the Grey Vale…"

"As I said, the Court is irrelevant," said Cedar. "Summer is known for being idle about the affairs of the families. They cared nothing at all when she was alive, and tortured her own people on a regular basis."

"But they care that I killed her. The bloody hypocrites." I began to walk downhill, cursing the Sidhe with every step. "I need to see my dad first, come up with another excuse about why I've been missing for probably weeks … and then tell him I can never see him again."

Cedar didn't respond for several moments. "It'll pass in time."

"It won't blow over. This is the Seelie Court we're talking about. They probably won't kill Dad, but they might use magic on him. Even seeing one of them might break the spell making him forget. Not to mention Robin's still alive, and under her power."

I didn't want to think about him. Let alone what Cedar and I might have had—that brief, fragile hope that had existed for seconds before it'd been extinguished.

Cedar took my hand. "I want you to know I'm here, what-ever choice you make. I have no Court, nor any other allegiance."

Oh hell. On top of everything else, his stepfather had been murdered, and he'd definitely lost his family now. I wasn't the only outcast. Not by a long shot.

I squeezed his hand in response. "I appreciate it. But you

know, being involved with me in any way is a hazard. We should go."

We crossed the field to the path leading into town, in silence. My mother was still out there, and even without much of an army, she could still amass enough force to take down the Courts.

And everyone knew the Sidhe could die. If word of what I'd done had spread throughout the Courts, they'd all know the Sidhe were capable of falling at the hands of a half-blood. *Then what will they do to the rest of us?*

I needed to lie down. I'd lost a ton of blood, I wasn't thinking clearly, and I wanted to see Dad so badly it hurt. Just to cling onto the last shreds of normality in my life, even if it was better for both of us that we no longer saw one another. That he forgot he had a daughter…

Cedar and I turned into the road leading to my house. No mercenary stood on duty.

"Shit." I quickened my steps, my heart sinking in my chest.

The front door lay open. No signs of a struggle, but the door to the flat opened at a push. It wasn't locked.

And Dad wasn't here.

I walked around the room. Dust had settled on every surface. He hadn't been here for days. The bedrooms and bathroom were empty. My nails bit into my palms. "She has him."

"No," said Cedar. "He wasn't in her prison. I'd have seen him."

"Then who…" I trailed off as the door opened.

A strange woman stood in my doorway. Human, with long dark brown hair and a blade in her hand. Blue light outlined her body, and her sword. *A faerie talisman.*

"Raine Whitefall, right?" said the woman. "My name's Ivy Lane. I've been told you need my help."

ABOUT THE AUTHOR

Emma is the New York Times and USA Today Bestselling author of the Changeling Chronicles urban fantasy series.

Emma spent her childhood creating imaginary worlds to compensate for a disappointingly average reality, so it was probably inevitable that she ended up writing fantasy novels. When she's not immersed in her own fictional universes, Emma can be found with her head in a book or wandering around the world in search of adventure.

Find out more about Emma's books at
www.emmaladams.com.

www.ingramcontent.com/pod-product-compliance
Lightning Source LLC
Chambersburg PA
CBHW020758190726
48285CB00006B/2080